PANGEA

AND ALMOST BACK

A WILD ADVENTURE RIDE!
- MICHAEL GERARD BAUER

D. R. HENDERSON

PANGEA
and almost back

D. R. Henderson

Glass House Books
Brisbane

Glass House Books
an imprint of IP (Interactive Publications Pty Ltd)
Treetop Studio • 9 Kuhler Court
Carindale, Queensland, Australia 4152
ipoz.biz/glass-house-books/
ipoz.biz/ipstore

First published by IP in 2021

Printed in 12 pt Adobe Caslon Pro on 16 pt Chalkboard

ISBN 9781922332486 (PB); ISBN 9781922332493 (eBook)

 A catalogue record for this book is available from the National Library of Australia

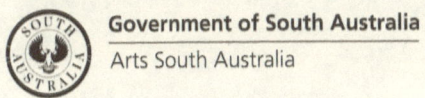 **Government of South Australia**
Arts South Australia

ii

for Liz

Acknowledgements

Author photo: Lucy Henderson
Cover and maps: Ty Brookhart
Book design: David P. Reiter

Firstly, thanks to three wonderful supporters of young adult literature—Arts SA, the May Gibbs Children's Literature Trust, and Asialink. The initial outline for Pangea was made possible through an Arts SA project grant. The first chapters were written while on a May Gibbs creative residency in Canberra. The broad outline, much of the research, and the decision to make Pangea an Asian adventure book was the result of an Asialink residency in George Town, Penang. For their hospitality and support during this residency my family are grateful to Khoo Salma Nasution and to her wonderful staff at the Sun Yat Sen Museum, in particular the late Ms Goh Mai Loon and the irrepressibly amiable Mr Yeap Ee Ban.

Secondly, thanks to my editors, including my lovely and insightful wife Alison, my university supervisor, Kerrie Le Lievre, and the meticulous editorial staff at IP, David Reiter and Krystal Nicol, who made the publishing process so enjoyable and the book so much better. I must also acknowledge the brilliant work of my multitalented illustrator, Ty Brookhart, for his work on the cover design.

And finally, thanks, in alphabetical order, to my generous band of readers: Kingsley Allen, Timothy Cooke, Mary Davidson, and, last but by no means least, Danielle Murphy.

Contents

PANGEA
and almost back

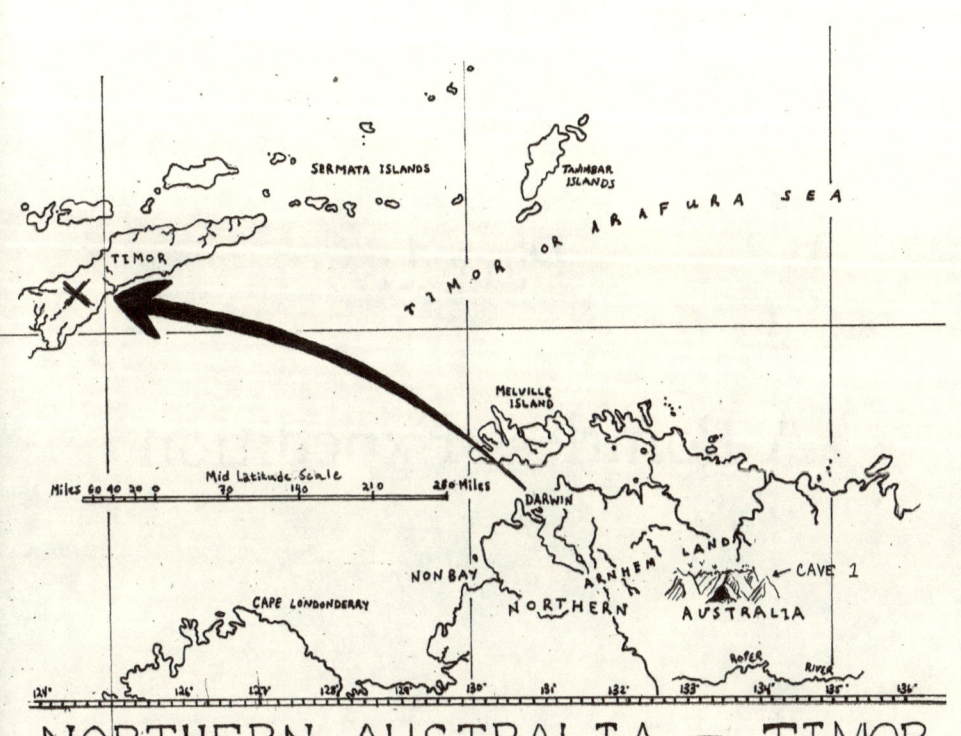

NORTHERN AUSTRALIA – TIMOR

Part 1:

A Pointless Expedition

1. Running Like Blazes, Timor, February 1942 AD

Just as Freddy O'Toole thought that things could not get any worse, the poison dart thumped into his backpack. *Blazes*, he thought.

'Run, Little Boss,' yelled his crusty manservant, Gruntenguile—not that he needed to.

'Good thinking! I would never have thought of that!' cried Freddy, glaring back and down at his little companion. They had been together for almost as long as Freddy could remember, but he still felt something like a no-returns punch to his heart every time he looked at Gruntenguile. He was a short, fuzzy-looking fellow with a grizzled beard like a badger's backside. He farted almost as often as he breathed and was, Freddy believed, the grossest and most useless manservant ever.

This opinion was actually quite unfair. Gruntenguile's work contract—scribbled in charcoal on a Gorgonopsian skull[1]—had only three words—'Keep Freddy alive'—and at that point of Gregorian time, Freddy had made it to sixteen and was still very much alive.

What's more, he was keen for it to stay that way, so he turned and ran.

Sweat sliding down the small of his back like a wet snake, he raced along the flooded trail they had been following for the past few weeks. Slashing his machete at groping vines to clear a path. His heart pounded in his chest. His lungs sucked the hot, sticky air in short, tight gasps. His leg muscles burned.

---

[1] In the unlikely event of ever meeting a Gorgonopsian—RUN. FAST!

Swoosh …

Thud …

Twang …

More poison darts, like back to front kamikaze mosquitoes, swooshed through the sticky air miraculously missing them.

'Don't look back, Little Boss. Just run!' cried Gruntenguile.

Really? I thought we might stop for a cup of tea, flashed through Freddy's mind but he was too short of breath to say it.

Thinking of smart Alec comments while running for your life is usually not a good idea. In the situation Freddy found himself, however, it was better than thinking about the things that might happen if the Snapahuti got hold of him. Things like having his head chopped off with a not-so-sharp axe and being enslaved in the afterlife—for all eternity—to the person who chopped it off![2]

Up ahead was a fork in the trail. Which way? Left or right? Blazes! They could not afford to get lost now. If they did, it would not matter if they escaped the Snapahuti. They could not survive for long, alone in the jungle with hardly any supplies. The only food in his backpack was a block of Cadburys Ration Chocolate kept cool in a bio-freeze bag. It had been given to him by Professor Dupler as he was about to leave on the expedition. An expedition about which the Professor had told him nothing except that it was best that he knew nothing. An expedition that seemed more pointless with each passing day. Still, in Freddy's heart, it carried a quiet hope that he dared not think, let alone say out loud.

[2] There are many reasons for headhunting, from just plain bad manners through to a genuine interest in macabre collect-ibles, but this was the one most common in the East Indies at that time.

He pulled a map from his trouser pocket and tried to read it, but he was running too fast. The dots and lines and words bobbed up and down in the opposite direction to his eyes. Frightened that he might lose it, he shoved it back.

'Gruntenguile, which way?' he gasped.

No reply.

He looked back.

Gruntenguile was gone.

Had he run too fast for Gruntenguile's stumpy legs to keep up? Or had one of the Snapahuti darts found its mark?

There was no way of knowing.

The only thing he knew for certain was that there was no going back.

He reached the fork. Left. A very short distance ahead, another fork. Turn right. No reason. Just instinct now. No time to think.

A branch ripped his army surplus shorts and cut into the pale skin beneath. Blood trickled down his skinny leg, making a slimy snaking trail in his muddy sweat.

All the while, the ferocious cries of the Snapahuties grew louder. Only the bends and forks of the jungle path, and his agility, kept him safe. Or so he thought.

Swooooshhhh!

A dart pierced his hat, pushing it forward. He grabbed at the hat and pricked his finger—luckily, not on the dart, but on the needle of a weird-eye hatpin that the Professor had given to him as he was leaving on the expedition. 'Blazes,' he cried, sucking the blood from his finger, and pulling the dart from his hat. He hurled the dart into the jungle, flipped his hat back on his head, and ran with an enthusiasm that only those who have been chased by a tribe of Snapahuti headhunters can fully appreciate.

He held his machete in front of him to stop the slap of low hanging branches. The sweat stinging his eyes blurred the way ahead to a jumping jumble of green. Every slender leaf seemed like a dangling viper. His legs felt like they were already being barbequed.

Another fork in the trail jumped out at him and this time his instincts told him to turn left.

Nosy gibbons with pointy white beards and sharp black eyes looked down from the treetops at Freddy. *Humans are so stupid*, they must have thought.

Even so, they chattered encouragement as he passed.[3]

Freddy would have happily given up a million years of evolution and sprouted a prehensile tail to join them up there. He no sooner thought this however, when he noticed a change in the world of noise beating about him. He stopped to listen. Clutching a dangling vine to steady himself, he held his breath. Cupping his hand to his ear, he turned around, thinking he could hear the beating of drums. Then he realised it was his heartbeat. The wet snake still slithered down the crook of his back.

Incurious insects scraped and scurried in the stinking leaf litter at his feet.

Outside that, it was silent. His pursuers must have stopped. Maybe they were regrouping and straining to hear him splashing ahead. Unsure of which path he had taken. Maybe discussing whether he would be best roasted or gently broiled.

His hand fumbled in his pocket and once more pulled out the map. It made no sense, as all he could see of his surroundings was the spot where he was standing and the trees towering above him and there was still no sign of Gruntenguile.

Freddy was about to give up when—somewhere ahead—he heard something.

[3] As much as the gibbons may have felt an affinity with Freddy, it should be noted that they are not, in fact, Hominids. They belong instead to the closely related Hylobatidae family.

2. Discovery

It was the sound of running water, and, if his ears were not playing tricks on him, it meant that the map Freddy was clutching so tightly was starting to make some sense.

As he bounded over a large buttress root, the forest suddenly opened up into a clearing of dappled light and ancient green rocks. Here the two great powers of the rainforest—sun and water—met and held each other in a clinging, choking embrace.

He knew he had to act quickly, but he also knew he had no time for mistakes. Breathing a great gasp of air into his lungs to calm his nerves, he looked around.

Taking the map from his pocket, he squinted to read it in the speckled light. His heart leapt from his chest and punched the dank air when he saw that there was a river right there in front of him just like the one running past the X on his map.

On the far side of the stream, a pile of boulders like giant steps ran up the side of the slope from which they had fallen. Checking his map once more, he noticed a cluster of over-lapping circles that he guessed were the formation of boulders before him. Scrawled in faded and smeared ink alongside the circles were the words—*Os Passos a Inferno.* Although he did not understand a word of Portuguese, Freddy did not like the sound of it.[4]

---

[4] Timor was colonised by the Portuguese in the sixteenth century. Although they mainly stuck to the coast, Freddy's map and the broken remnants of ten-gallon demijohns later found near this site suggest that at least one party of Portuguese ventured inland and quite possibly stumbled on the discovery that was now within Freddy's grasp.

A sharp cry shattered the silence behind him. The Snapahuti had picked up his trail. There was no time for thinking. Racing forward he splashed across the stream, jumped onto the first rock, and clambered upwards.

The ever-flooding stream had rounded and polished the rocks over countless centuries. The green slime that covered them did not make things any easier, but Freddy pushed on, clinging like an insect in a storm and wedging his machete into crevices for balance. Still he slipped often, and his pants and shirt were soon covered in the green slime from the rock, and his legs and arms in bruises from his falls. His back muscles twitched with the thought that a hail of poison darts might pincushion his body at any moment.

As he climbed, he made his way through the changing layers of the rainforest. He was almost at the canopy level when the steps ended. Here he found a ledge several yards wide and dotted with boulders that had fallen from the cliff, looming above. One of these boulders in particular caught his attention. It rested against the cliff face, directly in front of him. It was an almost perfect sphere and about the size of a sack of potatoes—or possibly even onions—and covered in black lichen. Freddy grabbed the boulder and rolled it backwards. It gave way easier than he thought, and, before he could steady its movement, it was tumbling down the cliff face and crashing through the jungle below. Startled cries from hundreds of hidden creatures shrieked through the sticky air.

Gu–gu–gu–gu–gu–gu–gu–gu–gu–gu–gu–gu–gu–gu–gu–gu–gu–gu...

The sound was awful even as it faded and tugged on Freddy's already tight nerves. The silence that followed was even worse. Freddy looked back to where the boulder had been and saw the dark entrance to a cave. That cave was the intersection of the X on his map, and it brought him to a sudden stop.

It was very like a cave he had already seen.

3. Darwin & Arnhem Land, northern Australia, September 1941 AD (5 months earlier)

Freddy had only ever been on one other expedition. Five months earlier, Professor Dupler had taken him on a field trip up the Alligator River.

He had not wanted to go.

'Why do I have to go?' he had whined.

'Yours is not to reason why, Freddy,' said the Professor. It was his usual response, and it always caused Freddy to reason why he could not reason why.

'But I'm scared of alligators,' said Freddy.

It was true. When he was younger, Freddy had taken the bother to write a list, which he had titled 'Reptiles to Avoid in my Lifetime'. It was a big list and included scientific names in brackets, as well as details that might prove useful if attacked. Alligators had made it to that list even though they were shy creatures who slept most of the time. Freddy did not like the look of them.

'Don't be ridiculous—there are no alligators in the Alligator River,' replied Professor Dupler, knitting his scrubby brows at Freddy's stupidity. 'They are *crocodiles*. You should know that—there is an excellent book on them in the library—I suggest you read it before we leave.'

Freddy had already read the book and knew quite well that they were crocodiles. The two species of alligator lived thousands of miles away in China and America. Freddy also knew that the river's white 'discoverer' Phillip King, had named the river in 1820 after mistaking the crocodiles for alligators. He just liked to bait the Professor every now and again, and the easiest way to do that was to pretend to not know something that was clearly explained in one of the hundreds of books in the Professor's library. As much as he did not like alligators or crocodiles, they were only a smoke screen. They were not the creatures he most feared.

Doctor Blight, Hoogleraar van Nutt, Lord Poonsonberry, and other random anthropologists joining Professor Dupler's expedition, were the creatures he really wanted to avoid.

He tried a different tack. 'But I'll be the only one my age that's going.'

'Not so,' said Professor Dupler, fixing his shiny-new glass eye on Freddy and smiling like he had splendid news. 'Doctor Wong is bringing her daughter.'

The air whooshed from Freddy like he'd run over a seven-inch nail.

'Lucy Wong! You can't be serious!'

Freddy was an only child who did not go to school. He therefore had very little contact with other children. The only other child he had seen much of over the years was Lucy Wong. Her mother, Dr Wong, had similar research interests to Professor Dupler, and they sometimes worked together. She was a nice woman with round spectacles and an expression that suggested that she could never quite believe what she was hearing from her mostly male colleagues. Unlike Professor Dupler's other acquaintances who saw children as a type of human tadpole, Dr Wong seemed to enjoy Freddy's company. Unfortunately, Doctor Wong never went anywhere without Lucy.

When he first met Lucy, he still believed there was good in everyone. On that occasion, the Professor had told Freddy to entertain Lucy while he and Dr Wong examined some skulls. Lucy was only a year younger than Freddy, so he thought that she might like to see his Buck Rogers comics. He was wrong.

'You are such a . . . *boy!*' she cried. She was right of course. There was no denying it.

The next time they met, he tried to impress her with how many push-ups he could do. He was not even up to twenty when she huffed out of the room. Another epic fail!

This time she said just two words: 'You *idiot!*'

Freddy was not sure if this was better or worse than being called a boy.

'You . . . girl,' Freddy replied—under his breath.

Further catastrophes followed. Now, just the mention of her name made Freddy so nervous he could hardly remember what she looked like apart from the fact that she wore braces, which reminded him of the barbed wire entanglements that lined trenches in World War One. Bits of food trapped in them looked like little corpses, shot trying to make it over the top.

*

Despite Freddy's protests, the next day he found himself hiking up the face of the Arnhem Escarpment. In patches, he was barely visible against the sandstone slope as he was dressed almost entirely in khaki. Specifically, he wore a khaki shirt and khaki army shorts that billowed out like little parachutes, making his hairy legs look insectivorous. The only thing that was not khaki was his hat. It was one of those towelling hats often worn by fishermen who rarely catch fish. It was faded green like a drought-stricken bush on his head and had a floppy brim to shade the sun. Gingerish hair stuck out in untidy clumps beneath it. The faintest whisper of a ginger cookie brush glistened with sweat between his nose and mouth.

Freddy's backpack was extra heavy as it contained not

just his things but also the Professor and Gruntenguile's.

Apart from the heat and the load on his back, however, things were not as bad as they could have been. Firstly, he had survived the Alligator River. Secondly, Lord Poonsonberry had been unable to make the expedition. German submarines were making it impossible for ships to leave England safely. It seemed to Freddy that Hitler was not such a bad chap after all. Unfortunately, however, there was no thirdly. Doctor Blight and Hoogleraar van Nutt had made the expedition. Another anthropologist, who Freddy had not met before, was also tagging along. He was a chubby man with a monocle clenched in his right eye, giving him the appearance of a lopsided Cyclops. The rest of his head sat like an egg in an eggcup on a neatly trimmed van Dyke beard. He had arrived at the last minute and almost missed the boat. Everyone else seemed to know who he was, but when he shook hands with Freddy, he did not offer his name. His fingers in Freddy's hand were like raw sausages. A fresh scar that looked like something you should not ask about ran across the top of his right cheek. Despite it being a considerable effort to join the expedition, he seemed even less enthusiastic than Freddy.

These gentlemen had hung about Freddy like one of Gruntenguile's finest farts for most of the hike, but they had now fallen behind. After the usual banter about the war, they had settled into a discussion on the origins of Gruntenguile.

'If I didn't know better, I would say Neanderthal,' said Dr Blight, inspecting Gruntenguile closely.

'More like ze missing link,' said Hoogleraar van Nutt.[5]

'I can assure you I am very typical of my tribe . . .

---

[5] This discourse between three of the world's most eminent physical anthropologists would, of course, in modern times be considered . . . well, just plain rude.

grrrnnt,' said Gruntenguile, in clear English, which sounded so strange coming from him. 'Just part of the usual variation in the species,' he added, staring a little longer than he needed at Hoogleraar van Nutt's nose stretching towards him like the Malay Peninsula.

Freddy tried to ignore the ravings behind him and looked ahead to where even greater danger lay. Most times he would have been jumpy about the taipans, death adders, and king brown snakes that were native to that area but, on that day, they were the least of his worries.

Up ahead, Lucy Wong, sucking on the same peppermint she had popped into her mouth on the boat (without offering one to Freddy), clambered over the rocks without so much as a drop of perspiration. (Freddy's shirt was dripping like a rusty tap.) *At least her braces were gone and, maybe in time*, thought Freddy, *her mouth might loosen enough to crack a smile.* She was dressed in jodhpurs with leather boots to the knees and a white shirt, which still looked freshly ironed. Her hair was tightly braided into two short devil horns that jutted out on either side of her head. She scampered like a mountain goat up the escarpment, stopping only to allow her mother to catch up. Doctor Wong was not very old, but she was limping and stopped from time to time, to rub one leg.

Normally she would have been walking with Professor Dupler, but, on this trip, they had hardly said a word to each other.

This might have been because another mysterious newcomer was stealing all of Professor Dupler's attention. Doctor Claudia Bufon had recently contacted the Professor to discuss his work. When he mentioned the expedition to Arnhem Land, she invited herself.

Professor Dupler, who was never impressed with anyone, seemed unusually taken with her. She wore green coveralls pulled tightly around her thin waist. On the river, she wore a white turban that had since been unfurled, but her black hair remained in a tight bob with the exception of a few loose strands that had wiggled free. She blew these to the side of her face as she spoke to Professor Dupler.

'Shouldn't that boy be in schoooooool?'

'School . . . school . . .' cried Professor Dupler stabbing the air with his cane as if being attacked by schools at that very moment. He was unable to say the word a third time. He pushed his pith helmet, which was much too large for his head, above his hairline as if needing to ease the pressure on his cranium at the mention of the dreaded word. 'Textbook loony-bins ruled by the disciples of straight lines that must never exceed the length of an exercise book! No, no, never! While he is with me, he will learn by my method, Doctor Bufon.'

'And what iiiis your method?' asked Dr Bufon.

'Watch and learn,' said Professor Dupler. Glancing up, he pointed with his walking stick to a bird soaring on the afternoon thermals. Then he turned to Freddy and asked, 'What bird is that, Freddy?'

'Red Goshawk,' replied Freddy, without a moment's hesitation. It was, after all, a very easy bird to identify.

'Erythrotriorchis radiatus,' said the Professor triumphantly, as if adding an exclamation mark to his point. 'It is my favourite raptor, Dr Bufon. Gaze on it while you can. It may not be with us much longer.'

Looking up, she saw the bird. Its burnished and dappled feathers looked magnificent against the bright blue of the dry season sky, but she did not look at it for long. Dr Bufon hated birds. They pooed on things and made horrible squawking noises at the most inconvenient times. Like in the morning when she was trying to sleep.

'Yes, but wouldn't schooooool get him out from under your feet?'

'The bird? From under my feet?' The Professor had always had trouble with the rambling nature of everyday conversation.

'Not the bird, Professor—the boy!'

'Oh, I see. Well—he's really not much bother . . .' he mumbled. 'I have a library of anthropological books for him to read and plenty of useful things for him to do and . . .'

'And what?'

'And the war. Until it's over I'd rather keep him close by.'

This surprised Freddy. He had thought that the Professor simply enjoyed annoying him.

'So *whyyy are you* the boy's guardian?' asked Dr Bufon.

'I am not really the boy's official guardian,' said Professor Dupler.

'*Reeeally?* Then whyyy have you got him?'

To Freddy, it sounded like asking why someone owned a cocker spaniel.

'His father was Colum O'Toole—'

Doctor Bufon's long and beautifully curved eyelashes flicked upwards. '*Reeeally?—the* Colin O'Toole!'

'Colum,' corrected Freddy under his breath.

'*The famous anthropologist?*'

'Yes, a rather eccentric fellow.'

'*Reeeally?*' said Doctor Bufon. 'I wouldn't know. I have heard of O'Toole, but I have not had the pleasure of meeting him.'

'Yes, a *curious chap*,' continued Professor Dupler. 'As I am sure you have heard. As bald as a Suri warrior on Donga day! And not much of a father, I have to say. He was always getting into fights. Worse than that, fighting was all he ever seemed to teach young Freddy. Backyard was chock-a-block with weights and ropes and all sorts of training gear.'

'*Really?* How do you know?' asked Dr Bufon.

'They lived next door.' The Professor shook his head. 'One Easter I hid some chocolate eggs in their backyard. I knew Freddy's father wouldn't think of it, but when I asked Freddy the next day if he had found any eggs, it turned out that his father had eaten them all, and made him pick up the wrappers. Worst damn father ever.'

'*Reeeally?*'

'Another time I insisted that he buy Freddy a birthday present and, guess what he got him?'

Dr Bufon scrunched her face to show that she had no interest in guessing games.

'A bottle of Blarney Whiskey! And a cigar! He was five years old for heaven's sake!'

Doctor Bufon arched her eyebrows.

'Another time I had to go over and calm him down he was in such a rage with young Freddy. The poor lad had lost something but when I asked what it was, he wouldn't tell me. That was the sort of *odd fellow* he was.'

During this conversation, Freddy's hand slid into his pocket and wrapped around his father's pocket watch. The face of the watch nestled in his palm while his fingers ran over the engraved names of his mother and father on the back—Jane and Colum O'Toole—and the date—1921. It was a habit of his whenever he thought of his father. He wished he could also think of his mother, but he could not recall her. She had died well before he could remember.

The Professor's story stirred a faded memory in Freddy. He could vaguely remember losing something but could not recall what it was. He could recall only his father's fury and the veins bulging on the side of his bladder-like head.

'I can't say I was surprised when he disappeared over Timor years later,' continued the Professor before waving his walking stick at another bird perched on a rock up ahead. 'Jabiru.'

Doctor Bufon nodded briefly at the bird. 'I believe O'Toole was working with you at the time?' she asked, returning her attention to the Professor.

'Yes. I was also part of the search party. We couldn't find a thing.' He paused before adding, 'Of course, as you know, the area where he disappeared swarms with headhunters. Freddy was only ten at the time, so someone had to look after him. I tried to track down some relatives in Ireland. The mother by all accounts had died when he was quite young in a car crash, although there was some confusion over the dates. Terrible record keepers, the Irish! I thought I might come across some distant relative at least but I kept drawing blanks. It was quite a murky affair. So, in the end, he just stayed with me. There wasn't anywhere else for him to go. That was six years ago.'

'I seeee. So how then did you *aquiiiire* that dreadful manservant?'

'Gruntenguile? O'Toole brought him back from one of his expeditions. Told me he had no choice. His tribe were about to sacrifice the poor blighter or some such thing. He's actually an illegal alien. The government doesn't know a damn thing about him.'

Doctor Bufon looked back at Gruntenguile before glancing at Freddy. He smiled at being noticed, and she screwed her face into something like a smile in return. She was a good-looking woman in a dark eyed, pouting lips kind of way, but her face was trowelled thick with makeup. Freddy felt uneasy under her cool gaze.

At that moment, the Professor and Doctor Bufon caught up with Lucy and her mother. The latter was sitting on a boulder resting her gammy leg. Freddy expected the Professor to say something to his old friend, but he stared silently ahead, avoiding her searching look.

'It appears you have had an accident since I saw you last, Professor,' said Doctor Wong.

The Professor raised his hand briefly to his glass eye. 'Yes,' he said. 'A branch flew back and skewered the old one like a pickle in a jar. Damn nuisance!'

It was not clear whether the 'damn nuisance' referred to the branch-skewered eye or Doctor Wong. This exchange however, was almost unremarkable compared to the exchange between Lucy and Dr Bufon.

'How's the war going *for you?*' asked Lucy.

'The same as for you my little . . . *daaaarling*,' replied Dr Bufon.

At the same time, a look passed between them, which was so searching and female that Freddy had no hope of understanding what it meant.

The rest of the climb was in silence. Conversations, feebly started, faded like the mirages shimmering and disappearing ahead. Freddy sweated so much he thought he might melt before he reached wherever it was they were going. Most of his solid body mass was still intact, however, when they at last stopped at a point where the ground levelled off some fifty yards or so before the top of the plateau. The entrance to a cave about the size of a car door stood before them. Spider webs netted the entrance, and spears of sunlight lit the yellow bellies of their weavers.

The Professor waited for the party to gather in tight. Everyone did apart from Gruntenguile who sat on a nearby rock and, to Freddy's annoyance, took out one of his *Buck Rogers* comics (which he had borrowed without asking), and began reading. The Professor coughed, stared down van Nutt who was still debating Gruntenguile's origins, and began. 'What you are about to see, I believe, is the most significant anthropological site ever found in this country. Current theories, as I am sure you all know, about the arrival of Aboriginals to Australia, guess at around 10,000 years BP. The earliest known artefacts found at places like Kow Swamp support this estimate. We also know that this arrival seems to have taken place in a series of waves—'

'I believe there are some, Professor, who now believe in a more ancient date of arrival,' interrupted Dr Bufon.

'Yes—yes,' the Professor nodded, 'but, what I am getting to Dr Bufon; what I am getting to . . .'

Dr Bufon's eyebrows arched upwards. Her eyes followed them. She blew the loose strands of hair from her face. Freddy saw this and a shiver ran up his spine like a quick little insect.

'What I am getting to,' continued the Professor, 'is that evidence in this cave suggests a date of arrival much more ancient than even the previous most generous estimates.'

The Professor stepped back, his new glass eye sweeping his audience. The eyes of his listeners boggled. It was thrilling news.

'How ancient?' asked Lucy.

'Now that's a good question!' replied Professor Dupler. 'Perhaps it's time to go inside and have a look.' That said, the Professor brushed aside the spider webs and disappeared into the cave like a sideshow magician.

At the same time, an overwhelming desire to enter the cave washed over Freddy. It had nothing to do with the Professor's speech. It was a feeling that somehow awakened inside him. Not a thought feeling, but a something in his gut.

Instead of following the Professor straight away, the rest of the party gathered around Dr Blight, who was closely examining one of the spiders through his field magnifying glass.

'Doss anyone know vot species is dis?' said Hoogleraar van Nutt, peering over Blight's shoulder. 'I hev not seen it before.'

The fellow with the van Dyke beard stepped forward and examined one of the spiders through his monocle.

Sweat dripped from the pudgy tip of his sunburnt nose.

'I am quite sure they are not poisonous, gentlemen.'

'How do you know?' asked Dr Blight.

'It's a long story but I can assure you, I have seen them before.'

As this discussion took place, Freddy jumped forward to follow the Professor. He would have been the next in the cave had he not been cut off by Lucy.

'Ladies first,' she said.

Freddy bit his tongue and let her go in front of him.

Inside, the cave was so dark that he could see nothing for a while. Some light filtered in through the entrance, but this was soon blocked by the arrival of the others who decided to brave the spiders.

Outside, Gruntenguile laughed at *Buck Rogers*.

The Professor did not switch on his torch straight away. He waited for everyone to squeeze into the cave. As they did, Freddy's eyes slowly adjusted to the dim light, and he started to make out a faint shape in front of him. As the outline of that shape became clear, he realised the incredible significance of the Professor's find.

'Blazes!' cried Freddy. 'It's a spaceship!'

Gasps of excitement and disbelief followed this news. Eyes strained to see Freddy's spaceship.

'Calm down!' cried the Professor. 'There is no spaceship! If certain people are not going to take this expedition seriously, they can jolly well march back down the escarpment right now and swim back to Darwin for all I care. And good luck to the crocs!'

'You pathetic moron!' hissed the spaceship so close to Freddy's face that he could feel her hot minty breath. His eyes had now adjusted sufficiently to the light to enable him to see two furious eyes in the middle of the spaceship.

'Blazes!' groaned Freddy to himself. It was Lucy Wong. Looking into her glaring eyes, he realised that he had only thought that she did not like him before. Now she really did not like him, and there was nothing he could say or do to make amends. Unless, of course, he could travel back in time.

Dr Wong entered the cave and put her hand on Freddy's shoulder. Freddy could not imagine how much that poor woman had suffered.

Luckily, the Professor switched on his torch at that point and held it club-like over his head. As Freddy's spirits sank, his eyes followed the beam upwards. He promised himself that no matter what he saw, he would say nothing.

When the light came to rest, it illuminated a sight so extraordinary that the small group inside the cave became as still as the stone walls that surrounded them. Only their mouths moved, springing open like cockles in a cooker. A few tried to gasp but the air needed to do so would not leave their lungs.

Three waves washed over Freddy at that moment. The first was the enormity of what he was seeing. The second was an understanding of what it meant. The third was a knowing as sure as the sunrise that his father was alive. These waves crashed over him in such quick succession they left his brain spinning in his head.

To steady himself, he glanced around at the others to see their reactions, but all he could see was bleary darkness. He was about to raise his eyes once more to the image on the wall when something caught his attention.

A pale glint of light reflecting off a glass eye.

4. Foot

Memories of that earlier expedition to the Arnhem Land cave stirred in Freddy's brain like a spoon in a half-boiled egg. He had felt then that he was somehow walking in his father's footsteps. He felt the same way now.

The cave entrance was too small for him to slide into with his backpack on, so he took it off and saw for the first time the poison dart that could so easily have ended his expedition. He shivered at what might have been before pulling the dart out and throwing it as far as he could. Next, he looked inside his pack for anything he might need. He was tempted to eat his chocolate bar before it was too late but decided to save it for later. Instead, he grabbed his Band-Aid, his note pad and pencil, and his toothbrush, and shoved them in the pockets of his army shorts. His torch was too large for his pocket, so he tucked it inside his shirt. Then he pushed his pack as far under a nearby ledge as it would go and rolled a rock into place to hide it. He had just finished when a low rumble shook the air and sent a shiver through the jungle.

Casting one last look at his backpack, he wondered if he would ever see it again. He thought one last time about eating his precious chocolate bar before deciding that he would save it as a reward for his return. He turned, stepped towards the entrance, and lay down in the slimy mud. Then, just as he was about to wriggle in, he saw something a couple of feet down the tunnel. It was a swirling mass of centipedes swarming over a U-shaped object. Looking closer, he saw that it was the heel of a boot. Reaching down, he dragged it out. It was an army boot of the type commonly worn by trekkers. There was nothing remarkable about it until he turned it around.

'Agggh!' he gagged. Holding the boot as far from his nose as he could, he peered inside. He could now see the cause of the stench. Inside the boot were the putrid remains of a rotting foot. Still gagging, he swung the boot as far as he could over his shoulder. Suddenly the tunnel did not seem like such a good idea but, at that very moment, something happened to change his mind. He heard the cries of the Snapahuti emerging into the clearing below. Then a new sound exploded across the jungle.

TAT-TAT-TAT-TAT-TAT-TAT-TAT-TAT-TAT-TAT-TAT-TAT-TAT ...

Since when did Snapahuti headhunters carry semi-automatic weapons?

A bullet pierced the brim of his hat, dislodging it from his head. He just managed to grab hold of it as he jumped, feet first, into the tunnel.

To the wide-eyed gibbons, still watching from the jungle canopy, it was as if the earth had swallowed him.

5. Other Bits

Freddy flew as if sliding down a wet slippery dip until a sudden levelling of the tunnel caused his backside to plug into the soft mud about thirty feet down. Wiggling his torch out from under his shirt, he switched it on. A bend in the tunnel meant that he could not see very far. Fortunately, that also meant that his pursuers could not see or shoot him.

He had no choice now but to continue squeezing and sliding down the tunnel. The problem was that he had expected the tunnel to widen, but instead it had quickly narrowed and now squeezed tight about him. He wriggled a few inches but then no more. He was stuck fast. Something sharp dug into the soft flesh of his backside. He considered the contents of the boot he had found near the surface and guessed at what it might be.

Fear overwhelmed him. Pushing and squeezing his burning muscles in every direction, he screamed aloud while the damp clay surrounding him swelled and pushed harder and harder against his tiring body. His madness only made things worse but still he pushed and screamed.

It was useless. All he achieved was the loss of valuable energy. Like the Phantom in quicksand, he was not going anywhere in a hurry. Finally, exhausted and defeated, he stopped.

He tried to block out everything that was happening and just breathe but it was not easy. Why me? spun in his head. Why was he, Freddy O'Toole, caught in that dreadful pickle; wedged in a narrow tunnel where he would surely starve or die of thirst, or, worse still, be slowly eaten alive by the army of bugs he could already feel creeping about him? Why had he not kept Gruntenguile in sight? Why had he not eaten that chocolate bar when he had the chance?

A noise came from somewhere above. A mixture of rough voices, evil laughter, and nasty activity. Strange how we can tell when people are up to no good. There is a certain tone that is unmistakable, and that is exactly what Freddy heard at that moment. At first, he thought it must be Japanese soldiers. The world was at war and the Japanese had been pushing closer and closer with each passing day, but the voices did not sound oriental. They sounded German. But what would the Nazis be doing in Timor so many miles from Europe?

The Snapahuti retreated to the thick cover of the jungle where they watched from the sweating darkness as a smaller group of larger men gathered around the entrance of the cave. Freddy did not know what they were planning, but he knew it was probably not anything nice. He was right. They were untying a bag containing a slither of highly poisonous snakes.

Freddy, of course, did not know this, but he knew he had to keep moving down the tunnel. Straining and pushing every part of his body in every direction, he searched for a weakness in the perfect, pounding pressure that surrounded him. It was no good. He could not move. To make matters worse, his machete was sticking out like a barb into the mud. He squirmed and heaved himself up the tunnel so that the sheath of the machete could lay tight against his leg, but he made no progress.

His torch was still pointing up the tunnel, and when he stopped to rest, he saw that something was moving there. For a moment, he thought he was seeing things because it looked like a bent line of white spots was sliding down the tunnel towards him. Then, as the spots drew closer, he realised what they really were: black and white banded snakes. His boyhood obsession with listing reptiles enabled him to identify them as Malayan kraits.[6] A single bite would give him a 50 percent chance of survival—if he received urgent medical attention. Maybe it was luck, maybe it was the encouragement provided by the poisonous snakes sliding his way, but Freddy gave one more determined wriggle and this time he felt himself slip a little further down the tunnel. It was only a foot or two, but it was something. Inspired by the movement, he hunched his shoulders as close to his body as he could and wriggled with renewed desperation.

Malayan kraits are shy by nature, but Freddy knew that fear and an instinct for survival would result in them making a meal of his face when they found it blocking the tunnel. They were now a few feet away and he could see their beady eyes, as cold as marbles, and flicking tongues, sensing something ahead. They slithered to within less than a foot when Freddy slipped again. A little further this time, but another cruel narrowing of the tunnel trapped him once more. The snakes continued to slide towards him. Within seconds, they were again within striking distance. Rearing their heads, their forked tongues seemed to lick their lips. Freddy closed his eyes for what he believed was the last time, when he heard a rumbling from the world above as the afternoon rains burst over the jungle. The snakes were poised, ready to strike. Water trickled into the tunnel, filling the space around Freddy. The thought ran through his mind that if he got lucky he might drown before the snakes struck. Instead of drowning him, however, the water made the sticky clay walls even more slippery, and he suddenly slid and popped out the narrow part of the tunnel like a rat from a drain. He rocketed down a muddy chute with the

---

[6] *Bungarus candidus*—kraits are a poisonous snake found throughout Southeast Asia.

Malayan kraits still sliding behind him. The only things to slow his slide were jagged rocks that cut into his already bruised and battered skin. Shock waves rattled through his bones to his skull and back down to his bum and then back again as the parts of his body competed for their share of the pain racing through him. *Please make there be something soft at the bottom of this, pleeeease make there be something soft at the bottom of this* was the only thought Freddy was capable of during that terrifying slide. Given the way his day was going, he felt that there probably would not be a soft landing at the bottom—but he was wrong!

6. Dog-Eat-Dog

As Freddy crashed into the putrid corpses and chiropter guano that covered the floor of the cave,[7] he could not help thinking that he lived in a dog-eat-dog world.

'Blazes,' he cried.

Under normal circumstances, he would have spent more time feeling sorry for himself, but the thought of the snakes and the murderous henchmen above got him moving.

Wishing Gruntenguile was still by his side, he tried to stand up, but the guano-rotted bones gave way under his feet, and he fell face first into the black stewing sea of guano. Rolling to his feet, he wiped his face clean with his hat and looked around. It was a massive cavern. Apart from this he knew only that it was somewhere in the middle of the Timorese jungle.

A faint scratching sound clawed the air. Eyes adjusting to the weak light, he saw that everything around him was crawling. Something scaly scurried up his arm.

'Cockroaches,' he cried.

His disgust at these ancient, black creatures was short-lived as a shower of mud and human bones, which he must have loosened in his terrifying slide down the chute, smashed into him almost knocking him over once more. A skull rebounded off his own and fell onto the guano at his feet. It looked up at him as if it was just as surprised as he was.

'Thanks for dropping in,' said Freddy

---

[7] *Chiropter guano* is more commonly known as bat crap.

The skull stared blankly back at him.[8]

Next Freddy saw a fading glow of light, which he quickly realised was the head of his torch sinking into the guano. Picking it up, he pointed the light upwards into the tunnel directly above him. He could just make out the white bands of the kraits still snaking their way towards him. It was time to get moving. He shone the torch around the cavern and, about twenty feet away, saw a stone ledge, raised about a foot above the sea of guano. It seemed to run along the edge of the cavern. He sloshed as quickly as he could to this ledge, clambered up, and shone his torch back to the spot from where he had fled. The snakes slid down one at a time. Even as they fell into the cavern, all he could see were the white bands. Breathing a sigh of relief, he watched them slither to the opposite side of the cavern, gorging on cockroaches as they went.

In the fresh silence, Freddy listened for sounds from above. He hoped that whoever was up there would assume that he was now dead. Not so long ago hardly anyone had known he was alive. Why did so many people now want him dead? He shook the question from his head. There were many things about his situation that he would have liked to change, but he needed to focus on the one big positive—he was alive. He knew that if things were going to stay that way, he needed to keep his wits about him.

He held the torchlight on the white dots of the snakes until they disappeared into the darkness on the other side of the cavern.

Feeling safe from the snakes, Freddy examined his poop-stained hat and poked his finger in the most recent hole. He wiped it across his pants, placed it back on top of his head, and shone his torch along the side of the cavern,

---

[8] The skull's former owner, if my further research serves me correctly, had never been fond of black humour and death had done nothing to change that.

illuminating rocks that had been drowned in darkness for he knew not how long. The beam slid slowly over a rippled rock wall that could easily have been the surface of a newly discovered planet.

Then, to his surprise, as the beam of light roved further along the wall, the surface suddenly changed. It no longer had the appearance of natural rock but of a man-made wall—flat, but not quite. Straining his eyes, he thought that he could see something on the surface. He made his way along the ledge for a closer look, probing everywhere with his torch as he went. Edging nearer he could see the wall more clearly, but it was not making any more sense. Staring hard at the surface of the rock wall, he allowed his eyes time to fully adjust to the light and sift through the haze of particles that hung in the air. He had made up his mind to be completely quiet in case his pursuers were still listening from above, but he could not help gasping,

'Blazes!'

The wall was covered in petroglyph carvings, scoured by the centuries but still visible. This was surely the reason the Professor had sent him on the expedition. This was the discovery the owner of the skull, now housing a family of cockroaches and sinking into the sea of guano behind him, had given their life to see.

He shone his torch upwards and guessed that the area covered by the carvings stood about twenty feet high. Then he lowered the beam.

Hundreds, maybe thousands of figures covered every inch of the rock. There were both men and women, but there was something brutish about them. Some were running with spears, others throwing spears, or leaping in the air, or lighting fires. The carving told the story of a hunt and the feast which followed, but something was wrong. Normally, these types of carvings were made by civilisations that were more recent, more 'civilised'. The scenes Freddy was looking at, however, were more typical of Stone Age cave paintings drawn with ochre and a heavy hand. Not carved in this precise manner.

The torch light continued to move over the figures until it discovered the object of their hunt. A huge beast rearing on its hind legs, spears spiking from its body. Freddy had seen similar cave paintings before in Professor Dupler's books, but this scene was different. The animal here was massive and towered over its attackers. That would not have been unusual if it were a woolly mammoth, but it was not. It was a lizard, something like a Komodo dragon (also on Freddy's list of 'Reptiles to Avoid in My Lifetime') only four or five times larger. Freddy would have been even more amazed had he not already seen something like it before—in the Arnhem Land cave.

He stared in amazement. It took a conscious effort and a shake of his head to return to his exploration of the other parts of the petroglyph. Dragging the torch beam away from the creature, he stretched it out along the wall until it faded into the darkness. Nothing. He was about to take another look at the hunted animal when a sudden shaft of light from a large crack in the overhanging rock, spotlighted an object on the edge of the torch beam. Curious to see what it was, he walked towards it.

Glancing up as he went, he noticed that the crack through which the light was creeping ran for some fifty feet through the rock in the roof of the cave. The sun had reached a point overhead perfectly in line with the tilted bedding plane. Water was dripping in from the sudden downpour, and the sound echoed eerily in the stillness of the cave.

Even as he drew closer, Freddy was not able to make out what the object was. The sun's rays were too bright after his time spent in near darkness, and his eyes could not pick out the detail. It was not until he was standing directly before it that lines and a shape began to appear. Everywhere else, the wall was covered by the curved lines of nature, but this object had the straight, angular lines of a device, but not a machine as Freddy or you and I know them to be.

On closer inspection, it seemed to be a crystal outcrop, spearing out from the wall at strange angles and lengths. In the centre of the cluster, a single transparent shaft stuck out like a sword about three feet from the wall. It looked in colour and transparency like quartz and tapered into a sharp, needle-like point.

Drawing his eyes away from the crystal, Freddy noticed that the carved figures surrounding it were kneeling before it as if it was a God. Above the sword was another petroglyph—an eye—human, but not quite. Freddy took off his hat and looked at the hatpin the Professor had stuck there at the start of the expedition. It was the same.

Freddy had lived with anthropologists his entire life. He had read most of the books in the Professor's library, and his mind clicked through his memorised inventory of weird artefacts, but he had never seen anything like this!

Bending forward, he ran his eyes along the edge of the crystal. It was razor sharp—as if honed by machinery. But if the object were man-made, he thought, it should be more ordered and mathematical, not the chaos of irregular shapes he saw before him. At the same time, the location of the crystal in the middle of the petroglyph suggested that it could not possibly have formed naturally. Later, Freddy would come to understand the absurdity of seeing things as either natural or man-made, but at that time, his mind could only make sense of the object by classifying it as man-made.

It was too weird. He glanced suspiciously around the cave. This had to be a joke. A brilliantly planned hoax! Like Orson Welles pretending the Earth was under attack by Martians.[9] Surely Gruntenguile was hiding somewhere in the cave and doing his best not to burst out laughing. Freddy shone his torch around the cave one more time but all he could see was ghostly, grey rock surrounded by darkness. He was alone.

Something cracked under his feet like a snapped twig. Pointing his torch to the ground, he noticed to his horror that he was standing on a mouldering pile of human bones. Some were almost white, but others were in varying stages of yellowing decay. Those ground into the mud beneath were blackened and so brittle they crunched under his feet like shell grit. Repulsed by the sight of the bones, he returned his attention to the sword-like crystal.

Just as a wave of understanding had welled within him in the Arnhem Land cave some five months earlier, a similar sense washed over him.

Deep down, he knew that what he saw before him was real. He knew also that what his instincts told him about the object was real. A creeping chill slid like a melting iceblock down his spine.

He was still staring directly at the tip of the sword when suddenly, something else quite unexpected happened. The already dim light suddenly faded as if a dark cloud had passed overhead. This was followed by a slight scraping sound, a sprinkle of rock particles, and an enormous thud of biomass. Freddy was pummelled to the ground by over 300 pounds of writhing muscle. His torch was knocked from his hand and flew some distance away. It threw a spotlight on Freddy and the giant snake, which had just fallen on top of him. His knowledge of snakes told him

---

[9] On October 30, 1938, Orson Welles broadcast an adaptation of H.G. Wells' novel, *The War of the Worlds*. Listeners tuning in after the show had started, missed the disclaimer at the beginning, and believed that Martians were actually attacking Earth. This is of course quite ridiculous as Mars has been uninhabited for eons.

instantly that, given its size and his location, it could only be a python. Despite the dire nature of the encounter, he also recalled the scientific name: Python reticulate,[10] from his list of 'Reptiles to Avoid in My Lifetime'—yet another failure! It was a massive beast, almost thirty feet in length. He knew he had to think quickly to survive but all he could think of was to scream, 'Blazes! What are the chances of that? What are the blazing chances of that? How often are you standing in a cave beneath the Timorese rainforest with a crack directly overhead, and how often does a 300-pound reticulated python accidentally fall through a crack like that?' He repeated this cry as he desperately sought and found the snake's head and grabbed hold of the neck just below the jawbone.

'How often do you get attacked by a slither of Malayan krait and a reticulated python in the same day? What are the blazing chances of that?' The words screeched despairingly through the cave as the powerful body twined around him. It was a huge, single-limbed, single-minded thing. If only he could grab his machete—but that meant releasing one hand from the snake's head, and that would surely have been fatal because he was struggling to hold it with two hands. If he let one go, the snake would have his head in one bite. Freddy fought suffocation and panic. His mind flew in all sorts of useless directions. Why was he, of the millions of people on Earth, the one standing in that spot, in that cave, at that moment? Why had he saved that chocolate bar for later?

The snake's head twisted and broke free of Freddy's grip. It reared above him and briefly caught the light still sneaking into the cave. In that instant, Freddy felt

[10] The reticulated python is the world's longest snake and reptile. They inhabit the jungles of Southeast Asia, and, although they do not usually attack and eat humans, there are a number of recorded instances. This particular snake must also have been somewhat disoriented after its fall.

totally justified in his long-standing dislike of reptiles. The lower body of the snake wrapped around his torso and squeezed tightly. Soon, his ribs would crack like sticks. The snake could feel Freddy's heart beating, and it would not relax until that beating stopped. The head plunged and the eyes sent darts of terror through every atom of Freddy's crushing body. Freddy was a thing to be destroyed: a dangerous living thing that could be a tasty dead thing. Freddy was running out of instants. He saw the descending flash of the fangs and just for the tiniest smidge of a second, the crystal sword protruding from the wall behind. His mind, almost frozen as it was with fear by now, seized upon that one small chance. Remembering that a snake's heart lay near the first coil of their body, he regained his hold on the snake and pushed it back with all his might. The giant snake swung back to break free of Freddy's grasp. It almost made it, but with one last remaining gasp of strength, Freddy forced the snake backwards onto the point of the crystal sword, which ran through the snake with a horrifying ease, piercing its heart and popping out the other side. The writhing of the python's body sent Freddy flying and his head smashed onto the floor of the cave. Had he not been so terrified he may have passed out. Instead, he lay barely conscious on the ground gazing in horror at the snake's pierced body and piercing eyes. He had survived, but what followed was even more amazing.

As he watched, the snake began to fade, as if the very atoms that composed it were pulling apart but at the same time contracting inwards to the point of the crystal sword. Freddy blinked in disbelief.

By the time he reopened his eyes, the snake had vanished.

7. The Crystal Sword

Freddy eyes remained fixed on the point of the crystal sword, which, just moments before, had ended the life of the giant python.

Or had it?

There was no blood. Not a drop. Everything was just as it had been earlier.

In the world above, the sun had moved on and light was fading. The grey storm clouds that had saved him in the tunnel a little earlier were now black battleships, booming and cracking over the drenching jungle. Water still dripped into the cave and filled it with a hypnotic trickling. As the darkness deepened, Freddy felt like he was sinking into a bottomless pit.

Dragging himself to his feet, he never once took his eyes off the tip of the crystal sword. His stomach churned and his heart thumped hard against his ribcage, but his brain was clearing. He felt weirdly as if he was seeing things from way above where he was standing.

'Blazes,' he whispered. 'I think I know what I have to do.'

'That would be a first.' The voice came from just behind him. Freddy wheeled around to see who was there. No one. Staring into the darkness, he strained his eyes for some sign of movement.

'Grrrnnt . . . down here, Little Boss.'

Freddy looked down and jumped back in surprise.

'Gruntenguile!' he cried. 'How'd you get in here with all those killers outside?'

'I used the stairs.'

'You what?'

Gruntenguile shone his more powerful light into the darkness on the other side of the cavern and there, sure enough, was a set of steps carved into the rock face. It even had a handrail on the outside.

'Thanks for telling me,' whisper-shrieked Freddy, remembering the killers listening above.

'And thanks for losing me back there in the jungle … grrrnnt,' said Gruntenguile.

'I'm sorry,' said Freddy. 'I must have been running faster—'

'Never mind, Little Boss. We are both here and you are still alive.'

'And I think we have discovered why the Professor sent us on this expedition,' said Freddy, turning to the crystal sword.

'Not quite, Little Boss. I think I am starting to understand what the Professor had in mind for us and, if I am right, this sword is just a door.'

'A door?' Freddy turned and looked at the tip of the crystal sword.

'I think you know what you have to do,' said Gruntenguile.

Freddy looked at Gruntenguile as if his head was spinning. He had always been a little crazy, but he seemed to have really lost it this time.

Even as he was thinking this, however, a feeling was growing in Freddy about why he was there and what he must do. His hand moved to his side and, without thinking, he felt in his pocket for his father's watch and ran his fingers over his parent's names for luck, and courage.

Standing in the hollow, water cascading darkness of the cave, he knew what he had to do. He had always known. It was just that the thought was too terrifying.

That was the problem—the thought. If he could just banish thought, then he could follow his instincts.

Freddy cleared his head. It was surprisingly easy at first. Gruntenguile and the rest of the world faded away and all that remained was the crystal sword. He stared at it until he imagined he could see the very last atom on the tip.

It was not the first time he had seen that deadly point.

He had stood before it in childhood dreams. Terrified, yet knowing. His gaze fixed on the pointy end of the sword. Slowly, then suddenly, the scene would zoom and turn inside out until it was not Freddy looking at the crystal sword, but the crystal sword looking at Freddy. Next thing he was running forward in an agony of slow motion towards the pin-sharp tip. The moment the point pierced his heart he would wake in a shiver of sweat.

Freddy recalled those nights and sensed what it meant.

He knew what he had to do.

Gruntenguile was right. The crystal sword was a door, and his heart was the key. It was so simple but—at the same time—so absolutely, beyond stupid terrifying. Not to mention totally crazy.

Freddy was about to step back from the sword when, suddenly, Gruntenguile placed both hands in the middle of his back and pushed him forward. The tip of the sword ran through Freddy's heart like a hot skewer through a marshmallow. He later told me—and I am quite happy to take his word for it—that it felt like every atom in his body was being sucked like grains of sand in a whirlpool into a swirling, blackening, cruel centre. Like a plug-pulled ocean. The pain surged beyond description until suddenly, his body was gripped, and shaken, and shredded, as if by the most vicious beast you can imagine. Then swallowed into a darkness like returning to the womb.

PANGEA

NORTH CHINA

EUROPE

NORTH AMERICA

SOUTH AMERICA

AFRICA

INDIA

·DOYLIAN LAIR·

AMAZONIA

ANTARCTICA

Part 2:

A Deadly Place

8. Pangea (Gondwanaland), 250Ma[11]

Freddy's first thought was that he was dead.

His next was that, if he thought he was dead, he probably wasn't.

The cuts and bruises from his recent escapades ached. His heart burned. Recalling the crystal sword, he shuddered. *Wait 'til I get my hands on Gruntenguile*, he thought.

Sniffing the air, he almost puked. It smelled like rotten egg gas[12], blended with body odour, and bat guano.

Next, he heard a faint rustling, like wind through leaves.

His hands rested on his chest over the point pierced by the crystal sword. He slid them slowly to the ground. Spreading his fingers, he felt the soil. Gritty and wet. Then he opened his eyes. The glare was blinding. He squinted and rolled to his side, shielding his eyes with one hand. Questions rattled through his head.

Where am I?

Why am I here?

Why didn't I ask a few more questions along the way?

Will that bio-freeze bag really stop my chocolate from melting?

More than anything, he wished that he had been able to squeeze a few more details out of Professor Dupler. Freddy had gone along with the expedition thinking that it might have something to do with finding his long-lost father. That had been enough for him.

---

[11] Ma is the preferred abbreviation for 'million years ago' used in this text. It is worth noting also that this date is an approximation and that time itself is considered an absurd concept on the more civilised planets. None of which, by the way, are in our galaxy.

[12] Hydrogen sulphide (H_2S).

Now he was not sure of anything. The understanding that had burned inside him when facing the crystal sword was gone. He wanted to be back home in Darwin. To discover that he had just had the weirdest dream after listening to one of Gruntenguile or the Professor's cock-and-bull stories.

The problem was that he was hurting too much for it to be a dream. Any movement caused pain in some part of his body.

Slowly, his eyes focused on a ghostly, shimmering world of green light. A fern drooping under the heavy rays of the sun swayed suddenly in a gust of dry wind and brushed his face. Further proof, he thought, that he was alive.

Something glistened above his head, like a drop of water on a leaf. Except, it was too big to be a drop of water. Freddy shook his head and blinked. Opening his eyes again, he could unfortunately see more clearly.

An eye stared menacingly down at him. Just to the right, another eye, just as menacing. The eyes belonged to the giant python he had so recently parted company with, in the Timorese cave.

Over three hundred pounds plus of twisting, crushing vertebrae and muscle collapsed on top of him for the second time that day. 'Blazes,' cried Freddy. 'What are the chances?' He screamed aloud in his despair. 'To have unbelievably survived! For this!' The only hope he had left was Gruntenguile. Surely, he knew what the crystal sword could do and would not be far behind him. Although not the biggest of fellows, he was surprisingly strong. He could do some serious damage to the python if he got his hands on Freddy's machete.

But, as precious seconds ticked by, it occurred to Freddy that if Gruntenguile did not follow him straight away, the chances were that he was not following him at all.

All he could do now was clutch the narrowing point of the python's monstrous body just below the jaw and hold on as best he could as his strength drained from his crushing body and arms. What energy he had left he used to scream for Gruntenguile, but to no avail. As both his grip on the snake and his life slowly faded, random thoughts spun in his head like bubbles in a whirlpool. The last of them was a huge pang of regret at not eating his chocolate bar. As he passed out, there was no way of knowing if he would ever wake again, but he did not like his chances.

Freddy would later describe that day as 'the day he couldn't die, even if his life depended on it.'

9. Koia

When Freddy woke, the only part of his body where he could still feel pressure was his right hand. Someone was holding it.

He did not want to open his eyes after his recent near-death experiences, but curiosity got the better of him.

At first, all he could see was white. A white sky, dirty in patches and stitched at the edges.

No, not a sky—a tent! A white hide tent and, to the side, slightly blurred, a human figure. His eyes sought and found a face.

As it came into focus, he wondered briefly whether he was in Heaven with an angel watching over him. Blazes! What were the blazing chances of that? A second glance and he was not so sure.

The face was not sweet and saintly like the angels he had seen in the *Illustrated Bible* in Professor Dupler's library. It was a strong face framed by thick, peach-coloured dreadlocks. The heat caused tiny pearls of sweat to speck her face and run in little rivers down her brow and cheeks. Bronzed skin stretched like silk over her shoulder blades and the tight muscles of her upper body. Beneath this, she wore a soft leather top like a corset fastened with a leather strap down the front.

'Koia . . .'

Her voice startled Freddy. It came from way down her throat. Looking up at her face, he noticed that it was strong-boned and beautiful. He shrugged to indicate that he had not quite caught what she had said.

'Koia,' she repeated. Then she smiled like someone who had just learned how.

Freddy raised his finger and pointed to her. 'Koia?'

She laughed and Freddy smiled, thinking that she was relieved to know that he was alive and well.

He then pointed to himself and said, 'Freddy.'

She nodded but strangely did not repeat the name to check if she had heard it correctly.

'Where am I?' he asked.

She did not reply, and Freddy guessed she did not understand a word of English. Maybe that would not be such a bad thing. Here was a beautiful girl who he could say absolutely nothing to offend. Freddy could have looked at her all night, but she bent down and roughly pushed his eyes shut to indicate that he needed to sleep. He was surprised by her strength and too weak to resist. He gave in without a fight. He was so exhausted from the events of the past few days that it was not long before he once more drifted into a deep sleep.

10. L for Lucky

Freddy's eyes flicked open.

Sweat ran across his face like little wet bugs. The tent he had been sleeping in was now more like a glasshouse than a shade. It glared above him like a giant light globe.

He could no longer smell his own foul odour or bat guano, but the air still reeked of rotten egg gas. Smoke from a fire was also wafting into the tent, along with another smell. It took him a while to tease it out from the more unpleasant odours. It was sweeter and somehow familiar, and it soon set his stomach growling. It was the smell of roasting flesh—maybe chicken. It reminded him of how long it had been since he had eaten. It blew in on a hot breeze, which gently whipped the door of the tent, making a flapping sound as regular as his heartbeat. When this noise suddenly stopped, Freddy glanced in that direction to see why. The hide door was drawn and a head, blurred by light, and Freddy's drowsiness, peered through the opening.

Freddy's head still ached and for a moment, he was confused and could not remember where he was. His mind racing and stumbling, he squinted at the intruding face. Blinded by the light flooding in, he could not see clearly. Still, something about it looked familiar. It looked a little like the girl who had been holding his hand, only older.

'Who are you?' he cried, dragging himself onto his elbow.

The face disappeared and the flap of the tent was left once more to the mercy of the wind. Freddy kept staring in that direction until it was flung open again, and this time the face of the girl who had been holding his hand earlier appeared.

Freddy calmed a little. 'Good morning,' he guessed. 'How's the weather?' It was a ridiculous question especially considering he believed she could not understand a word he said.

Koia confirmed this by making no reply. She walked across and sat on the edge of his hammock. Then, placing a bowl and cloth on a side table, she grabbed his hand as before. Freddy tried to stay calm, but it was not easy.

'I . . . I'm feeling better,' he lied.

He was in fact still pretty battered and bruised. A bandage was wrapped around a large puncture wound just below his elbow. There was also a large cut under his left eye, which, though covered in a foul-smelling poultice and his Band-Aid, would leave a permanent L-shaped scar.

L for lucky, he would later claim.

She smiled, once more like someone who was not used to the expression. Still, it made Freddy feel better. He pulled himself up so that his back rested on the crumpled animal skin that had been his pillow. His body did not ache quite so much, and he was less drowsy than the last time he had woken.

He looked around the tent, but the tail of one eye never left the girl. She was really no older than he was. Maybe the same age.

Koia placed the bowl and cloth on a small table on the other side of Freddy's hammock. She sat on a stool opposite. Then, reaching over Freddy, she grabbed the cloth, and dipped it in the bowl. Her biceps bulged as she wrung it out before padding it across his brow.

'Can you speak English?' he asked.

She did not reply and continued at her work as if Freddy had said nothing.

As she wiped his face, Freddy cast his mind back over his recent adventures. He had imagined he was on a safari through the jungles of southern Asia where somehow, somewhere, there was a chance he might find his father. Maybe he was held captive by Sulu sea pirates, or chained in a POW camp, or maybe even hiding from the world for who knows what reason (he was a *curious chap* after all) in the blurry jungles of Sumatra. He did not expect whatever it was that was happening now. Nothing seemed right. Even the air did not smell right. These thoughts crashing around his head soon grew too big and crazy for him to make sense of, so he gave up, and focused on his nurse instead.

She was wearing the same leather corset, loosely tied at the top. Freddy had lived a bachelor's life with both Professor Dupler and his father for sixteen years. He was not used to being so close to a girl. For the past few years, he had been studying the bare-breasted photographs in the Professor's anthropology books with more curiosity than they warranted from a purely ethnographic standpoint.[13] Outside the occasional encounter with Lucy Wong and her mother, however, he had no firsthand experience of girls.

Freddy blushed and looked down. This drew his attention to the fact that she was wearing a short skirt made of the same soft leather. Her legs were athletic and her feet bare and hard as though she often went barefoot.

When Freddy looked up again, he found himself gazing directly into Koia's icy-grey eyes. His pulse flat-lined, but he tried to hold her gaze. 'I'm feeling better,' he repeated. 'I might get up and move about. Maybe have something to eat. Start getting my strength back.'

Koia ignored him and continued to rub his face with the damp cloth. It was cool and refreshing and Freddy was enjoying being pampered after the many recent attempts to kill him. Her hands were strong. He could feel this through the cloth. She moved her attention to his neck and chest

---

[13] Ethnography is the study of different cultures.

and began working her way down his body when Freddy suddenly realised that he was naked. Absolutely starkers! Where were his clothes? He sat up, pointing to his naked upper body while repeating the word 'clothes' until Koia finally understood his meaning. Laughing, she pointed to a wooden stool in the corner. Lying on top of it were his clothes. They looked clean but there had been no effort to fold them, and they lay in a crumpled heap. On top sat his towelling hat. It was clean of crap and, apart from the holes, which were still better in the hat than his head, it was looking in better nick than the last time he had worn it. Freddy's machete leaned like an old friend on the side of the stool. Beside that lay all his worldly possessions: a note pad and one and a half pencils, his scruffy toothbrush, and his pocket watch.

'Blazes,' sighed Freddy.

Turning back to Koia, he pointed to the opening of the tent to indicate that he wanted her to leave so that he could dress. She seemed puzzled that Freddy should feel it necessary that she leave the tent. Finally, with his animal skin bedsheet draped around him, he led her to the entrance and ushered her outside.

'Come back later—I need to get dressed,' he explained.

Koia briefly stood her ground at the door of the tent and, once more, Freddy felt her strength.

If she had chosen to resist, he did not fancy his chances. Instead, she smiled and stared deep into his eyes until he thought he might melt under her gaze. That look convinced Freddy that there was something funny going on. Frightening—but at the same time—interesting. He had never felt such a connection with another person.

Koia released her hold on him and slipped out of the tent. For a while, he just breathed. Then, needing to focus on inanimate objects for a while, he turned around and inspected the inside of the tent.

There was not much to see. The hammock he had occupied for the past day or so stood in the centre. Instead of a mattress, a piece of the same white hide as the tent was stretched between two branches that had been shaped with an axe and strapped together with lengths of plaited hide. Alongside the bed was the small table with the bowl of water and wet cloth. Next to that was a three-legged stool. The only other things he could see was a collection of weapons. Most of them were spears similar to those used by indigenous tribes in Freddy's time, but there was also a double-bladed axe unlike anything Freddy had seen before. The spears were wooden and primitive. The axe was solid metal from handle to blade. The spears seemed to be for hunting, and all indigenous people needed to hunt. The axe seemed to have a different purpose altogether. Freddy picked it up and ran a finger down the side of the blade. It was deadly sharp, and the feel of cold metal sent a shiver galloping across his scalp. He returned the axe to the exact position it had been before and made his way to his clothes.

Rummaging through the pile, he found his underpants and blushed at the thought of someone else having washed them. He hoped it had not been Koia. Apart from that thought, it felt good to be putting on clean clothes. It was like putting on his old self. Once he had dressed, he checked his watch. It was still ticking so he popped it back into his pocket, looked towards the flap of the tent, and braced himself.

He had been resting for two, maybe three days. The inside of his tent, and Koia, were all he had seen of wherever it was that he now found himself. He made his way to the opening and pulled the flap of the tent aside. He should have waited for his eyes to adjust a little but, instead, he took a couple of steps before stopping to look around.

First, he looked up at the sun to get a feel for the time of day. It was visible only by its glare in a hazy sky, but he guessed it was mid-afternoon. Beneath the sun, grey, pine-like trees surrounded the clearing in which he stood. The wind played an eerie tune in their stunted branches. Lowering his gaze even further, he saw that about thirty tents similar to his own edged the clearing.

Then a sudden cry made him look to the middle of the camp where many of the inhabitants were gathered. They were sitting, or standing, or walking, beside a long fire pit that glowed and smoked in a hollowed bed about three feet wide and thirty feet long.

Above the fire pit, a line of charred stakes on each side supported the roasting meal he had smelled earlier. This meal stretched the full length of the fire pit. It was his old wrestling chum, the reticulated python.

11. Polydora

Freddy did not think that he could ever feel sympathy for the giant snake. But the two occasions that it had tried to skewer his head like a melon bite with its knife-sized fangs seemed a long time ago now. As much as he hated reptiles, he had to admit that it was a beautiful creature.

As he stared, a woman strode over to the roasting snake, drew a large blade from a scabbard at her hip, and cut a big chunk of meat from its side. She bit into the flesh with a ferocity that reminded Freddy of the beast she was eating.

Freddy then ran his eyes over the other inhabitants of the camp. The first thing that struck him was that they all looked similar, and it slowly dawned on him that there were no men, only women. *The men must be out hunting*, he thought.

The women were dressed like Koia in two-piece outfits made from soft leather in various shades of tan. Like most indigenous groups, they were lean and healthy.

Near the fire, two groups of young girls were standing about a cricket pitch apart, throwing spears at each other. They dodged and caught each other's spears with great skill and yelled in a wild tongue that sounded like nothing Freddy had ever heard before. The adults ignored their dangerous game.

It soon occurred to him that even among the children there seemed to be no boys, except possibly, among the very youngest, where it was hard to tell anyway. By the time he had made this realisation, everyone in the camp had noticed him. One by one, they turned and looked at him as if he might be even tastier than the snake.

Freddy had left his tent confidently. Koia's care of him had made him feel that he was in a safe place. Now he was not so sure. He stood and stared while the women stared back at him. Drums started in the distance and Freddy jumped at the sound.

Toom . . . Toom . . . Toom . . . Toom . . . Toom . . . Toom . . .
TOOM!

He had a vague sense that this beat may have been in the background from time to time, as he lay semi-conscious, but he could not be sure. The beat repeated. Six smaller beats followed by a large angry thump as if the drummer had just discovered a bug crawling across the skin of the drum.

Toom . . . Toom . . . Toom . . . Toom . . . Toom . . . Toom . . .
TOOM!

He was still standing dumbly looking at the faces looking at him when Koia came from nowhere and grabbed him, her fingers digging deep into his shoulders. Turning him around, she pushed him towards the tent. She clearly wanted Freddy out of the way, but as sensible as that seemed, Freddy resisted. He could not go any longer without some answers to the questions that were now spinning in his head. Standing before the crystal sword a few days earlier, he had some sense of what might happen, but he would never have acted on that sense. If Gruntenguile had not pushed him, he would have still been standing there.

He was lost, alone, and completely clueless.

'Who are you? Where? What? *When?*' The last word shrieked from Freddy and drew even more attention. The children and many of the women came closer to hear his raving.

'*When? When? When?*' Freddy screamed the words into the hot air where they mixed with the rhythmic *Toom . . . Toom . . . Toom* of the drums.

Toom . . . Toom . . . Toom . . . Toom . . . Toom . . . Toom . . .
TOOM!

Thwack!

Freddy turned and saw a long metal-tipped spear quivering from the timber frame of his tent, an inch or two from his left ear. He stared at the cold, barbed point of the spear before slowly running his eyes along the length of its shaft to the throwing end, and beyond that to the direction from which it had been thrown. Twenty yards away, staring at Freddy with impish eyes, stood a girl of little more than twelve years of age. She was covered in dirt and had she not been smiling, and her teeth flashing white, she would have been hard to see.

The older women laughed at the astonished look on Freddy's face.

Koia controlled herself enough to only smile as she forced him through the opening and into the tent. 'Polydora,' she explained.

Freddy took this to be the name of the filthy brat who had thrown the spear at him.

Koia led Freddy to his bed. 'I don't need any more rest,' he protested. 'I'm really okay. If people could just stop trying to kill me—'

Koia was not a good listener. She forced Freddy towards his hammock and pushed him onto it. He tried to resist but she was too strong, and he fell helplessly onto the hide, which creaked under his weight. Then, to his surprise, Koia jumped on top of him, straddling his body. The inside of the tent was fuzzy after the bright light of the outside world. Having this wild girl sitting on his pounding chest made things even fuzzier. Her dreadlocked hair fell on his face. The soft animal fur that was his pillow elevated his head, and he found himself once more guessing at Koia's age. Her dreadlocks tickled his nose and he felt strangely terrified of sneezing. Her grey eyes looked deep into

Freddy's. They pierced his heart as ferociously as the spear might have pierced his skull a few moments earlier.

The events of the past few weeks had made Freddy accustomed to uncertainty but even when the python was crushing him, he had at least known what he should try to do. His heart raced so fast it was suddenly using all the oxygen in his body, and he thought he might pass out.

He had just made a decision that he needed to do something—he didn't know what—when Koia bent forward, cupped her hands behind his head, and pulled Freddy towards her. Freddy had watched enough Clark Gable films to know what was coming next.[14] He closed his eyes and leaned forward.

'Ouch!' They butted heads.

'I'm terribly sorry—' Freddy began, but she placed her hand on his mouth, and pushed herself back into an upright position. Her eyes tried to catch Freddy's but he blushed, avoiding her gaze by staring at the roof of the tent. Outside the drums were still beating:

Toom . . . Toom . . . Toom . . . Toom . . . Toom . . . Toom . . .
TOOM!

Toom . . . Toom . . . Toom . . . Toom . . . Toom . . . Toom . . .
TOOM!

Raising her eyes, Koia looked around as if she was not quite sure how she had come to be on top of Freddy. A hot gust of wind blew in from outside, ruffling her hair. This seemed to rally her thoughts and, looking down at him, she whispered, 'Tonight!'

With that, she leapt off the bed with the same cat-like agility she had jumped onto it.

Freddy remained on his back like roadkill, watching her leave the tent, her hair falling the full length of her back.

The glare of the outside world lit the inside of the tent

---

[14] The most famous and suavest actor of his era, best known for his role in *Gone with the Wind*.

for a moment, and then the flap fell back and resumed its incessant flailing. Freddy was once more alone, his heart beating at a million thumps a minute.

Freddy had been wrestling with thoughts about girls as something more than an anthropological fact for some time. At least once, he had even caught himself thinking of Lucy Wong. He had dismissed those thoughts by imagining that when an opportunity presented, it would somehow take care of itself. Now it seemed like he was right.

Even so, there was something really odd about what had just happened. It ate away at him until he realised what should have been so obvious. She had actually spoken a word in English. She had said, 'Tonight!'

The word reminded Freddy of a song that had been driving him nuts over the radio for the past couple of years:

Someday, when I'm awfully low,
When the world is cold,
Will feel a glow just thinking of you,
And the way you look tonight...

He sang the song wistfully, and terribly out of tune for a while, before returning to the point of Koia using an English word.

Maybe he had not heard her correctly. Maybe he was so wanting to hear a familiar word that his mind had jumbled the letters to make them sound familiar. Perhaps she had really said, 'toohoohoo' or 'timitee' or any number of weird tribal woman words that could have meant anything. Maybe, 'We're having python stew for tea,' or 'How about tidying the tent!'

Freddy thought about these things until his brain hurt, but he was still no closer to an answer. Time slipped by and outside the sun dipped below the horizon. Inside the tent, it was like a light switching off. 'Tonight' seemed to be racing towards him at an ever-increasing speed.

Suddenly the flap of the tent opened, letting in the last pale light of the day. Freddy's heart leapt into his mouth. He turned and smiled only to find the spear-throwing urchin, Polydora, grinning at him from her filthy face. She was really quite cute in a primitive kind of way, but Freddy gave her a haughty look. She was carrying a tray with a bowl in the middle in one hand and a candle in the other. She placed the bowl on Freddy's table and set the candle alongside. Leaning over and looking into the steaming bowl Freddy guessed the contents—stewed python— not one of his favourites. He would have killed for that chocolate bar he had left in his pack.

Polydora stood looking at Freddy for a moment with a mixture of amusement and curiosity. She had the same icy-grey eyes and the same peach-coloured hair as Koia. Raising her hand slowly to his head she ran her fingers through his red mop of hair.

'It's called hair,' said Freddy, growing tired of his novelty.

Polydora laughed, stood up, and walked towards the flap of the tent where she stopped, and, swivelling around, threw an imaginary spear at Freddy. He ducked. Polydora's laughter rung in his ears until it became lost in the beating of the drums.

'Filthy urchin,' said Freddy. Then he turned his attention to his python stew.

It looked disgusting, but he needed to keep his strength up. He had no spoon, so he raised the edge of the bowl to his mouth. Then, remembering a trick Gruntenguile had taught him for taking medicine, he held the bowl with one hand and used the other to pinch the bottom of his nose. 'Bottoms up,' he said, before closing his eyes and pouring some of the stew into his mouth. For a moment, he remembered what he was eating, and it almost slithered back up his throat. The first mouthful was the worst. After that, the rest of the bowl disappeared pretty quickly. When it was gone, he would not have said no to seconds, but he was not keen on sticking his head outside the tent and asking.

Instead, he lay back on his hammock clasping his hands across his belly, which was stretched tighter than it had been for days. There was nothing else to do now except wait for Koia.

To while away the time, he tried to remember the second verse of the song he had recalled earlier. He was just remembering a few more words and tapping out the rhythm on the bottom of his hammock when two arms wrapped around him, and a hand holding a cloth soaked in a vile-smelling chemical clamped down on his nose and mouth. In his few seconds of awareness before passing out, he heard a voice. He was almost certain it was one he had heard before.

'I hope this isn't a mistake,' it said.

He passed out before he could hear a reply.

12. Sure Death Swamp

When Freddy came to, his first thoughts were not about his kidnapping. They were about Koia.

Was it night yet?

Tonight?

He could not kid himself for long. The heat of the sun on his face soon told him that the night was long gone. Apart from that, he had no idea what time of day it was. He tried to roll over but could not move. Leather straps ran across his chest and legs. This made him think that it was best to keep his eyes closed for a while.

The only thing that seemed certain was that he was in a vehicle made with little regard for passenger comfort. It was also very hot. It must have been over a hundred degrees Fahrenheit. Sweat stung his eyes and slid like mercury across his temples, soaking his matted hair.

Straining his ears, he heard nothing but the creak of the cart and the dry wail of the wind. He was just about to open his eyes when a voice cut the silence. Thankfully, unbelievably, it spoke in English. It came from somewhere just forward of where he was lying. He held his breath to catch each word. Apart from Koia's 'tonight', they were the first words spoken in a language he could understand for several days.

'I'm still not sure this is a good idea. I can't believe he will be any use to us,' said the voice. It was clear and confident, and the same voice he had heard in the tent. Freddy felt even more certain that he had heard it before.

'Useful or not, I do not think that we could just leave him there.' The accent was strange.

Why not? thought Freddy. As far as he was concerned, things had been going pretty well.

'Yes, but I know him.'

It took all of Freddy's willpower not to open his eyes at this news. At the same time, an icy shadow drifted over his heart. Freddy did not know that many people.

'Yes, yes,' continued the first voice, 'I know he's here, and I know that says something, but . . .' The speaker searched for the right words.

'But what?'

'He's just not right for this. Maybe if he were really smart, or really sensible, or really *something* . . .'

'So we should have left him to his fate?'

'This is a dangerous game we're playing. Maybe we *do* have to make hard choices like that. The stakes are high in this game, and we can't afford to mess things up. People will die anyway. We just have to make sure that the right people live. I don't think he's the right people.'

'The fact that he's here at all is surely enough to make him the right people.'

Silence.

Freddy kept his eyes closed. One or both of them may have been looking back at him. He held his breath until a sudden jolt threw him upwards. The leather straps dug into him, and he thumped down on the wooden boards. He needed no more convincing that he was travelling in a cart. There was also no sound of a motor, and this suggested that it was being pulled by some beast (or beasts) of burden.

Then, after a few minutes, the voice that Freddy was now convinced he knew said something truly incredible.

'I still have my doubts! Yes—he did travel back 250 million years, but he knows nothing. Everything is instinct without thought, and, if we had left him to his instincts back there, you know what would have happened.'

250 million years?

Travelled back—250 million years?

Even before his father's disappearance six years earlier, Freddy's life had been mysterious. His father's work had always seemed shady—his behaviour shadier. He had no circle of friends. He had no relatives. A fact that came home to roost when his father disappeared, and he was left in the care of Professor Dupler and Gruntenguile. The Professor's expedition to the Arnhem Escarpment the previous year had caused this fog surrounding Freddy's life to thicken like a London pea souper with Jack the Ripper on the prowl. Freddy had put his faith in the Professor even though he seemed shadier than his father. His secrecy over this expedition had meant that Freddy had no idea where or when he was or why he was even there. All he had was the hope that he had carried in his heart for six years. The hope that somehow, somewhere, he might find his father.

Opening his eyes, he found himself lying in the tray of a wooden buggy like the kind you sometimes see in movies about the Wild West. His head was near the backboard. He raised it gingerly as it was still sore from the bumpy ride. The first thing he saw was his hat, which was hanging over one foot. There was no sign of his machete, but his other things were scattered about near his feet, on the floor of the cart. Beyond that, as he had guessed, two people were sitting in the front of the cart. A set of horizontal braids—in outline, not unlike Buck Rogers' spaceship—immediately confirmed his fear as to who one of them was. Freddy groaned.

'So you're awake at last!' said Lucy Wong, without turning around.

'Did you just say, "250 million years back in time"?' Freddy asked.

Lucy turned around to face him. Freddy had last seen her five months earlier on the expedition to Arnhem Land, but she somehow seemed more that five months older. She had turned fifteen since then and, though Freddy could not say what it was, something about her had changed. The man next to her held the reins and looked ahead. He was wearing a khaki shirt over which two bandoliers of shotgun shells made the letter X across his back. A sheath, running halfway down his back, held a sawn-off shotgun. A sweat-stained fedora hat shaded his face.

'Roughly,' said Lucy. 'Where did you think the time portal would take you?'

'I don't know,' said Freddy. 'This may sound stupid, but I really don't know anything about this expedition . . .' Freddy trailed off, reluctant to tell the truth to Lucy about Gruntenguile pushing him. 'Besides, it's not like it had "CAUTION—TIME PORTAL—LICENSED OPERATORS ONLY" written on it or anything.'

'When you do things, you should know why you do them and what the possible consequences might be,' said Lucy.

Of the two beings Freddy had encountered from his old world in the past few days, he preferred the python.

'Can we take a few steps back?' asked Freddy, drawing a deep breath.

'Don't tell me you're going to start asking some questions?'

'Yes,' said Freddy, 'and I'm going to start with this: What the blazes is going on?'

Lucy looked sideways at the driver.

He gazed ahead for a few moments before saying, 'We have to tell him sometime.'

Lucy was silent for a while, and when she spoke again her voice lacked its usual conviction, as if she doubted it was worthwhile telling Freddy at all.

'You have become a player,' she said.

'What?'

'You really don't know?'

'No, I don't,' said Freddy. 'That's why I'm asking.'

'A little late, isn't it?'

'I would have thought so,' said Freddy, 'but, according to you, I am 250 million years earlier.'

The driver turned and smiled at Lucy. 'Touché,' he said. Freddy could now see that he was olive skinned with a Mexican bandito moustache. 'I think you should slow it down a bit,' he continued, 'You know the dangers of finding out too much too soon. Besides, it might be better for now if you two just learn to stop bickering. If we are not united, we don't stand a chance.'

You tell her, thought Freddy.

The driver turned back to face the road or whatever lay ahead. Lucy made a face at him before turning around and asking Freddy, 'Any more stupid questions?'

'How about, why have you kidnapped me?'

'You mean, why have we saved your life?'

Freddy hated people rewording his questions. 'Saved my life? I was getting along pretty well back there, thanks very much—until you showed up.'

Lucy turned to the driver, her mouth open, her hands choking an imaginary idiot.

'Do you see what I mean? He is a fool, and we are even bigger fools for saving him.'

'What do you think you were saving me from?' asked Freddy. 'An attractive girl, not afraid to express her feelings?'

'We rescued you from Amazons, you fool. They have no feelings. They reproduce by conceiving with males, sometimes captured in battle and—'

The driver looked sharply at Lucy. She swallowed the end of her sentence before continuing. 'Usually their captive males must meet certain physical standards, but they must be getting desperate. After conception—which they can achieve in just one night—the male is ritually slaughtered. His flesh eaten and his skin used to produce the leather that they wear. Your little Amazon's outfit was most likely her last lover. If we left you there, you would have been next season's outfit—maybe a handbag—within days.'

The man with the reins turned around for the first time. He wore a faded orange bandana to protect his neck from the searing sun. Beneath that, the top buttons of his shirt were open, revealing a wiry carpet of chest hair and a medallion hanging from a gold chain. It was catching the sun, and Freddy could not make out its shape. The driver nodded at Freddy. 'Pangea is a deadly place. Trust us, you were in great danger.'

'Pangea?' Freddy's knowledge of geography was pretty good, but he could not recall any place called Pangea.

'It's what he calls this place,' said Lucy. 'But, if I were you, geography would be the least of my worries.'

'She's right,' said the driver. 'There are many dangers in Pangea, and you were facing one of the nastiest. From the drums and the preparations in the campsite we had every reason to believe that last night was to be your last.'

Freddy looked up at them in disbelief. He did not want to believe anything bad about Koia. What they were telling him seemed crazy, but, then again, everything that was happening seemed crazy.

'But there is no anthropological evidence for Amazons. They are a part of Greek and later Roman mythology. Besides, didn't they cut off one . . .?'

'Breast?' asked Lucy.

'Yes.'

'It seems not.'

Silence followed as Lucy and the driver shared a series of headshakes and nods. This ended when the driver pushed the reins into Lucy's hands. Then he jumped into the back of the cart and untied the straps from Freddy's feet and chest. As he did so, the medallion that he wore fell out of his shirt and hung directly in front of Freddy's eyes. It was a ring with a quarter-moon crystal as the centre-stone. Freddy felt sure he had seen it, or one just like it, before. He was about to say something, but his instincts silenced him. He took his eyes off the medallion so as not to arouse suspicion and looked instead at the moustachioed face of the man bending over him.

'Thanks,' said Freddy.

The man reached out his hand and introduced himself. 'My name is Haji,' he said, 'and I believe you are Freddy O'Toole.'

Freddy was flattered to be recognised so far from home but still felt uneasy about the ring.

Haji tried to pull Freddy into a sitting position but suddenly grimaced and let him go before clutching his back. 'Bad back,' he explained. Standing up, he stretched and gave Freddy a look-over. 'That's a nasty cut you've got under your eye,' he said. 'It's going to leave a scar.'

'You should see the other guy. I mean, python,' said Freddy, glancing towards Lucy.

Her back stiffened harder than the boards of the cart.

Glancing at them both, Haji smiled before returning to the front and taking up the reins once more.

Stretching his muscles, Freddy squinted up at the filthy sky. It reminded him of London smog as he had seen it in Sherlock Holmes films. He doubted that he was anywhere near London, however, because the only thing he could hear was the clunking of the wheels and the squeak of the wooden axle. The lazy silence beyond that told him they were somewhere deep in the country.

Squinting at the glare, he sat up, placing one hand on the cart to steady himself.

At first, he was disappointed. They were travelling through arid terrain similar to the country he was familiar with in northern Australia. Dry, flat plains, pimpled by rocks. The horizon shimmering with heat. Not a tree in sight. Only the skeletal remains of bushes that seemed to be losing a dogged fight for life. Then he turned his gaze to the other side of the cart, and his understanding of everything changed forever.

They were traveling along the edge of a massive swampland. Above the swamp hung a stewing haze of insects most of which were the size of birds in Freddy's time. Freddy gripped hard on the top paling of the cart. Then he saw something even more remarkable. Plodding along the boggy edge of the swamp were three elephantine beasts. The sight of these creatures told Freddy more than his two travelling companions could have in a thousand words. They were the same or at least similar to the creatures on the walls of the Arnhem Land and Timorese caves. Those discoveries seemed a long time ago to Freddy now, but they did not seem like 250 million years ago.

'Estemmenosochus,' said Haji. 'Their meat is considered a delicacy by the Tribals. They seem slow enough but try catching one! That particular species is *Estemmenosochus uralensis*, the "crowned crocodile".'

Freddy could not take his eyes from their hideous faces—scarred by combat and crowned with satanic antlers. Even from that distance, he could see the cruel outline of their pincer-sharp teeth. One of the beasts looked up at the cart and Freddy almost tore the top rail off, but he need not have worried. The beast's curiosity was soon satisfied, and it turned back to its grazing. Feeling somewhat reassured that the crowned crocodiles were not going to attack, he took his eyes off them and noticed another, smaller species of animal. They were mostly grazing in the middle distance, although some had strayed to the edge of the swamp. They were big lizards, a couple of yards long, with Count Dracula fangs protruding from their scaly lips.

'What about those smaller lizards?' he asked.

'Diictodons,' said Haji as casually as if he were naming a breed of cow grazing in a paddock. 'If you watch them closely you will notice that they are very mammalian in their habits.'

'Dinosaurs?' asked Freddy. 'That portal has taken me back to the age of dinosaurs?'

Lucy turned around, dropping her chin at Freddy.

'No,' replied Haji, 'you're not that lucky. We are much further back than that. We are near what geologists call the Permian-Triassic boundary. We are on the Permian side of that boundary—the end of the Lopingian Epoch, to be precise. There are no dinosaurs at this time. There won't be for another 20 million years. These beasts—half-mammal, half-reptile—are much older than dinosaurs.'

'Do they eat meat?' asked Freddy.

'Yes and no,' said Haji. 'The Diictodons are herbivores.'

'So they just eat grass?' asked Freddy.

'There is no grass yet. They eat vegetation.'

'What about the big . . . crocodile things?'

'They are also herbivores but they can be very aggressive if you enter their space.'

As if to confirm that point, one of the crowned crocodiles turned on a particularly cheeky Diictodon that had grazed too close. This sent that animal scuttling to the water's edge where it splashed clear of the slower moving crocodile. The scene was so playful that Freddy smiled, but, suddenly, just as the crocodile gave up its chase, the water exploded in front of the hapless herbivore. A creature like a tadpole, only the size of a hippopotamus, spouted from the water. It threw open a massive mouth and swallowed half the Diictodon in one vicious, blood-splattering bite. A brief struggle and a thrashing of water followed but before Freddy had time to blink both predator and prey slipped back into the now red-stained, bubbling swamp. The crowned crocodile kept grazing as if nothing had happened.

'Blazes! What was that?' cried Freddy.

'You are a lucky boy! You don't get to see that every day. That was an Eryops—a primitive amphibian. It is one of the reasons we usually avoid Sure Death Swamp. But don't worry, we are quite safe at this distance. They are reasonably slow and clumsy on land.' Freddy kept his eyes on the surface of the swamp for a while to make sure that was the case. He would have kept his vigil a lot longer if he had not remembered his curiosity as to what was pulling the cart.

When he looked to the front of the cart, he was no less surprised. 'And that?' he gasped.

'That is a Moschops,' said Haji. 'They are one of the dinocephalians, meaning, "terrible heads". We try not to mention it in front of her. We call this girl Mossie. Not very original I know, but we have a lot on our plate. They are meant to be extinct, and they might be if they had not been domesticated. That is something we did not consider back at the Academy.'

The beast pulling the cart had a head like a pit bull terrier and a powerful body like a bison. A thick layer of matted fur ran along its back all the way to a long, pointed tail, which flicked at primeval insects attracted, for reasons best known to them, to its backside. It had no hooves, only four reptilian toes at the bottom of each stocky, slow-moving leg.

Freddy closed his eyes, shook his head, and looked at everything again. Nothing had changed. 'So when you said, "250 million years back in time", you really meant "250 million years back in time".'

'We most certainly did,' said Haji.

Freddy fell back onto the floor of the cart. He had only just turned sixteen. There were over a hundred lots of his lifetime separating him from the birth of Jesus. That was a lot, but it was at least comprehensible. There were almost fifteen million lots of time equal to his lifespan separating his birth from the time he appeared to be living and breathing in at that very moment. That was incomprehensible!

He looked up at the glaring sky. A sky that had existed millions of years before humans, and yet here they were. He touched the side of the cart to confirm its existence. In the background, the Diictodons bleated like sheep.

Crawling to the front of the cart, he picked up his father's watch. Flipping it open, he was relieved to see and hear that it was still ticking. The minute hand pointed somewhere near the twelve, and the hour hand was approaching ten, but that meant nothing. He turned the watch over and looked at his parents' names on the back, running his fingers over them like a blind man reading Braille.

Looking back, Haji guessed at Freddy's feelings. 'It's good that you are suffering some shock now,' he said. 'Time shock affects everyone in some way. Some never recover. The enormity of it is just too much for them. It's a bit different for me. I'm a palaeontologist. I'm like a kid in a candy store here.'

Freddy felt more like the kid who had just eaten the candy store. Leaning over the side of the cart, he threw up the entire contents of his stomach in one hit. His organic matter, or at least the stewed organic remains of the python, splattered over the barren Pangean soil. Watching his steaming vomit soak into the desert, Freddy wondered if he had just changed the natural history of the Earth.

Then he passed out.

13. Doylian Lair

It was late afternoon when the cart came to a stop with a head-banging jolt.

'Are we there yet?' asked Freddy, rubbing his head.

'Time to hop out and save the world,' cried Lucy, leaping from the cart

Groaning, he pulled himself up and crawled to the front to gather his few belongings. Then, grabbing the side of the cart, he shaded his eyes and looked around.

Lucy was unhitching Mossie from the cart. She was dressed in much the same way as she had been for the excursion to Arnhem Land the previous year. Jodhpurs, with riding boots and a shirt so crisp despite the heat that she could have been an advertisement for laundry soap. To shade the sun, she had tied a bright checked handkerchief between her pointed braids. She had soaked this with water from her canteen to keep cool. The main difference in her attire to the earlier expedition, Freddy noticed was a holster strapped to a wide belt and further secured by two more leather straps, which ran around the inside of her leg; one just above the knee, the other around the upper thigh. These straps pulled the holster down low on her hips. These also seemed a recent addition to Freddy. Inside the holster sat a Colt 45 pistol.

The sight of this weapon came as a shock to Freddy who was more used to seeing Lucy as a nasty little girl with a face full of braces. He was not ready for her to be a nasty young woman with a Colt 45.

Freddy also had a better look at Mossie and decided that its suborder name, dinocephalian, meaning terrible headed monster, was not far from the mark. Mossie was much more lizard-like than he had thought at first glance. Two bony ridges stretched back from her eyes, and, as she chewed on a plant, Freddy noticed razor sharp teeth— well-suited to the tough Permian vegetation. Despite her appearance, there was gentleness in Mossie's movements and an obvious bond between her and Lucy, who she playfully nuzzled as she went about her work.

Lucy led Mossie to a large pen that was really just a narrow, steep-sided ravine jutting back from the main jaw of the canyon towering above them. Timber rails secured the front of the pen, and once Mossie was inside, Lucy slipped these back into place and returned to the cart.

'How are you feeling?' she asked, noticing Freddy's pale face propped over the side of the cart. For the first time she sounded like she was not about to spit on him at the end of the sentence.

'I'm not sure,' he said. 'How about you?'

Lucy narrowed her eyes at Freddy. She placed one hand on a hip and the other on the handle of her pistol.

'I have had plenty of time to come to terms with things. I have known about Pangea for some time.'

'How long?' asked Freddy.

Lucy angled her head to the side as if the spaceship on top was preparing to land. 'You will have answers to your questions soon enough. There is a lot that you need to learn, but it will be better for you if you take it slowly. You have already been sick from time-shock. It will be enough for now if you can get down from that cart.'

Anxious as he was for more answers, he knew she was right. He also did not want to seem too clueless by pestering her with further questions.

Pulling himself up into a crouching position, he vaulted over the side of the cart. Seconds later, he wished that he had looked before leaping because he jumped right on top of something. It let out a terrified squeal and leapt into the air in fright, dragging Freddy's legs from under him. He landed heavily on his already battered backside. Looking up, he saw a stocky creature like a pig with the face of a chubby budgerigar, squealing down the canyon. Looking around, he saw even more of these creatures and wondered how he had not noticed them before. They appeared quite docile when not being jumped on.

'Lystrosaurs,' explained Lucy, unable to hide a smile.

'Of course,' said Freddy, trying to resurrect some lost dignity. Not an easy task when you are lying flat on your back and smelling something you have never smelled in your life before, but which you very strongly suspect is fresh Lystrosaur poop.

Lucy enjoyed Freddy's embarrassment, then turned her back on him, and walked up the canyon.

'What about my machete?'

She kept walking.

'Blazes! You're armed well enough,' cried Freddy, pointing to the Colt 45 strapped to her hip. 'Haji said this was a dangerous place, but you've taken my only weapon.' Freddy paused before saying the last word because up to then it had simply been a tool for slashing through vines and a walking stick for rocky slopes. He had liked the jaunty, buccaneer-feel of it slapping against his leg but had not, until then, thought of it as a weapon.

Lucy stopped in her tracks before turning and tramping to the front of the cart. Reaching under the front seat, she grabbed the machete and threw it at Freddy. Then she stormed off.

'Thanks,' said Freddy, reaching down and picking up his machete. It felt good to have it back in his hand, and he swung it about his head a couple of times like a pirate before lacing it through his belt.

The sun had been fierce all day but just then, a shadow crept across the ground and shaded him. Looking up, he saw a grey storm cloud towering upwards, smothering the sun. It was a relief from the heat but made the humidity worse. Beyond that, an even darker cloud crouched low and menacing.

The now-familiar smell of rotten egg gas still fouled the air. He was also starting to notice something else. The air seemed thinner as if there were less of something, and he guessed it was oxygen. Since waking up in Koia's tent, he had been breathing more deeply. At first, he had thought it was because of his injuries.

Squinting into the shadowy canyon, he saw that Lucy had reached a pile of boulders and rubble. In the midst of this pile, he noticed a dark space, which he guessed was a cave. A wisp of smoke hazed the entrance.

Stepping forward he picked up his hat, which he noticed had landed in Lystrosaur poop. Luckily, it was the same colour. He popped it back on his head and followed Lucy up the canyon.

By the time he reached the cave, she was already inside. *Thanks for waiting*, he thought. The opening was large enough for him to enter standing up, which he did slowly, giving his eyes time to adjust to the darkness. A downdraft from the back of the cave blew the smoke of a small fire out the entrance and directly into his eyes. By the time he was inside, he was half-blinded. He squinted, rubbed his eyes, and dimly made out four shapes seated around a fire. Two of them were his recent travelling companions.

Lucy sat on a ledge to the side, taking off her boots. Haji tended a pot suspended over the fire from a metal tripod. A spark from the fire briefly illuminated his face and the ring on his necklace, which had once more fallen outside his shirt.

The third person sat well back from the fire and was no more than a shadow.

The fourth person caused Freddy to scream.

14. Psychic Surgery

'Gruntenguile!'
      Seated on a camp chair in front of the fire, with a cup of tea in one hand and a cream biscuit in the other, sat Freddy's crusty manservant.

'Where have you been? How did you get here? Why did you push me into that crystal sword?'

'No need to thank me, Little Boss. All young people need a bit of a push every now and again.'

'Not into a crystal sword, they don't! And why didn't you follow me and help out with that giant blazing py—'

'Whoa—slow down, Little Boss . . . grrrnnt, take a seat.'

'He's right,' said Haji. 'Why don't you sit down and have a cup of tea?'

Freddy was not ready to calm down just yet. Miming Gruntenguile pushing him into the crystal sword, he glared at him for an explanation.

'Here's your tea,' said Haji, handing Freddy a steaming cup. 'And welcome to Doylian Lair.'

'Thank you,' said Freddy, grabbing the enamel handle and grimacing at its black contents. He preferred milk and sugar but guessed it was not worth asking for them.

He sat down, glaring at Gruntenguile all the while. He only took his eyes off him when he put his hand down in the middle of a scurry of scaly bugs. Jumping back to his feet, he brushed the bugs from his hands and sleeves, spilling most of his tea.

'Nothing to be alarmed by,' said Haji. 'They are Blattopterans—Permian cockroaches. The most common creature in Pangea. You'd better get used to them.'

Freddy sat back down as Haji placed the billy pot on a rock near the edge of the fire to keep it warm.

'Where did you get to?' said Freddy, returning his attention to Gruntenguile, 'I'm guessing you already knew where that crystal sword would take me. Why didn't you follow?'

'I would have, but are you sure you wouldn't like a biscuit with that tea? We've got your favourites—Monte Carlos.'

Freddy wished he could have said no to the biscuits, but he was starving. 'Thank you,' he said.

'What Gruntenguile is reluctant to tell you,' said Lucy, 'is that the crystal sword means of time travel that you used is no longer—how should I say?—the preferred means.'

'What? You mean there are alternatives,' said Freddy, turning to Gruntenguile. 'Nobody told me that!'

'I should also tell you that the crystal sword portals have a ninety percent safety rating,' continued Lucy.

'Ninety percent sounds pretty good,' said Freddy.

'No, you fool. The ninety percent refers to their fatality rate.'

Sounds numbed and stars spun on the edge of Freddy's vision. 'How did everyone else get here?' he asked.

Gruntenguile dunked his Monte Carlo and pointed with his non-dunking hand over his shoulder.

Squinting into the darkness at the back of the cave, Freddy could just make out a round object like two dessert bowls placed rim to rim.

'It's a GT Turbo,' said Lucy. 'They have a zero-fatality rate. They are very reliable and quite comfortable. Some of the later models have built-in sound systems.'

'Mine's got a massage seat,' added Haji. 'It's *fantastic* for my bad back.'

'Well, thanks for telling me about them now,' said

Freddy, vaguely wondering what a sound system and massage seat were while glaring at Gruntenguile.

Gruntenguile looked at his biscuit.

'You allowed me to travel by that incredibly dangerous and unpleasant means, while you travelled like Buck Rogers in some luxury time-space disc thingy?'

'Well, the thing is, Little Boss—the GT Turbos are quite small. They only carry one person. For us both to get here, one had to use the old portal. But that is neither here nor somewhere else, Little Boss. You are living proof that they work just as well . . . grrrnnt.'

Freddy was about to ask Gruntenguile how he could have taken such an incredible risk with his life, but he was interrupted.

'You will soon learn that there is much more to Pangea than just getting here, young man.' A ghostly echo followed the voice from further back in the cave.

Freddy squinted into the darkness as the speaker moved closer to the fire, sat down, and pulled his knees in tight to his chest. A sudden spark showed him to be a man with more skin than he needed—like he had recently lost a lot of weight. When the fire died down, all that remained visible was a grey outline and the reflection of the fire on his monocle.

'Don't be so dramatic, Count Schnauzer—the boy will learn this game soon enough,' said Haji.

'Maybe he will,' said Count Schnauzer. 'But, first, I'd like to know what's going on back home. In our time.'

'Anything in particular?' asked Freddy.

'He means about the war, you—' Lucy was cut short by a look from Haji.

'Oh,' began Freddy, 'not great. The Japanese are still coming. They've invaded Java, and bombed Darwin just as I was leaving on this expedition. The Nazis have mounted a successful counterattack in Africa. Not much good news—'

'Tell me—why haven't you signed up, young man? It's easy enough to fake the papers.'

Freddie looked hard into the darkness surrounding the speaker. It was something he had thought about, but the truth was that the Professor had kept too close a watch on him. Freddy shrugged.

'Are you afraid of fighting?'

Freddy was about to jump up and say how he had single-handedly wrestled a giant python, but he thought better of it.

'Because, if you're afraid of fighting,' continued the mysterious Count, 'you have come to the wrong place.'

Freddy could now only just see the tiniest twinkle of firelight from the Count's monocle. Recalling a saying of the Professor's that 'it is better to say nothing, and be thought a fool, than to speak and remove all doubt', he remained silent.

Lucy stood up to say something, but the Count had not finished. He held up his finger to silence Lucy and turned to Freddy. 'What skills do you bring to Pangea, young man?' he asked.

'What do you mean?' asked Freddy.

'I mean—can you do anything . . . special?'

Freddy did not know how to answer. 'You mean, like sing?' he said at last. 'I know some Frank Sinatra—'

'No, I mean like this,' said the Count, stepping for the first time into the full glow of firelight. Then, as Freddy stared at him, he plucked the monocle from his eye, threw it into his mouth, and swallowed it whole.'

'Really,' said Haji, 'you are such a show-off! What on Earth do you hope—?'

'I am just showing the boy what anyone who is really useful here can do.'

The Count opened his mouth wide for Freddy to check that he was not hiding the monocle under his tongue. Freddy stood up and looked inside, but there was nothing there apart from a couple of gold fillings and a bloated tonsil. The Count's breath reeked of tea and stale Blattopteran stew.

Freddy stepped back as the Count unbuttoned his shirt and placed a hand over his eyes. At the same time, his other arm began moving like a snake grafted to his body. The fingers on the end of that arm pinched together at the tips making a shape like a snake's head. The Count then twisted this hand into the fatty folds of his stomach. Unsure what was going on, Freddy smiled nervously at Lucy. She nodded for him to keep looking, so he returned his attention to the Count. The Count's performance looked quite ridiculous until, after a few seconds, as sure as Freddy lived, the Count's hand cut into his flesh. Blood oozed and a coil of gut popped out for a moment. This did not worry the Count as his hand kept moving and twisting about inside him. Freddy's attention shifted to a bump on the Count's stomach. This bump moved in searching circles until it suddenly swelled as if the hand beneath had suddenly clenched into a fist. Slowly, the Count drew his arm back out of his gut. Freddy had recovered enough by now to look for mirrors or anything else that might be tricking his senses, but he could see nothing—only the steaming hand of the Count holding his slimed and bloodied monocle.

'No, I don't mean singing,' said the Count, placing the bloodied monocle back over his eye. A trail of blood slid slowly down the side of his face.

Without wasting another word, he returned to his former place in the shadows.

Haji clapped the Count's performance. 'Psychic surgery—one of the Count's many party tricks.'

The fire crackled and the water in the billy made a tinny fizz. Freddy felt his own stomach, blew into his cup, and glanced around the cave. His eyes rested for a moment on Gruntenguile, but he had nothing to say.

'No, I have no special tricks. I'm not even sure why Professor Dupler sent me on this expedition,' said Freddy at last. 'I guess Gruntenguile has said the same.'

'I have, Little Boss. I have told them that I know nothing other than my job, which is to keep you alive,' said Gruntenguile.

'And how well do you think you're doing?' fumed Freddy.

'Are you dead?' asked Gruntenguile.

'No,' said Freddy.

'Then I'd say I am doing very well.'

'How many times do I have to tell people that bickering gets us nowhere?' cried Haji.

For a while the incessant scratching and scratching of Blattopterans was the only sound in the dank stillness of the cave.

'I'll tell you what I know, but it's not much,' said Freddy. 'Professor Dupler sent us on this expedition. Neither of us knew anything . . . although—' Freddy turned once more to Gruntenguile. 'How did you know about the GT space-time thingy back there? And the other entrance to the cave?'

'I may only be your manservant, Little Boss, but the Professor did tell me about the cave and the portals. If you had only stuck with me, you could have entered by the stairs yourself.'

'How did you know how to operate that?' Freddy jerked his thumb in the direction of the GT Turbo.

'They are simpler than a car, Little Boss, and their location and time coordinates are pre-set—that is how I ended up here.'

'What more did the Professor tell you?' asked Freddy.

'Just the same thing that he told you. That someone

here would be able to tell us what to do next.'

Freddy turned around and faced the mixed gazes of his companions both old and new.

'Well,' he said finally, 'as you just heard, my manservant knows more than I do! I should have asked more questions about what I was getting into, but the Professor said that it was a secret expedition.'

'Yes,' said Lucy, 'but you do realise that the point of a secret expedition is that it is a secret to everyone else—not the people who are actually on it?!'

It was a good point, and it took Freddy a little while to muster a reply. 'Well, let's just say that I'm more used to weird stuff happening than most people. My father was the anthropologist, Colum O'Toole.' Freddy paused to see their reactions to his father's name but was blinded by a spark from the fire. 'You may have heard of him?'

'We have Freddy,' said Haji, 'but I'm afraid he is as much a mystery to us as he is to you.'

Breathing in his feelings, Freddy continued. 'The only reason I agreed to come on this expedition was that I thought that it might have something to do with finding him. I guess you all know that his plane disappeared over Timor on March the fourth, 1936.' Freddy remembered the day Professor Dupler had told him as clearly as his last breath.

The fire lit Freddy's face and splattered his shadow across the craggy walls.

'If you want to stay alive here, Freddy, you will need our help, and if we are going to help you, we need to know as much as you can tell us about why you are here—in this cave, 250 million years before your time. Is there anything else that stands out in your memory about your father, or mother? Any small detail you can recall may be able to help us,' said Haji. 'At the moment our biggest danger lies in not knowing who we can and cannot trust.'

'I can't remember my mother at all. I can remember my father, but whenever I think about him its like when the curtain closes at the end of the movie—I know that sounds stupid.'

'When did that ever stop you from saying anything?' encouraged Lucy.

Count Schnauzer snorted from the back of the cave.

'Just tell us what you can remember about your father,' said Haji.

Freddy nodded, and gathered his thoughts before starting again. 'He was a . . . "curious chap",' he said, recalling Professor Dupler's description.

'What do you mean by that?' asked Haji.

The fire sparked. Freddy's shadow danced.

'There was one time . . .'

'Go on,' said Lucy.

'It was when I was quite young. I remember losing something—I can't even remember what it was, but what I do remember is my father going berserk. Like Doctor Frankenstein in a power blackout. I think I was so scared that I blanked the thing—whatever it was—right out of my mind for years.'

Haji looked to Gruntenguile.

'Grrrnnt . . . it was before my time,' he said.

'Where's all this getting us?' cried Schnauzer. 'All children lose things. They're incompetent by nature. I can't see how this boy is any use to us! I can't believe—'

'Let him at least tell his story,' said Haji.

'There's not much more to tell. Before my father disappeared, he brought Gruntenguile back from an expedition somewhere . . .'

'Grrrnnt.'

'Since then I have lived with Professor Dupler. Nothing much of interest ever happened until last year when he took me on an expedition to a cave on the

Arnhem Escarpment. I guess Lucy has already told you that there were cave paintings there, which were quite amazing. They depicted creatures like those we observed earlier today.' Freddy turned towards Haji.

'Estemmenosochus,' he said.

'But it wasn't just the paintings. When I was looking at them, I had this really weird feeling, and then I sensed that someone was looking at me.' He glanced at Lucy. 'At first I thought it was you. I thought you might be death staring me over the spaceship comment, which was an innocent mistake by the way. Anyway, where was I? Yes, I knew it wasn't you because I could see your . . . silhouette, and you were looking upwards. Anyway, I kept looking, and that's when I realised that it was Professor Dupler. It was strange that while everyone else was looking at the cave paintings he was looking at me. Then, when we got back to Darwin, I woke one morning and he was sitting on the edge my bed—'

'Creepy,' said Lucy.

'It was,' said Freddy. 'Anyway, he told me straight out that he had observed me at the cave and knew that I had instinctively understood the paintings we had seen there—'

'When you say understood—what do you mean?' asked Haji.

'I knew that the paintings were proof that this . . .' Freddy gestured around him, 'was possible. I knew that time travel was possible the way the Wright brothers knew that air travel was possible, and, because of that, the Professor sent me on this expedition. He was never clear on the details and only ever said that it would be somewhere in the East Indies which, as you know, covers a rather large area.'[15]

---

[15] The East Indies covers over 24,000 islands between India/Malaysia and Australia.

The storm cloud that had been building earlier had come to nothing. Dry dust eddied into the cave. It was the hottest part of the day and the fire was still burning. Freddy was roasting.

'All I knew was that I would be told what to do when the time came.'

'Please tell me that you at least feel stupid about that,' said Lucy. 'It is quite important to me that you admit that.'

Freddy wanted to tell Lucy that all he really cared about was finding his father, but the look on her face gave him no encouragement. He turned to Haji and continued. 'We were meant to receive further instructions, but so far, nothing. In the meantime, I've been almost eaten by an oversized python and an oversexed Amazon.'

That was as much as Freddy thought he could tell them. Looking through the flames into the glowing embers of the fire, he did wonder at his own stupidity, but he would never give Lucy the pleasure of hearing him say it out loud.

When he looked up, he was surprised to see that no one was looking at him. Instead, they were staring at something behind him. He turned around to see what it was.

Something was standing in the entrance of the cave, staring at him.

15. Escape to the COY

'What *is* that?'

The creature to which Freddy referred stood awkwardly on two legs as if it would have preferred four. It was puffing and slicked with frothy sweat.

'Don't worry,' said Lucy. 'It's a Spotter. Most of them are on our side . . . we think.' She quickly pulled her boots back on as she spoke.

The Spotter looked like a hairless dachshund on two longer than expected legs. Its tongue, flopping from its mouth like something it was eating rather than part of its body, gave it an appearance of imbecility not entirely undeserved. Thick, toilet-brush hair sprouted from the top of its head. Freddy later learned that this hair came in a variety of bright colours. In the case of this Spotter, it was a bright green, which clashed with its otherwise filthy appearance.

'It's okay,' said Haji, 'it's mine.'

'So, what are they?' asked Freddy.

'Flea-bitten mutts not to be trusted,' snorted Count Schnauzer.

'Grrrnnt.' Gruntenguile stiffened at the reference to flea-bitten.

Haji and Lucy frowned. 'It's hard to explain in a hurry,' said Lucy. 'Let's listen to what it has to say.'

The Spotter took a cautious step towards Haji who reached into his back pocket, grabbed two capsules, and offered them to the Spotter in his outstretched hand. The Spotter sniffed the capsules before snatching them like a mouse stealing cheese from a loaded trap and throwing them in its mouth.

Turning to Freddy, Haji explained, 'Nutrition capsules—those two will keep him alive for a month.'

This proved to be incorrect because, at that moment, as Freddy was staring directly at the Spotter, the sharp end of a spear burst through its body and a spurt of black blood splattered across Freddy's hat, which lay on the ground at his feet.

Freddy stared at the tip of the spear dripping black blood in front of him. He had seen one exactly like it before. It had been in Koia's tent. The Spotter collapsed and would have fallen face down on the cave floor had its body not been propped up by the end of the spear as it fell forward. Freddy looked around to see what the others were doing and noticed that they were not there. He panicked, and his adventure would have almost certainly ended there if Gruntenguile, remembering his work contract, had not raced back to save him.

'This way, Little Boss,' he cried. 'Follow me.'

Gruntenguile took off at a surprising speed for a biped with such short legs. Freddy ran close on his heels. The tunnel was as dark as a black cat's gizzards at midnight. Freddy kept as close to Gruntenguile's head as he could. Behind them, a horrible cry echoed through the cave and grew louder with each stumbling step.

YiiiiiiiiiiiiiiiiiiiiiiiiiiiiiiiYiYiYiiiiiiiiiiiiiiiiiiiiiiiii

The battle cry of the Amazons.

Very few have lived to describe that blood-curdling cry.

All Freddy could recall of that escape was a blind scramble and a fear of being shish-kebabbed by an Amazonian spear at any moment. Leaping and scrambling over the rocks that littered the cave floor his instincts once more served him well. To stay alive he had to stay with Gruntenguile. How Gruntenguile knew where he was going he did not know.

In the echoing darkness above, creatures fluttered, and Freddy wondered if the ancestors of bats existed at that time. He hoped so, because he did not want to imagine what else they might be.[16]

After a minute or two, maybe more, Freddy caught a glimpse of a light up ahead. It grew brighter with each stride and soon he could see the walls of the cave and the grey shapes running ahead of him. The cries of the Amazons, however, grew louder. They seemed like a landslide about to swallow him. He looked back to see how close they were. This was almost a fatal mistake. Up ahead, one of the grey shapes had fallen. The eagle-eyed Gruntenguile could see that it was Count Schnauzer and bounded over him. It was every creature for themselves, and his job was to keep Freddy alive—not the Count. When Freddy turned around, he mistook the Count for a rock. Leaping to avoid a trip, his foot clipped the Count's head as he was trying to get back to his feet. This had two effects. The first was that the Count collapsed to the floor of the cave and lay there in a state of concussion for the next few minutes. The second was that Freddy tripped and rolled forward. He was halfway through his third roll when he thudded into a wall.

The cries of the Amazons were deafening by now and, looking back, he could see the light of their crude lanterns swaying in the darkness. The halos of light were growing larger by the second and fierce shadows formed in them. Before he had time to think of standing, two small but firm hands grabbed him by the back of the shirt and pulled him up with astonishing strength just as a spear struck the spot where he had been lying.

'Gruntenguile?'

---

[16] I have investigated this, and I doubt very much that they were bats as the oldest bat-like fossil dates to the Palaeo-cene—a mere 60 million odd years ago. Despite further re-search, I have no suggestions as to what they may have been.

'No, it's me,' cried Lucy. 'Just lie there and try not to get yourself killed.'

What followed was even more of a blur.

Everything turned upside-down . . . the whole world yelling . . . the criss-crossed surface of a large basket . . . a burst of gas and a bright plume of flame like a flower opening.

In the midst of all this, Haji yelled, 'Cut the ropes! Cut the ropes! Cut the ropes!'

Looking up, Freddy saw a huge billowing shape fluttering above him. It was then that he realised that he was in the basket of a hot-air balloon.

Bodies brushed about him in the darkness. He hoped they belonged to his companions and that they knew what they were doing.

The only voice he could make out in the din was Haji's. He was screaming. 'Damn you, Schnauzer, cut the ropes! How many times have we done this drill?'

Freddy heard all of this lying in the bottom of the basket, feet trampling over him and his heart hammering hard against his ribs.

Haji kept yelling, but there was no reply. Freddy tried to get up but fell back as the basket began to rise and sway. At the same time, it shuddered with the thumping of spears. In the darkness, he heard a muffled cry. He did not realise until later that it was Count Schnauzer coming to his senses amidst a throng of screaming Amazons.

The basket was tied by two sets of ropes. The first secured it to the ground. Lucy had already untied those ropes. The second, longer set of ropes acted as a safety device and held the basket at about forty feet. It was Schnauzer's job to untie them, but he had fallen before reaching them. This meant that the balloon would come to a wrenching stop forty feet in the air when they pulled tight. Freddy struggled to his feet once more and, looking over the side of the basket, he saw that these ropes were already pulled tight. Squinting into the darkness he saw the reason for this. Amazons, as nimble as monkeys, were halfway up the ropes. Knives gleamed in their white clenched teeth. Their furious eyes seeming to fly from their sockets towards him. Lucy shook one of the ropes, but they kept climbing. Haji and Gruntenguile were busy working on one of the burners, which was flickering and seemed in danger of going out. Quicker than thinking, Freddy unsheathed his machete and leant over the side of the basket. He slashed one anchor rope and then, racing to the other side of the basket, slashed the other, just above the outstretched hand of the first of the Amazons. She fell to the ground with a terrible cry followed by shouts in the Amazonian tongue that did not bode well for their next meeting. Freddy and Lucy flopped to the floor of the basket, and at the same time, Haji and Gruntenguile overcame the problem with the burner.

The flame roared and the balloon floated upwards with a serenity that was weirdly at odds with everything that had just happened. As it ascended, it pulled a canvas cover from the roof of the cave and light flooded in from the furnace of the sky above.

Freddy lay in the bottom of the basket sucking in as much of the oxygen-depleted air as his lungs could take. Someone grabbed his arm. It was Lucy.

'I'm glad I gave that machete back to you,' she puffed. 'You may not be as useless as I thought,' she added, smiling.

It was not a big smile, but it made Freddy feel as good as it was possible to feel under the circumstances.

Below them, the Amazons squinted into the blinding sunlight as the balloon soared upwards.

The sun was going down, but the light still seemed bright after the darkness of the cave. It also seemed like freedom. For the first time in days, Freddy relaxed and allowed himself to smile. Even Gruntenguile smiled, and that was unusual because he often said that smiling invites disaster, and in this case, he was right. More Amazons were waiting above and one of them leapt from the cliff face. It was an enormous leap but not quite enough. She fell short, just managing to get a handhold on the side of the basket. Lucy sprang to her feet and pounded her hands to make her let go, but she was too quick and grabbed hold of Lucy's forearm. Freddy was slower in getting to his feet. When he looked over the side, he recognised the attacker immediately. It was Koia. Her face striped with yellow war paint, she looked quite upset. It suddenly occurred to him that he had stood her up the night before.

'She's dragging me out of the basket,' screamed Lucy. 'Use the machete. It's her arms or my life.'

Freddy turned, grabbed his machete, and leant over the side of the basket. He swung the blade down but foolishly looked into Koia's eyes as he did so. She had such beautiful grey eyes, like a cool pool on a hot day. Suddenly the blade was hanging in mid-air. He could not do it. He had stood her up on their first date, and now he was about to chop her arms off. What sort of a boyfriend was he?

Lucy slipped further out of the basket.

'What are you doing Freddy? Cut her arms off, now! I can't hold on!'

Still he hesitated. Lucy's waist was now teetering on the edge of the basket. She was about to topple over the side. He had to do something and, reluctantly, he knew what it was. 'I'm sorry it had to end like this,' said Freddy. He swung the machete towards Koia's straining forearms, but, at the last moment, she let go and dropped into the darkness of the cave below. Freddy watched her as she fell and hoped that she would land safely. It did not seem likely, but she was tough.

After watching Koia disappear into the darkness of

the cave, he turned to Lucy. She was lying breathlessly on the floor of the basket.

'You hesitated,' she said. 'I hope you had a good reason.'

Freddy did. In his heart he could not believe that Koia was as bad as Lucy was making her out to be. She had nursed him after he had been almost crushed to death by the giant python. She had cooled his brow with a damp cloth when he was too weak to move. Plus, there was just something about her! Maybe she did intend to slaughter him and skin and tan his hide, but relationships are never easy. Freddy guessed it was not a good idea to share any of these thoughts with Lucy.

'Have you ever chopped someone's arms off with a machete?'

'They're Amazons; you either kill them or they kill you! And what did you mean by, "I'm sorry it had to end like this?" Did you know her?'

'Of course not. I was just—'

Luckily, before he could finish, Haji stepped between them and raised a hand in front of each of their faces. 'Enough!' he cried. 'I think you should know, Freddy, that Doctor Wong almost lost her life to Amazons on her last visit. Luckily she managed to escape but she was struck by a spear just below the knee.'

Freddy recalled Doctor Wong limping on her way up the Arnhem Escarpment. 'I am sorry to hear that,' said Freddy, turning towards Lucy.

She glared suspiciously at him.

'You two must learn to get along and trust each other,' continued Haji. 'There are so few of us, and we have just lost Count Schnauzer.'

At the mention of Count Schnauzer, they all looked over the side of the basket into the darkness of the cave below, which was still ringing with the wild cries of the Amazons. Freddy did not want to think at that moment what fate may have befallen the Count.

'I never really trusted Count Schnauzer,' said Lucy, 'but, you're right. There's so few of us left. Everyone becomes precious.'

'Grrrnnt,' agreed Gruntenguile. In their brief time together, the Count had called him a flea farm on several occasions, and a meddling monkey (under his breath) at least once, but he was nonetheless mildly upset that he had been captured.

'It's too late now. There's nothing we can do,' said Haji. He turned back to the burners and opened both valves a little. More gas farted from the bottle to swell the flame and they soared higher into the gloaming sky. At the same time, Lucy cranked a diesel engine into action and gyro blades, secured by a network of cables to the sides of the balloon, began rotating.

'Where to now?' asked Freddy.

'Northern Gondwana,'[17] said Haji. 'To the land that in our time—our other time—we call Africa.'

'But that will take weeks … maybe months. What will we eat?'

'Don't worry,' said Haji, 'I have plenty more nutrition capsules. Each one will last us a couple of weeks. More if we're just sitting about not using any energy. Plus, we have a small desalinator.' He pointed to a spaghetti of pipes in the rigging. 'It will turn the seawater into drinking water. If that breaks down, I have a supply of hydration capsules.'

'What about going to …?'

---

[17] Gondwana was the southerly part of Pangea. It broke away from the northerly part known as Laurasia as recently as 200–180 Ma. It included the current-day land masses of Antarctica, South America, Africa, Madagascar, Australia, and both the Arabian and Indian Peninsulas.

'To what?'

'The toilet.'

'You don't need to go so much when you are on a diet of nutrition capsules, but when you do go . . .' Haji held up a rope ladder. 'Don't worry,' he said. 'I've thought of everything . . . everything I can think of that is.

Welcome aboard the COY.'

16. Tethys Sea

'Where's Freddy?'
Lucy woke, and straight away noticed that she could only see two of her three companions. Gruntenguile was still sleeping. She did not need to look to find him because he was snoring loudly from both ends. Haji was already up. He stood on the edge of the basket, his moustache waving in the wind, staring at the northern horizon. In answer to Lucy's question, he pointed down.

'What? He's fallen overboard?'

'Calm down, I'm just exercising.' Freddy's slightly strained voice came from below the basket. Popping her head over the side and looking down she saw him clinging to the lower rung of the rope ladder doing chin-ups. His biceps strained. They were hardly Joe Louis[18] guns, but they had lost their boyish softness. He took one hand off the rung to wave at her. 'I like to exercise in the morning if I can,' said Freddy, smiling at Lucy. There was something charming about the worried look on her face, but it did not last long.

'What on Earth do you think you're doing?'

Freddy was sure he had just told her. 'Exercising—there wasn't any room in the basket . . . so I came down here.'

'Get back up here this instant,' she cried. 'As if there aren't enough dangers in Pangea without you inventing new ones!' She stormed in two steps to the other side of the basket and sat down.

'I'd finished anyway,' said Freddy, though not very loudly. Climbing the rope ladder, he clambered back into the basket.

[18] World Heavyweight Boxing Champion from 1937 to 1949.

Haji grinned at each of them in turn.

Lucy took out a notebook and a RAF issue Biro from her shirt pocket and began scribbling furiously.[19] Freddy wondered whether she was keeping a journal of his idiocy. He had thought when he turned sixteen that it was the start of a new, less idiotic Freddy O'Toole, but it seemed he was wrong.

A couple of things to say to her crept towards his tongue, but they died a cowardly death before making it all the way there.

Instead, he turned and leaned on the side of the basket next to Haji.

The first thing he noticed was that Haji's shirt was buttoned all the way to the top. It raced through his mind that he might be trying to hide the quarter moon ring he had noticed earlier. It could just as easily have been because it was cool at that altitude. Even so, he was hesitant to start a conversation with Haji. Back at the cave he had told him everything, but Haji had told him nothing.

He glanced back at Lucy. He had at least known her longer, and maybe she was the one he should trust. She paused in her writing and bit the tip of her pen as if she were struggling to find the words to describe Freddy's stupidity.

Freddy turned around again, and this time he looked at the horizon. Billowing, tar-black clouds smothered the entire northern sky. He had noticed this earlier and had thought it was a big storm brewing. He put on his hat and stood next to Haji.

Haji turned to face him but seemed suddenly taken aback. 'Where did you get that pin?' he asked, staring at the eye pin on Freddy's hat.

---

[19] Invented by László Biro, these pens were first used by the Royal Air Force in World War Two. How Lucy got her hands on one is anybody's guess.

'Professor Dupler gave it to me. Why?'

'No reason,' said Haji, although he stared at it for a while before turning and pointing to the west. 'By the way, that's where we're heading. Normally I like to stay in sight of the coast, but that would take too long. The land which will become your Australia is now way south of us.' Haji swung his arm in that direction. 'Much of the southern half of it is covered in ice. India joins it to the west—'

'I beg your pardon?' Freddy was quite sure that India was some 6,000 miles northwest of Australia.

'I'm sorry,' said Haji, noticing Freddy's surprise. 'You are not familiar with the theory of continental drift?'[20]

Freddy shook his head.

'Continents move, Freddy. They float over the Earth like giant plates and sometimes crash into each other to form great mountain chains like the Andes and the Himalayas.' While he spoke, he reached into his shirt pocket, pulled out a crumpled map, and handed it to Freddy.

Freddy turned the map to face the sun so that he could see it more clearly. It was hand-drawn and showed a large body of land in appearance not unlike a human skull facing upwards. Across the land was scrawled 'Pangea', a name Freddy had already heard on several occasions. Either side of it were two named bodies of water. To the east, beneath the spot where the jaw would have hinged, was the Tethys Sea, to the west, the Panthalassic Ocean.

'That is the Earth as it is *now* with the seven continents we know, in our time, joined as one. We are somewhere here, over the Tethys Sea,' said Haji, pointing to a spot on the map. 'We should reach land somewhere around here, which is now the continental shelf of northern Africa.'

---

[20] The theory of Continental Drift emerged after World War Two.

Freddy snuck a sideways glance at Haji before turning to Lucy and twirling a finger around the side of his head.

Lucy shook her head. 'Haji is from a time after our own,' she said, as if that were a satisfactory explanation for insanity.

For a few moments, Freddy did not know which lunatic to look at. It then occurred to him that if he had travelled through time, it was surely possible for people in other times to do the same thing. If that was possible, maybe continents could float around the Earth bumping into each other.

Freddy turned back to the western horizon and glanced at Haji out the tail of his eye. He was still leaning into the breeze, his slightly closed lashes shielding his eyes. His moustache rippling like grass.

'Okay,' said Freddy at last. 'I've told you everything I know. Which amounts to blazing nothing ... but ... I am here in this place where you tell me all the world is joined in one great lump, 250 million years before my own time, and I still have no idea why Professor Dupler sent me here.' Freddy looked straight at Haji as he said this, but his face gave nothing away. 'So—what about you, Haji? Why are you here? I think it's time *I* had some answers.'

Haji kept gazing into the distance as Freddy spoke. Before answering, he looked first towards Lucy and then back to Freddy. His hand slipped inside his shirt and played with the ring hanging there. 'I ... don't know everything about this game,' he said at last, casting another glance at Lucy. 'But I can tell you some things.

'Firstly, I should confess that we do know quite a bit about your guardian, Professor Dupler, and his research.

'This research over the past few years has focused more and more on the "sixth sense". This is not new, of course— it has been the subject of research across several scientific disciplines since the early nineteenth century. Back then, it was called mysticism and was not so highly regarded. It was—and still is—considered the science of crackpots.'

'Crackpots?' smiled Freddy, still mulling over Haji's theory of floating continents.

'Professor Dupler, we believe, was very close to a breakthrough in finding out about . . . all this.'

Lucy joined in. 'My mother had been closely watching the progress of the Professor's work for several years. But recently, there was a change. The Professor quite suddenly became strangely secretive. My mother suspected that he had made a discovery of some sort. She had hoped to learn more about the state of the Professor's research on the excursion to Arnhem Land last year, but the Professor was very tight lipped. He wanted to share the discovery in the cave but nothing more. He would not even tell my mother how he found out about the cave. It was like he no longer trusted anyone.'

'Except Doctor Bufon,' said Freddy.

'Hmm,' a shadow drifted over Lucy's face at the mention of Doctor Bufon. 'We noticed also that the Professor had a new glass eye.'

'So?'

'A glass eye is often a sign that someone is playing this game, Freddy.'

'Why?'

'We're not sure. There's a lot going on here, and we've only just scratched the surface. The eye on your hatpin, by the way, is another sign.'

'What does it mean?' asked Freddy, taking off his hat and examining it closely.

'It is a sign that someone is a Searcher—that someone knows about all this. It is a way of making contact with other Searchers.'

'He must have got this around the same time he lost his own eye,' said Freddy. 'When he returned from that expedition, there was a change in him. It was like he was close to something. On the expedition to Arnhem Land last year I think he was worried about your mother finding out too much before he had worked it all out himself.'

'Yes,' said Lucy. Then, looking cagily towards Haji, she continued. 'But what the Professor did not realise was that my mother already knew.'

'What do you mean? That your mother knew about the portals in Timor?'

'No! My mother knew nothing of *those* portals. What I am saying is that my mother knew of *two other—GT Turbo—portals*. My mother is a member of a secret society—as in secret to *others* not to *themselves*. They have known about all this'—Lucy drew a circle about her with her hand—'for over a decade. She is a Doylian.'

'Doy what?'

'In 1882,' said Lucy, 'a group called the Society for Psychical Research was founded in London. The purpose of that group was to conduct scientific studies into psychic and paranormal phenomena. This group was further divided into more specific committees, who investigated particular topics such as apparitions, haunted houses, and telepathy.'

Freddy tried to keep a straight face as Lucy continued. He never in his wildest dreams imagined that she, of all people, would be into that sort of mumbo jumbo.

'My mother became a member of the Telepathy or Thought Transference Committee as it was called back then, while studying at Oxford just after the Great War. Some years later, this Committee appointed a group to investigate two brothers who worked in the carnivals up and down England at that time. My mother was a member of that group. These brothers claimed to have lived in previous times, and they told amazing stories about their experiences. From a distance, they appeared to be charlatans, and the sceptics in the Society were keen to prove them fakes. The problem was that my mother's group soon discovered reasons enough to believe they might be genuine. For years they tried to get the claims of these men properly investigated but the Society was run by sceptics. All they ever wanted was to debunk any claim that challenged the current laws of science. After years of in-fighting, Sir Arthur Conan Doyle led a mass resignation from the group in 1930. A short time later, Doyle formed another group, which continued its investigations in the utmost secrecy. To others, not to themselves. That clandestine group was known, only to its select members, as the Doylians.'[21]

Doylians? Freddy recalled the name from the cave. It sounded like some fancy club where dapper gents wore cravats, smoked big cigars, and talked about India.

'Hmm ... the Doylians—if I'm getting this right,' said Freddy, 'then discovered some of those GT ...'

'Turbos.'

'Then travelled back 250 million years to now?'

Lucy nodded.

Gruntenguile gave a semi-conscious grunt that told Freddy he would soon be awake.

Freddy looked quizzically at Lucy. Surely, she was joking. 'It's not just us,' she continued. 'There are other Searchers with less noble intentions playing this game, and many more who wish they were not playing at all—'

'Where are they?' interrupted Freddy.

---

[21] The choice of this name seems to confirm the ongoing leadership of Sir Arthur Conan Doyle of Sherlock Holmes fame. Doyle led this mass resignation from the Psychical Research Society in 1930 purportedly over the exposure by sceptics of several fraudulent spiritualists including William Hope. The name of the air balloon, COY, was most likely an acronym of the *City of York*, an air balloon alongside which Arthur Conan Doyle was photographed in 1901.

'Many live in Babel—a floating village on the wild coast of the Panthalassic Ocean. I have never been there, but I hear it is the strangest gathering of desperate, cut-throat villains you will ever see.'

'Do you think my father could be there?'

'Anyone could be, but don't get your hopes up. We're not going anywhere near Babel. It's too dangerous. Its approaches are protected by the most ingenious and cruel booby traps ever invented.'

Looking to the horizon, Freddy wondered whether he was only kidding himself. Was there any chance that his father was still alive?

'Besides that,' continued Haji, 'the world is bigger, Freddy, than just us, and what we want. There's no point finding your father if we can't save the world first.'

'Maybe some other time,' said Lucy, sensing Freddy's disappointment. 'But for now, we must stick to our core mission. Someone has sent those portals into the future for a reason, and that reason, we believe, is that something is happening here in Pangea that could end all life on Earth. Our mission is to stop it.'

'Stop what?'

'That!' said Haji.

Turning, he saw Haji pointing towards the black haze choking the northern sky.

'What is that?' asked Freddy. 'At first I thought it was a storm, but it never goes away.'

'Here in Pangea, they call it the Dark Cloud.'

'*Who* calls it the Dark Cloud?'

'The several higher species of alien creatures that inhabit the planet at the moment.'

Freddy stared at Haji. This was even crazier than floating continents.

'Three centuries ago an alien spacecraft—the *Atlantis*—crash-landed on Earth. It contained several species, but the master species are the Zynes. You have already met several of the other species.'

'Amazons?'

Haji and Lucy nodded.

'That Spotter, the creature the Amazons speared?'

Haji and Lucy nodded.

'Most of the species here are also telepathic and translingual.[22] The "sixth sense" Professor Dupler has been investigating. This makes them quite easy to communicate with.'

'What do these aliens look like?'

'They are mostly humanoid, and you could easily overlook them in a crowd. There are exceptions though. A Yiaaak, for example, is—'

'—hard to describe,' said Lucy. 'I try not to be a specist, but it is not easy where Yiaaaks are concerned. Don't worry, though, you are unlikely to see one—most of them are in prison.'

'What for?' asked Freddy.

'Visual assault—it's a crime in the *Atlantis*. No one is allowed in Zyne society unless they are visually *acceptable*.'

Was she serious? It was getting hard for Freddy to tell, and he was still racking his brain over any other unusual beings he might have met.

These thoughts were cut short when a familiar grunt and an explosion of butoxious odours alerted him to the fact that Gruntenguile was awake.

---

[22] This refers to the ability of the tele-communicator to use the language of any creature with whom they are communicating.

17. A Festival . . . of Sorts

'The master aliens—the Zynes,' continued Haji, 'are responsible for the Dark Cloud. They have built a machine in the north—the Probe Tower—to capture energy from the Earth's core to repower their ship. That tower is causing the Dark Cloud and, unless something is done about it, life on Earth will end.'

'How do you plan to stop something as big as that?' asked Freddy, staring at the Dark Cloud glowering over the northern sky.

'The Zynes,' said Haji, 'live in their crashed spacecraft, the *Atlantis*, which lies in the foothills of the Central Pangean Mountains. It is off-limits to outsiders except for once a year when they hold a festival . . . of sorts. The inhabitants of Pangea are divided, and this festival is the Zynes' way of bringing everyone together. It's like a national holiday. There is a tournament at this festival, and the best performers are granted an audience with the Alpha Zyne. The winner of the tournament gets to ask the Alpha Zyne for a prize of their choosing. It can be anything they like. Our plan is to join one of these teams and, if that team wins, we will request a visit to the Probe Tower.'

'And if that team wins, and if your request is granted, what do you do when you get there?'

Haji looked over Freddy's shoulder to the Dark Cloud and did not reply.

'What do we do when we get there?' repeated Freddy.

Haji clutched the ring beneath his shirt. 'That was Count Schnauzer's area of expertise,' he said.

'So you only have half a plan?'

'At the moment it is better than no plan and, at the moment, there is enough to do just getting a place in the tournament. It's not the sort of thing you turn up to uninvited.' Haji let go of the ring and ran his fingers through his hair. 'That is why we must first meet up with a group of Tribals. Without their help we will not even be able enter the *Atlantis*.'

'Tribals? Who are . . .?'

Haji turned first to Gruntenguile, but he just grunted, and looked the other way. No one could appear more disinterested in what was going on around them than Gruntenguile.

He turned next to Lucy. 'Perhaps you should answer that question,' he said. 'How would you describe them, Lucy?'

Lucy was cleaning her revolver. She looked through the barrel at Freddy as she replied. 'They are a sub-species of the Zynes, although . . .'

'Although what?' asked Freddy.

'Well, I can't say for sure, but I have heard they have some powers that are superior to even the Zynes—seventh sense powers—which they only ever use in extreme circumstances.'

'How did these Tribals get to Africa?'

'They were originally called Subzynes. When the Zyne spaceship crash-landed . . .' Lucy swayed her head as she pretended her hair was crash-landing. Freddy pretended not to notice. 'The tight social structure between the Zynes and Subzynes fell apart. The Subzynes had always been the workforce of Zyne society. They respect the technical genius of the Zynes, but when their spaceship crash-landed on Earth some of them lost faith in the Zynes. They abandoned the spaceship and set up their own groups south of the Central Pangean Mountains. These Subzynes became known as Tribals. They live not unlike more recent hunter and gatherer societies.'

'What about the rest of them?'

'Most of them still live around the spaceship. Like peasants around a medieval castle, I guess. They farm for the production of nutrition capsules and biodiesel for the Zynes' machines.'

'Why do the Tribals who have left the *Atlantis* go back for this tournament?'

'Food is scarce, and the Zynes reward all competitors with nutrition capsules—enough to keep their groups going for a year.'

'And what do the Zynes get in return?'

'They win,' said Haji.

'But what exactly is this tournament? Is it like a sports day?'

'Hmm . . . something like that,' said Haji.

'Okay,' said Freddy, 'so we win this sports day, request a trip to the Probe Tower, shut it down—even though we don't know how because we've lost Schnauzer—and save the world. That sounds great, except for one minor detail. We all know life on Earth continues to exist—millions of years from now! How can it end now, when it continues to exist—in our time?'

Lucy gave Freddy one of her more searing looks. 'It's a little more complicated than that and, to be honest, I don't understand it properly myself. It's like, where does the universe end? We know it can't end because there would have to be something next to where it ends, but still we can't imagine it. It is the same with time. Before the Arnhem Land expedition did you think that time travel was even possible?'

Buck Rogers flashed through Freddy's mind.

'What else don't you know about time?'

109

Freddy did not know what to say. In his desperation, he glanced at Gruntenguile, but he remained silent.

'I know that what we have just told you sounds crazy, but crazy stuff happens all the time, and what we really understand of the universe amounts to a flea's hair in a herd of elephants.'

Gruntenguile grunted.

18. Aloft

There is a lot of time for thinking when you are drifting for days and nights on end in a basket. Especially when you only have three companions and different reasons to doubt each of them.

Often, Freddy thought about his father.

Was he in Pangea?

It made some sense that he was. Firstly, being in Pangea would explain why no trace of him had emerged in the past six years. Secondly, his father was an anthropologist, and what anthropologist worth their salt would not want to research a lost civilization 250 million years before their own time?

Determined as he was to think things through, one question blocked his way every time. Why would his father abandon his own son without notice to embark on such an expedition? This question always left him floundering.

Each day the weather was the same as the day before and the day before that, and Freddy knew just what it would be like tomorrow. Hot and humid. The balloon wilted into tired preternatural shapes above them. The horizon shimmered to the west; billowed into a darkening cloud to the north.

Only three times was the weather any different, and, on each occasion, the change was violent and terrifying. Cyclonic storms sometimes hit Darwin, and Freddy remembered a big blow in 1937 that had caused a lot of damage and some loss of life, but it was nothing to the storms over the Tethys Sea.

When the wind began to rise and the dark clouds banked in the distance, Haji turned up the flame to rise above the clouds. At crazy altitudes, they shivered and watched the storm raging below. The thunderclaps were like cannon fire, and the lightning bolts split and lit the sky for miles. It was impossible to sleep during those storms, and, for days afterwards, Freddy and his companions dozed in the lazy sun like dogs.

Time moved slowly. Like their shadows, which rose before them at dawn, and crept imperceptibly behind them as the day wore on. The long afternoons were the worst. They stretched as endlessly as the ocean surrounding them, before dying through a seeming lack of further interest into the night.

Nights thickened quickly. Stars tried but failed to penetrate the haze that still hung in the air even in the midst of the ocean. Sometimes, just after the setting of the sun, in the western sky, Freddy could just make out the Evening Star. When that disappeared, it became an alien sky. The Milky Way was a blur of light so faint that Freddy wondered whether he was only imagining what he knew should be there. He looked hard for the Southern Cross but could never find it.

Despite the darkness and the gentle rocking of the basket, Freddy found it hard to sleep when all he had been doing all day was sitting or standing. At those times with everyone else sleeping peacefully at his feet Freddy felt lonelier than he had ever thought it possible to feel. Lonelier than he had been when, lying in his bed as a child, he had tried to push back the darkness of time to catch a glimpse of his mother. Lonelier than when his father had disappeared. Lonelier than when Professor Dupler had ignored him for days on end as he agonized over his research. This loneliness gripped him so tightly that it was hard to think his way out of it. Sometimes he thought of Koia and tried to convince himself that she really did not intend to turn him into a line of leather accessories. Sometimes, possibly because of her proximity, he even thought of Lucy. There were days when she hardly said a bad word to him and, as the voyage continued, the time between her bad words seemed to stretch further and further.

For the entire journey, they did not see a single island. The horizon stretched around them so tightly it looked like it might break under the strain. The sea rolled endlessly beneath them sharing its secrets only with the wind.

According to Haji's floating continents theory, Turkey, Iran, Tibet and India would later tear themselves away from Antarctica, and float across that sea on their way to the northern hemisphere.

'Blazes!'

'Yes, and at the same time Europe and Africa, and the Americas will tear apart, creating the Atlantic Ocean.'

During Haji's floating continents lectures, Freddy stuck to the principle of not antagonizing a lunatic.

'It really is a living planet, Freddy,' said Haji.

Freddy did not see it that way. To him even the water seemed dead. As if the black cloud that was choking the northern sky was somehow bleeding into it.

But one day, they did see some life.

Just over a month into their flight, a black shape like a dotless question mark reared out of the water, like the periscope of a giant submarine. Freddy was the first to see it.

'What's that?'

Lucy hopped up and stood alongside Freddy. Gruntenguile and Haji did the same, and they squeezed in tight on the western side of the basket causing it to dip downwards. They squinted into the sun trying to make out the object ahead. They drew nearer and it became more distinct. As they drew level, it looked upwards, and Freddy could actually see its eyes as it turned to look at them.

'Is that what I think it is?' asked Freddy.

Gruntenguile grunted.

'Apparently there are still some of them left,' said Haji. 'The Scots call one of his ancestors the Loch Ness Monster.'

'But this is not a monster, said Lucy, so close to Freddy that he could feel her electricity. 'It's a plesiosaur.'

The way Lucy said this made Freddy turn and look at her. Closer than he ever had before.

'What?' said Lucy.

'Nothing,' said Freddie. 'Only I think you're right. She's not a monster.'

'How do you know it's a she?'

As they floated directly overhead, they cast a shadow over the shining creature. In retaliation for this outrage, it whipped its neck back and sprayed them all with diamond drops of snotty water.

Arching its neck, it took one final look at the strange aliens in the wicker basket, held aloft by nothing more than hot air. Its upper lip slid over its sharply pointed teeth as if it was smiling, before it slid silently back into the slimy sea.

Part 3:

An Unnecessary

Cataclysm

CENTRAL PANGEAN MOUNTAINS

19. Aground, Seven weeks later

Days before the African coastline appeared, the Central Pangean Mountains reared over the clouds to the northwest, like a land in the sky. Words pale before some sights, and one such sight was these magnificent mountains. In our time, they stand ten thousand miles apart. Worn down to the Appalachians in North America and the Atlas Mountains in northern Africa. Beautiful in their own way, but not a shadow of the mighty range that crowned central Pangea. They soared far higher than the modern-day Himalayas. Winds played wild, howling symphonies over their slopes and soaring peaks.

At the base of the range, a mighty scar like a rift valley ran for hundreds of miles to a metal monstrosity teetering on the edge of the continent.

This monstrosity was the *Atlantis*, the largest creature-built construction the Earth has ever known. It loomed ever larger as the *COY* drifted nearer.

Everything looked small next to the Central Pangean Mountains except the *Atlantis*.

They finally reached the ship in the early evening just as thousands of lights lit its side like the Milky Way.

'How long is that thing?' asked Freddy staring at the galaxy of lights fading into the evening darkness.

'Ten, maybe twelve miles across,' said Lucy.

'Wait until you see it up close in the light of day,' added Haji.

'Where do we land?' asked Freddy. A curious full moon was out but it was still not going to be easy landing the *COY* at night.

Lucy turned away from the ship and pointed in the opposite direction. 'A little way to the south. All the challengers have set up camp there. The more fancied teams are further out. The less fancied teams are closer to the entrance to the *Atlantis*.'

'Where's our team?' asked Freddy.

'Our team are the Spring Tribals. They are camped right next to the drawbridge,' said Lucy.

Powered by the gyro blades they circled the many challenger's fires several times before deciding on a landing spot. Haji opened the deflation port, and they began a slow glide to the ground. At first, the raucous noise of a gathering rose to meet them, but as they drew nearer, it hushed to silence. They had been seen.

'What are these Tribals like?' asked Freddy, feeling more nervous once the silence set in.

Reaching up, Gruntenguile patted Freddy's back. 'It's okay, Little Boss. No need to worry . . . grrrnnt.'

'How do you know?' whispered Freddy.

Just then, the basket hit the ground with a jolt, and the balloon collapsed gracefully around them as if exhausted after its long journey. The basket tipped and sent them spilling over the ground. Freddy felt a momentary rush of relief. Then he looked about and saw that they were surrounded.

'Spring Tribals,' whispered Haji.

The best way to describe them would be to say they all looked—if not exactly like—very similar to Gruntenguile.

Freddy turned to Lucy. 'Over the Tethys Sea, when you said I had already met several species of alien, were you including Gruntenguile?'

Lucy nodded.

'Is that true, Gruntenguile?'

'It depends on what you mean by an alien. The fact that my ancestors come from somewhere else makes me no less an Earthling than you—'

'Silence!' A sharp voice returned their attention to the Tribals who shook their spears like so many exclamation marks to the order. Among them, prancing excitedly, were a few sweat-shiny Spotters. Their rough, saliva-dripping tongues dangling ridiculously from their panting mouths.

Like Gruntenguile, the Tribals were all short, though not quite as short as pygmies. They were also extremely hairy, and this was made even more obvious by the fact that they were wearing nothing more than loincloths and crude animal skin capes similar to those still worn by indigenous groups in many parts of Freddy's world. Their faces were humanoid with the most notable difference being that, like Gruntenguile, they had bigger foreheads, which shaded their eyes and gave them a slightly threatening appearance. Like the slow-chewing beasts Freddy had already encountered in southern Pangea, their skulls seemed doubly thick as if bashing heads was the favourite pastime of the Permian period.

At first, Freddy was reassured by the fact that they looked human. Then he reflected on the humans who had tried to kill him in recent times, and he was not so sure.

After an awkward pause, one of the Tribals stepped forward. He was no taller but much stouter than his companions.

'Follow me,' he said.

Though small, his voice commanded attention. His face was horribly scarred, and there was a dent above his right eye as if he had been struck with a heavy and hard object. His hair was tied in a knot around what appeared to be a human tibia bone although Freddy did not want to jump to uncharitable conclusions.

A gap opened in the circle of Tribals, and Gruntenguile followed the Tribals' leader through this gap, signalling for the others to follow. They made their way to an open area surrounding a large fire. At the head of this space sat an old man who, by his venerable appearance and lack of activity, Freddy guessed must be their chief. As they approached, his expression was somewhere between a smoky-eyed stupor and sleep.

The Chief looked Freddy and his companions over one at a time. First, he had what seemed to be a very agreeable exchange of glances with Gruntenguile. This seemed to put him at ease.

He inspected Lucy for much longer. This could have been because she looked so remarkably un-hairy in her present company. Her large, brown eyes seemed to be bulging out of her head when seen next to the hollow gaze of the Chief.

Next, he greeted Haji.

'You said you would return, and you have. And not a day too soon.'

'I was not sure that I would make it in time,' said Haji.

'And who is this?' asked the Chief, finally turning to Freddy.

'This,' said Haji, 'is Freddy O'Toole.'

The Chief stepped towards Freddy who fidgeted under his gaze. Remembering his manners, he took off his hat as the chief continued to stare at him from the darkness of his eye sockets.

'How do you do?' asked Freddy.

'Don't talk!' hissed Lucy.

'Your friend is right, Freddy. Tribals never talk more than they have to before eating. Let's sit and feast a while—then we will talk.'

The Chief walked back to the stump that served as his throne, leaping onto it with surprising agility. He pointed for Freddy and his companions to sit on the ground in front of him.

After months in the air, the ground felt hard and alien beneath him, but Freddy was glad to sit and just look.

His eyes were getting used to the moonlight, and what he saw about him was the strangest sight in his life to that moment.

Describing any group of beings is like painting the ever-changing ripples of sand on a beach. After every brushstroke, a gust of wind, or scuttling crab, or a high breaking wave, changes the scene forever. Seen from a distance, creatures—human or otherwise—may look the same but each is different and changable in their own way. This was especially the case with Tribals and particularly so when they were celebrating. It was a rollicking gathering and, after a short break caused by the new arrivals, it soon settled back into full swing.

They sat in family groups on stumps (some precariously) arranged in a rough circle about three or four cricket pitches across. Tribals are an active and chatty species. Swivelling, and rolling, and bobbing, most were in at least three conversations at the one time. There was a lot of drinking from gourds and an unbelievable amount of farting, all of which was met with a vast repertoire of fart jokes and guffaws of laughter. They were as quaint a race of beings as can be found anywhere, and as near to leprechauns as you are ever likely to see. Freddy could not look at them without smiling.

His smile soon grew even wider. As he was watching the Tribals' antics, a leafy tray of roast meat appeared in front of him. After months of nutrition capsules, the smell of just roasted meat was overpowering. He soon became so lost in his enjoyment of the feast that Lucy took it upon herself to tap his head with a rib bone to regain his attention.

'Ouch! That hurt!'

She pointed to Haji and the Chief. 'Pay attention,' she said.

'I can tell you—it's going to get worse,' said Haji wiping the fatty juices from his mouth and shining moustache with the sleeve of his shirt. 'We—the Doylians that is—believe that the Earth is headed towards an unnecessary cataclysm.' The words hung in the air for a while, and Freddy thought that 'unnecessary' seemed like such a prim word to be using in the circumstances.

Seeing Haji's mouth full of meat again, Lucy continued. 'Unless, of course, we do something about it,' she said. There was steel in her voice. Her eyes as usual caught more than their share of firelight.

'It is not the first time I have heard this from Wanderers,' said the Chief.

Lucy leaned towards Freddy. 'Wanderers are outsiders like us who have arrived from future times.'

I never would have guessed, thought Freddy looking back to the Chief. He found that gentleman staring at him strangely and guessed that he did not like others thinking when he held the floor.

'Our former masters, the Zynes, are a very powerful species. They see this world differently from you Wanderers. That is why many Wanderers find themselves in the *Atlantis* Brig[23]—waiting to become useful. What makes you think you will be any different?'

It was a Tribal custom for the Chief to be the shortest man, but, despite his size, the chief's voice rang through the still night air, causing eyes to turn in his direction. He was impressively dressed for the feast, wearing a thick fawn-coloured hide, which, by its luxurious fur, Freddy guessed had previously been worn by some beast in the frozen wastes of southern Pangea. His beard when he was standing, almost touched the ground despite being

---

[23] A brig is a term usually used for prisons onboard ships. The term appears to have been introduced to Pangea by Port Royal pirates many years before Freddy's arrival.

fashionably tied in parts around sabre-like teeth. His forelock was even more impressively wrapped around the polished femur of a Thrinaxodon. The Tribals considered these hairy, sharp-toothed carnivores lucky, and evolution would prove them right. To add to his grandeur, the Chief also sat on a taller stump, his feet dangling almost a foot above the ground.

The Chief waited so long for Haji's reply that Freddy expected Lucy to jump in and answer for him but instead she sat with her eyes trained to Haji as if she had no more idea what he was going to say than anyone else.

'The cause of the Dark Cloud that threatens us all lies to the north of the *Atlantis*—it is the Probe Tower that the Zynes are using to drain the Earth's energy. If we don't shut it down soon, it will be too late.'

The Chief waved his hand at this nonsense. 'No one goes to the north. The land of the Dark Cloud is too dangerous. Besides they only let Tribals as far as the *Atlantis*, and that is only allowed during the tournament starting tomorrow.' The Chief turned and bowed his head slightly to a battered individual who sat on the stump next to him. He was the same Tribal who had greeted them earlier and led them to the Chief. 'Beyond those great mountains,' continued the Chief, pointing his bone to the ghostly peaks, 'the land is heavily guarded. It is covered in Zyne bases, and their technology is far superior to that of any Wanderer we have met.'

'We agree with you,' said Haji. 'If we are to get to the north it must be with the Zynes' approval and ...'

'The only way for that to happen is to win the tournament and request the Alpha Zyne to take you there.' The Chief finished the sentence just as Haji hoped he would.

'You took the words right out of my mouth,' said Haji.

'I appreciate the capacity of your species to value hope over sense, but what you are suggesting is ridiculous. For hundreds of years—ever since our ancestors and other Tribals left the *Atlantis*—we have competed in the Tournament of Blood. No one ever beats the Zyne champions. They are unbeatable. As advanced as Zynes are technologically, they love nothing more than fighting. When Tribals get together, we eat and dance. When Zynes get together, they fight. It is an instinct in them like breathing. And, like all things that are instinctive, they do it well. The only challengers ever to get close have been the odd Wanderer but, whenever that happens, there is always a rule change, or disqualification, or something. The main rule of the Tournament of Blood is that the Zynes must not lose.'

Freddy's ears had been pricking through this exchange. He had been led to believe that the tournament was like a sports day. This was the first time he had heard it referred to as the Tournament of Blood, and he did not like the sound of it. He had been expecting high jump competitions, three-legged races, and half-price fairy floss on the way out. 'Tournament of Blood' did not sound like that.

'We Tribals have a saying to describe plans like yours: "It is a beautiful spaceship—but it does not fly".' Haji's teeth froze over his bone.

The Chief smiled at him. The kind of smile that stupidity in its rarest forms always inspires. Tribals within easy hearing chuckled, some pointing their half-eaten bones at Haji. One even repeated before bursting into laughter, 'It is a beautiful spaceship—but it does not fly.'

'Every Tribals group in the Lowlands,' continued the Chief, 'enters their greatest warrior in the Tournament of Blood, and each year they are not just defeated but humiliated. Raaktu has fought for the past five years.'

Once more, the Chief pointed to the battered individual alongside him. 'Here, he is a champion; in the *Atlantis*, he does not stand a chance. Thankfully, he has the heart of a Lycaenops and is still prepared to fight, but to think of winning against the Zynes. It will not happen. The idea is too ridiculous.'

For a moment, Haji looked defeated, but he was used to things not being easy.

'I agree with you,' he said. 'I do not think that Raaktu can win either. This year, you need a new champion.'

'Who? No other fighter comes near Raaktu. Besides, there is no time to find anyone else.'

The animation of their discussion had attracted attention. Those seated nearest the Chief stopped their chatter and held their farts.

The question of who should represent them in the Tournament of Blood was a great talking point among Tribals. Raaktu, their current champion, sat quietly on his stump. Staring at the bone in his hand, he chewed as if not listening, but Freddy could tell that he was hanging off each word. In paying attention to Raaktu's reaction, however, Freddy did not hear Haji's reply to the Chief's question as clearly as he might have.

'Freddy,' said Haji.

'What?' asked Freddy.

'Freddy,' repeated Haji, 'I nominate Freddy for the Tournament of Blood.' Then, turning to Freddy, he added. 'I would have volunteered myself only my back is still killing me. I'd do anything for a good massage.'

Haji's nomination rippled around the circle of Spring Tribals until it met itself on the other side. There was a second or two of reflection and surprised farting. Then a mighty roar erupted. One of the interesting things about telepathy is that groups can share the same feelings almost instantly. Even the Spotters, who had been lying

125

on the edge of the circle catching bones thrown by their masters, sprang to their feet and danced, although not sure why. Once stated, Haji's solution seemed obvious to everyone. Raaktu had been defeated year after year. Surely, it was time to give someone else a shot. In truth, not one of them thought Freddy had a grasshopper's chance at a frog party, but a full moon was up, and their bellies were full of meat and a good few draughts of gingko wine as it turns out. Besides, it felt good to be cheering.

In the midst of this uproar, Lucy fell backwards off her stump.

Freddy would have laughed had he not just been nominated for the Tournament of Blood. He looked at Raaktu. The light of the fire at that moment highlighted his scars and the crater over his right eye. He expected him to object to losing his job, but instead he gave Freddy a gracious nod as if to say 'well done and good luck to you', and kept eating.

The Chief hopped off his stump and raised his hands to silence the crowd. The Tribals hushed quickly although some of the Spotters continued to dance about until brought to order by sharp commands and bones hurled at them by their masters. 'A new nomination has been made for the Tournament of Blood. For the past five years, ever since the ... unfortunate accident, which ended the career of our previous champion, Crakka the Courageous ...'

Freddy wanted to hear more about this unfortunate accident, but the Chief rolled on. 'Raaktu has been a great champion, and, although not victorious, he has fought with great honour!' The Tribals cheered and those near Raaktu slapped his carpeted back. The Spotters kicked up their bony heels. 'But,' roared the Chief, once more silencing the gathering. 'It is time for a new champion. The Wanderer, Haji, has nominated Freddy—Fearless Freddy O'Toole, as that champion.'

The Tribals' joy swelled, and a tipsy ululation erupted around the circle. It grew and spun like a hula-hoop, and Freddy's head spun with it. It felt like the swirling noise might lift them all up into the night sky.

'The question is Freddy—do you accept?'

Every instinct in Freddy's body screamed no, but he could not stop his head nodding yes.

The Chief slapped his back and Freddy choked on his steak.

'Tomorrow,' cried the Chief, above the cheers of the Tribals, 'our new Champion marches into the *Atlantis*! Tonight—we raise our gourds and toast—a fair fight!'

20. The Atlantis

'What exactly is this tournament?' asked Freddy. 'I am guessing that Raaktu's face was not messed up like that by tripping in a three-legged race!'

'Look,' said Lucy, 'I know it looks like we haven't been entirely up front with you about this tournament—'

'—of Blood,' interrupted Freddy.

They were speaking on top of a small hill overlooking the *Atlantis* on one side and the Spring Tribal encampment on the other. As he spoke, Freddy wound and shook his pocket watch. It had stopped somewhere over the Tethys Sea.

In the early dawn, the *Atlantis* seemed even bigger than it had at night. Made almost entirely of the alien metal, adamantium,[24] it had survived a space flight begun before the creation of the Earth; 3,000-degree Fahrenheit temperatures while hurtling through the Earth's atmosphere; and a smashing crash-landing, which had gouged a scar in the foothills hundreds of miles long. A patina of grey-green tarnished its otherwise smooth plated surface.

Soaring to dizzying heights, it faded into the swirling clouds that shrouded the Central Pangean Mountains. Rows of rivet heads, the size of truck tyres, ran for miles along its side.

'So what sort of fighting is it—because that's what it is—isn't it?'

'Yes, it is. But I don't know of anyone who has died, recently. It is more of a ritual than anything.'

[24] The invention of adamantium is usually attributed to Dr Myron MacLain. His connection to events described in this book remains unclear.

'Why would Haji think that little old me—Freddy O'Toole—a boy—might win a fight against alien warriors, when Raaktu has been smashed for the past five years?' asked Freddy.

'He had his reasons.'

Freddy looked doubtfully at Lucy. When you have been deceived to the extent that you suddenly find yourself about to battle gladiatorial aliens 250 million years before your own existence, it is very difficult to know who you can, and cannot trust.

'What reasons?' said Freddy.

'Well, you do know how to fight.'

'What do you mean?'

Lucy's voice dropped to a whisper. 'You know what I mean.'

Freddy's eyes looked beyond Lucy into the haze of the coming day but his mind drifted elsewhere. It took him to his backyard, 250 million years into the future to when he was only six years old. He was living with his father then, and they were lying on the thick bladed grass under their clothesline. They were not reading or looking up at the clouds. Instead, Freddy had his father in a headlock. Squeezing as hard as his little arms would allow him.

'*Harder Freddy! Harder!*' his father cried.

'*What if I hurt you?*'

'*That's the point. Now—squeeze harder!*'

The sweat on his father's shiny head made Freddy think he was squeezing his brains out.

'I can't . . .'

'Can't what?' said Lucy, grabbing Freddy's arm.

Freddy looked down at Lucy's hand on his arm. 'It doesn't matter,' he said. 'How do you know my father trained me?'

'My mother has been in this game a long time. Knowledge is everything. But that's not the only reason.'

The sun was rising, and its rays reflected off the *Atlantis*. Freddy squinted, and waited for Lucy to continue.

'There is another group of . . . beings we have not yet told you about, Freddy. There are some in our time—not many—who are Crossbloods—the offspring of time travelling Zynes and humans. Your father was unusual enough for us, and others, to think that he may have been a Crossblood.' Lucy waited for Freddy to say something, but he was determined not to, so she continued. 'That would make you also a Crossblood.'

'You thought that would help me win the Tournament of Blood?'

'There's more to it than that. You see, the Zyne champion has been beaten before.'

'But the Chief said that the Zyne champions have never been beaten,' said Freddy.

'That is the official line, but the Chief knows full well that he has been beaten. By someone very close to you.'

'Who?' Freddy's chest tightened as he asked this question because he already sensed the answer.

'By your father.'

Freddy gasped but his amazement was cut short by a commotion in their camp.

Woooooofff!

Sticks gathered for a fire had exploded in a giant woof of flames as Gruntenguile ignited them by pyrokinesis.[25] He did not know that Haji had doused the sticks in biodiesel a few moments earlier and was looking for a match. The explosion singed the tip of Gruntenguile's beard and eyebrows. It also caused Haji to look up from his pocket search and see Gruntenguile's near miss and, beyond that, Lucy and Freddy deep in conversation.

'Lucy,' he yelled, 'we could do with a hand down here.'

'Sure,' shouted Lucy, 'I'm on my way.' Then, turning to

---

[25] The lighting of fires using psychic powers.

Freddy, she said. 'I have to go. Good luck.'

'Wait!' cried Freddy. 'There's just one more thing I have to know. How long ago was that?'

'Do you mean—was it after your father disappeared?' Freddy nodded.

'No—it was before that.'

'*Before?*'

'I'm sorry.'

Freddy did not hear her apology.

'How could I *not know* stuff like that about my own father? How could I live with him all those years, and not know that?'

'I don't know, but I guess if people don't tell you things—' Lucy weirdly cut short her own sentence before suddenly staring at Freddy like something was hanging from his nose.

'Why are you looking at me like that?' asked Freddy.

'It just occurred to me that you have never asked me about my father.'

Freddy stared at her. She was right. It had never crossed his mind that she even had a father. If he had thought about it before the expedition, he would have most probably imagined her the result of some form of demonic conception.

As he stared, a dreadful noise, like every creaky door that had ever been were opening at exactly the same time, erupted behind him.

'What about your father?' Freddy screamed so that Lucy could hear him over the creaking.

'This is about the dumbest time possible to ask that question, Freddy.'

'Why?'

Lucy pointed behind him to the *Atlantis*. 'Because, they're lowering the entrance ramp. It's time to get ready.'

21. A Secret Weapon

The Spring Tribals camp was alive with activity. As it was closest to the entrance ramp, all of the other challengers were gathering there as well as a swelling crowd of spectators. Every Tribal fit enough to make the journey to the *Atlantis* plus every Subzyne from the agricultural districts were jostling for a spot to watch the challengers enter the *Atlantis*. That was all they would be able to see. Their species was only allowed on board the ship if they were part of a competing team.

The entrance ramp was still descending from the clouds. Freddy had seen a newsreel showing the giant US aircraft carriers such as the *USS Enterprise*, and he described the ramp to the *Atlantis* as being at least ten times longer. The noise it made grew louder and he clasped his hands tighter over his ears. Lucy and Haji, he noticed, had brought hyperseal earplugs that blocked the sound.

'Sorry,' screamed Lucy. 'I just didn't think to bring another pair.'

As horrible as the sound was, it was nothing compared with the clang of the metal ramp as it finally smashed onto the rocky slope.

Haji removed his earplugs and walked over to Freddy. 'Are you ready?'

Freddy was not ready, but he nodded anyway.

'In that case I think it's time to show you our secret weapon. I'm hoping it will give us a psychological edge.' Haji smiled at Freddy, and Lucy looked surprised.

'I swear I don't know anything about this,' she said.

Haji raised his hand and waved. This caused a sudden commotion in the crowd and a general parting of the way, starting at the back and slowly stretching to the front row like a zipper. Once it reached the front, Gruntenguile emerged leading a broad shouldered, dull-eyed beast by a short rein.

Mostly the crowd gasped in surprise, but a few nodding old-timers knew straight away what was happening. The beast was the finest domestic Moschops to be found at short notice in the Subzyne agricultural districts. Its back legs bulged with mighty muscles. Its chest was so deep it was almost dragging on the ground, and, although the front legs were not as impressive, they were just as powerful and quite long. This gave the Moschops the appearance of being a two-legged creature from the front and pushed its chest forward like an overweight wrestler. At that stage of the Permian you could normally play a tune with a little rubber mallet on a Moschops' ribs, but this beast was in such fine condition they were barely visible. The overall effect would have been even grander if its expression were more enthusiastic. Instead, it gazed gloomily out of its deep-set eyes as if it would rather be somewhere else.

'What do you think?' asked Haji.

'Great—the Moschops is going to fight for me?'

'That's good, Freddy,' laughed Haji, 'and you're going to need your sense of humour. No! My plan is to create a mental edge by having you enter the arena riding this mighty beast like Hannibal marching into Rome.'[26]

'Number one, Hannibal never made it to Rome; and number two, this "mighty beast" looks a little . . . lacking in enthusiasm.'

'Don't worry about that,' said Haji. 'It will make you appear ten feet tall.'

---

[26] Hannibal was the great Carthaginian leader In the Second Punic War against Rome (spring 218–201 BC). Hannibal's secret weapon was the use of war elephants, and, Freddy was right, he never made it to Rome.

A rope circled the beast's neck, and reins threaded through eyelets in this rope ran along the neck to where they joined a spit-slathered metal bit on which it exercised its tongue. A rope ladder that was to act as a saddle ran around its chest. Haji nodded towards this and, grabbing hold of it, Freddy attempted to mount his steed. Unfortunately, as he placed his weight on one rung the whole thing slipped around.

Lucy and Gruntenguile scrambled to the other side and held the rope steady. Freddy tried again and was soon standing shakily on the shoulders of the Moschops. He gave the crowd the thumbs up. This meant something very different in the Permian, but they politely accepted the gesture as a cultural misunderstanding.

Freddy sat down and waited.

The other part of Haji's strategy was to enter the *Atlantis* last. With this in mind, he led the Moschops to the side of the ramp, and they waited there for the other combatants and their entourages to pass. As they did so, Gruntenguile gave a brief rundown of each of the groups.

'Desert Tribals—they're as skinny as a stick but as tough as Gorgonopsian leather.

'Swamp Tribals—they don't know the meaning of fear.'

Freddy recalled the Eryops exploding from Sure Death Swamp weeks earlier.

'Cave Tribals—they are almost impossible to beat in the dark but are not so good in normal light.' To confirm this, the last of the Cave Tribals bumped into his teammate from behind and they fell like dominoes.

'Pirate Tribals—those are from the Panthalassic Ocean. I wouldn't trust them as far as I could throw a Pygmy Tribal.'

Most of the challengers filing past were scarred veterans like Raaktu. Their noses flattened and twisted in all manner of violent ways and dents in their craniums. Some had chunks bitten from their ears; some did not have ears. Many of them limped already from injuries sustained in previous tournaments.

This evidence of the event's brutality did nothing to calm Freddy's nerves.

At the same time, however, he could not help feeling some pride. He was about to enter the *Atlantis* just as his father must have before him if Lucy was to be believed. Surely, that meant something. These thoughts crashed about in his head as he watched the remaining challengers pass.

They were not all Tribals.

One of the last groups was led by a sturdy human fellow, a little over six feet tall. He was dressed in the style of the ancient Greeks and carried a short, well-worn broad sword at his side. His thick hair and wild beard were black and his skin pulled tight by powerful muscles that started at his neck and went all the way to his toes.

He nodded at Freddy as he passed. 'Agrosios,' he shouted, thumping his fist into his chest. 'Agrosios the Angry!'

Thinking that such an impromptu expression of enthusiasm deserved a reply, Freddy thumped his chest and shouted, 'Freddy ... Freddy the ... Fearful ... I mean Fearless.'

'That should terrify him,' said Lucy.

Agrosios was accompanied by two much less impressive men. They were weasely in build and wore tweed flat caps of a type not trusted where Freddy came from. They also had Zyne eye tattoos under their right eye.

'Quite a solid lad, eh Guv?' said one of these men, glancing up at Freddy.

'Forgive my associate's bad manners,' said the other. 'Reggie and Bertie—at your service. If you'd care for a little wager, we're your men. At what odds do you rate your boy up there?'

Their accents were working class English.

'We give him some chance, but I am afraid we are not gamblers,' said Haji.

'Well, the best of British to you,' the first speaker replied. They touched the peaks of their caps at the same time and stepped onto the ramp.

It appeared that they were now the last of the challengers.

'That must be it. Let's get this thing over with!' said Freddy. He had been sitting on the Moschops' neck with his legs dangling each side but now hopped up into a standing position. He was about to shake his reins and yell 'giddy-up' when one last group of challengers emerged from the crowd behind them. When Freddy looked back and saw who it was, his heart fell like a little rubber ball from his chest and bounced down the rocky slope.

It was Koia.

She was dressed in the usual fashion of Amazons in a light leather skirt and bodice. The gap between the two revealed a stomach ripped with muscles. Across her shoulders, she wore the white skin of an Antarctic Gorgonopsian, which she had slain single-handedly. Balanced over her shoulder was the double-bladed axe Freddy had last seen in the tent in the Amazonian village.

'After you, ladies,'[27] said Freddy, rather gallantly he thought, waving his hand for them to pass.

Koia and the Amazons surrounding her shook their spears and shouted fierce Amazonian insults. It looked like the Tournament of Blood would start right there and then before they had even set foot on the drawbridge.

A sharp command sorted the matter. 'Go now!'

Turning around, Freddy saw what he thought was his

---

[27] If you ever encounter Amazons—do not call them 'ladies'. They just don't like it!

first Zyne. He looked simply like a blonde-haired man of good build and height, but at the same time, there was an indefinable something about him that was not human. Freddy could not put his finger on what it was, although it may have had something to do with looking too extraordinarily handsome. His face was a perfect mix of the best features of every film star Freddy had ever seen. In his hand, he held a lasernator. They were the preferred weapon of Zynes and could be set from tickle to terminate.

Freddy stared blankly until the Zyne, thinking that he was a bit slow on the uptake, repeated his instruction with a few more details. 'You are to go now, blood-head! The Amazons, as is the custom of our tournament, enter last.'

'What did he call me?' asked Freddy.

'It's just a name for someone with red hair ... grrrnnt,' said Gruntenguile. 'They don't get too many around here.'

Gruntenguile pulled on the Moschops' lead and stepped onto the ramp. Lucy and Haji followed on either side.

Freddy could feel Koia's eyes burning dagger-like holes in his back. Looking ahead, he tried not to think about what she might be thinking.

There was now a big gap between Freddy's group and Agrosios, and the Zynes did not like this gap. They urged them to go faster but a Moschops has only one speed,[28] and that is not fast. Even so, Freddy could see that Haji's strategy was working. There was a dignity in his lumbering advance that was very impressive. The Subzynes gathered around the foot of the ramp looked up at Freddy in wonder and maybe even a little hope. He thought they might cheer, but they remained silent. There were too many Zyne guards.

Freddy glanced at these guards out the tail of his eye as he made his way past. He hoped to see a reaction to

---

[28] Unless it is being chased by a Gorgonopsian.

his grand entrance but there was none. Their faces were as unflinching as the ramp at his feet.

He felt more uncertain with each step. The clouds lifted, and he could soon see the entrance more clearly. Above it stared the eye symbol of the Zynes. The same as the one he had seen in the Timorese cave. The same as the eye on his hatpin. Freddy watched it warily until he was directly beneath it and about to enter the Atlantis. Once he reached that point he lowered his eyes and was momentarily blinded.

The inside of the craft was much brighter and open than he had imagined. The *Atlantis* was made for both space travel and habitation on arrival. The upper skin was therefore retractable, and it was now open to the grey light struggling through the cloudy sky. The raw, icy slopes of the Central Pangean Mountains soared and spied over the rim.

Ahead lay a grand metal avenue, which ran towards the centre of the ship. On each side of this avenue, banks of pipes, like endless submarines, ran for miles. Metal gangways ran along the top and edges of these pipes, and they were crammed with cheering, screaming, fighting Zynes. It looked like riots were breaking out.

'An interesting aspect of Zyne culture,' yelled Lucy, noticing Freddy's startled expression. 'Fighting is their favourite pastime—that's why they're so good at it!'

It was so like Lucy to say something like that.

More Zynes wearing goggles and flying caps flew above them on air bikes not much bigger than their backsides. The avenue, the pipes, everything, led towards a central stem that towered into the mists above everything in the centre of the *Atlantis*. The tallest structure on Freddy's Earth was the Empire State Building. It stood 102 storeys and 1,454 feet to the tip of the antennae mast in the middle of New York. The Alpha Tower in the centre of the *Atlantis* soared three times that height. At the very top sat a saucer-shaped nerve centre known as the Control Disk. It served as the cockpit when the *Atlantis* was in flight mode, and the administration centre when landed. It could also separate and fly independently of the main ship.

Scattered along the entrance avenue, massive screens telecast images of everything that was happening. Freddy was so amazed he forgot his mixed feelings about his companions.

'Blazes!' he cried, nodding to Haji and Lucy.

'It's really something,' said Lucy. 'But you haven't seen anything yet.'

A fresh eruption of cheers greeted each new group of lowland challengers. Each seeming louder than the one before.

Zynes were busy beings. They worked with a cool and clinical sense that everything they did was moving them forward to some grand, ultimate thing. None of them, if asked, could clearly say what that thing was but that did not seem to bother them. It was only once every year at the Tournament of Blood that they got to really let loose.

An extra volume of cheers, like a freak wave, marked Freddy's progress along the thoroughfare.

'This Moschops was a good idea,' yelled Freddy.

Gruntenguile did not have the heart to tell Freddy that Zynes cheer and boo the opposite way around from modern humans. He grunted agreement.

Smiling at the crowd, Freddy pumped his fist, and the cheering grew louder.

'They're going to burst if they cheer any louder,' yelled Freddy. 'Maybe they heard about the python.'

'That must be it . . . grrrnnt,' said Gruntenguile.

'How are your legs holding out up there?' asked Haji. 'There's a way to go yet. Maybe you should sit down.'

'Sit down? No way! This crowd loves me!'

The Alpha Tower became less of a blur in the distance. The outline of the distant pipes that edged the avenue slowly sharpened to a puzzle of angular shapes. As they neared this point, Freddy noticed a large cage hanging in the air. It cast a webbed shadow over everything beneath it.

Reaching the front of the Alpha Tower, they discovered that it was surrounded by a large open area, paved like the rest of the ship with solid sheets of adamantium. The challengers were directed one to the left, and the next to the right and so forth, until eventually Freddy and Koia stood in the two innermost spots looking directly towards the tower. It was made of the same crystal as the crystal sword.

The pipes that had extended all the way from the edge of the ship turned at right angles when they reached this open space and provided a viewing platform that surrounded the tower. Only the seriously rich Zynes in the southern part would see any first-hand action. Everyone else had to be content with watching on one of the many suspended screens.

Bollards were scattered about the open space. Unknown to the challengers, the Zyne champions had been training in ways to smash opponents into them for months. Lights of every colour imaginable, and some Freddy had never seen, cut the arena into gaudy fragments. Randomly moving and pulsing, they gave the queasy sense that the entire space was alive, blurring and distorting things for the challengers and directing the attention of the spectators.

On the outer edge of this space ran the tournament's most famous feature and the one that had inspired its popular name. It was a straight, square-banked channel brimming to the top with what appeared to be blood.

'Don't worry,' shouted Haji, noticing Freddy's horrified

look. 'It's not real blood—just a bit of theatrics. The eliminated challengers are thrown in and washed from the arena. The crowd loves it!'

'That is so disgusting,' said Lucy. She would have said more, but a flourish of noise and a blinding flash of lights on the side of the tower stole her attention. The gaudy beams that had been pulsing about the arena suddenly froze on a metal panel inserted into the tower directly above the challengers. Just as suddenly, that panel dissolved, and a group of guards and officials stepped out onto a balcony that magically appeared before them.

'The official party,' said Lucy, peering around the chest of the Moschops, who was looking sideways, up and down, for something to eat.

The guards shielded the main party as they emerged but then stepped aside. Freddy could now see the officials, although not clearly due to the bright lights. Those lights then flashed to the side and Freddy's eyes fell on a man standing in front of the rest.

'The Beta Zyne . . . grrrnnt,' said Gruntenguile.

The Beta Zyne was older yet more oozingly handsome than any of the Zynes Freddy had already seen.

'And, of course, there's no need to introduce his special guest,' said Lucy.

Freddy could only just hear Lucy over the hubbub of the crowd. He had been so struck by the appearance of the Beta Zyne that his eyes had not yet wandered to the other members of the party. They did now.

Standing to the right, and just behind the Beta Zyne, was a woman; the only woman outside of the Amazons and Lucy that he had seen since entering the *Atlantis*.

And Lucy was right in saying that she needed no introduction.

22. A Change of Rules

'Doctor Claudia Bufon!' gasped Freddy.

The last time he had seen her she had been wearing green coveralls. What she was wearing now looked like it had been poured onto her body in a molten state. Black high-heeled boots extended to her knees. Above that, she wore black leather pants and a tight-fitting silver bodice. A pistol belt angled across her waist, and she stood slightly side-on as if the holstered pistol—a Walther P38 semi-automatic—was her favourite accessory. She also wore a black aviator's cap with goggles strapped to the front suggesting that she may have been observing them from an air bike as they were making their way down the central avenue. The butt end of a lasernator strapped to her back protruded over her left shoulder. Black gloves concealed her forearms and flared out at her elbows. Above that, to Freddy's surprise, her right arm was covered in more tattoos than a Maori sailor.

Stepping forward she rested one gloved hand on the handle of her pistol. A sliver of hair, like a dangling viper, dissected the right side of her face.

'What's she doing here?' asked Freddy.

'I'm not sure,' said Lucy. 'But I'm guessing that, whatever it is, it's not for the greater good.'

Despite Lucy's surprise at seeing Dr Bufon, Freddy looked suspiciously at her as he clambered down from the Moschops.

Lucy threw her hands in the air. 'I don't know how many times we have to tell you, but we don't know everything. We are just small players. It now appears that Doctor Bufon is a much bigger player.'

'We're as surprised as you are,' added Haji.

'And do you mind if I make a suggestion?' asked Lucy.

'Go ahead,' said Freddy.

'If you must gawk at her—close your mouth.'

Any moral high ground he had taken from Lucy was taken back, and Freddy was wondering how that had happened when the Beta Zyne stepped forward to speak. The crowd fell silent.

'Zynes . . .' Freddy could not see a microphone, but the words boomed over the ship as if spoken by a giant. 'Once more we find ourselves gathered for our festival. Our annual Tournament of Blood.'

The crowd booed and Freddy wondered how they could be so unkind to their second highest leader. He wondered also why the Beta Zyne was speaking English. He later realised that he was not speaking at all but sending his thoughts telepathically in as many languages as was necessary.

'Welcome also to our Lowland Subzynes'—Zynes refused to accept Tribals as a name—'and Amazons, all of whom we hope will one day forget their petty issues and re-join us here in the *Atlantis*. I hope it is sooner rather than later . . . or too late. We may not be here much longer.' He paused to allow time for these last words to sink in. 'I see also that some Wanderers have found their way to our festival. Some of you are here to test your strength against our champions. Welcome to you. Our tournament is open to all and we'—a crooked smile broke across the Beta Zyne's face—'hope you enjoy the experience.'

Zyne humour is famous throughout the universe for not being very funny to non-Zynes. In some parts, what Zynes call humour is considered gloating cruelty. The Zynes crowding around the arena laughed like a gutbust of Chthonosauri.[29] Gruntenguile looked at Freddy, and grunted.

The crowd died down as the Beta Zyne continued.

'As is our custom we will waste no time in getting our tournament underway. Let me start, however, by going over some rules. Firstly, only one-on-one fighting is allowed. Any breaking of this rule may result in lasernation and disqualification.'

'Unless you are a Zyne ... grrrnnt,' added Gruntenguile under his breath.

'If there are an odd number of combatants,' continued the Beta Zyne, 'challengers must wait for an opponent to become available. And finally, and most importantly, combatants are only eliminated once they have been thrown into the Channel of Blood.'

The challengers looked towards the bloody channel bordering the arena. Some nodded; others were too frozen in fear to do so.

'It is now time to hand in any weapons in your possession. They will be returned to you after the tournament.'

Freddy drew his machete from its sheath. It had become like an extra limb, and he was reluctant to part with it, but he had no choice. Lucy handed her Colt 45 over with the same reluctance.

The Beta Zyne smiled and shared a look with the crowd that only a Zyne could truly understand. 'We also have a slight change to the rules this year,' he announced.

Little rivers of sweat ran down the side of Freddy's face and the back of his neck.

'This year's tournament we have decided will be a team event.' The Beta Zyne ran his eyes along the line

[29] Tribal names for many Permian species such as 'big-ugly-creature-that-eats-you' were superseded by modern scientific names following the arrival in Pangea of Doylian palaeontologists such as Haji.

of challengers. 'Your team will consist of your chosen Champion, of course, plus two extra members of your group randomly selected by our impartial judges.' The Beta Zyne smiled and a grey shadow seemed to cross his face.

Screaming and booing followed, and Freddy assumed that Zynes were also not fond of last-minute rule changes.

'But Guv—' One of the two flat-capped Wanderers began until a Zyne guard pointed a lasernator at his nose. Whatever words he intended to say died in his throat.

Two teams of judges suddenly appeared at both ends of the line and began selecting the extra combatants. Their strategy was soon clear. They picked the two smallest and seemingly weakest members of each group. The crowd roared with each new selection as they steadily worked their way towards the centre. They reached the Amazons first and straight away selected a young girl who looked familiar to Freddy. Then, with a jolt, he realised that it was Polydora—minus a few pounds of dirt. Koia and an older Amazon pleaded fiercely with the judges that she was too young, but Polydora seemed keen to compete. She let out a fierce war cry when the judges stuck to their decision. The second choice was tougher for the judges as all the remaining Amazons looked as strong as Koia. Eventually they chose the older Amazon who had stood up for Polydora. She had a roughly shaven head and looked slightly shorter, but this may have simply been an illusion caused by her lack of hair. Her name was Aella, which in the Amazonian tongue means 'whirlwind'.

A moment later, the other pair of judges arrived at Freddy's group. Haji stepped forward. 'Pick me,' he said, but they did not even look at him. They walked straight past and picked Lucy instead. Having observed that their criteria for selection were smallness and apparent weakness, she was furious. She aimed a kick at the shins of the nearest judge but miscalculated and made contact higher than she expected.

'You just picked the wrong girl,' she screamed.

Gruntenguile grunted and then laughed. Tribals find injuries to the reproductive organs almost as funny as farting.

Even some of the Zynes laughed as the judge limped, red-faced towards Gruntenguile.[30]

'You have just picked yourself onto the Spring Subzynes' team,' snarled the judge. 'I hope you find that as amusing!'

Gruntenguile grunted. It would be easier to keep Freddy alive if he was competing.

'At least there are three of us now,' said Freddy. 'One for all; and all for one!'

As he said this, he looked towards Lucy, and was glad he did because she looked invincible with her brown steady eyes and war-like braids.

In the moment that he took his eyes off them, the judges disappeared. This coincided with the even more remarkable appearance of Dr Bufon. During the judges' deliberations, she had descended on one of the sky steps that connected the various levels of the *Atlantis*. These steps automatically levitated to wherever they were needed. They were not cheap, however, unless you were a high-ranking Zyne. All you needed then was an official chip in your boot. Nearer the ground, the steps levelled off to a point just a body-width away from Freddy. He did not see her approaching as he was looking at Lucy. When Dr Bufon suddenly spoke, he was taken by surprise and, turning quickly, found himself looking directly into her smoky-green eyes.

---

[30] Zynes rarely laugh at misfortunes that befall other Zynes. Humour for Zynes is more about bad things happening to 'lesser' species. ('Did you hear about the Yiaaak that got hit by a space truck? He looks a lot better now.')

'Look who proved to be useful!' said Dr Bufon. Her voice: half surprise, half ridicule.

Freddy had never been at ease under the cool gaze of Dr Claudia Bufon, and he felt even more awkward under the extraordinary circumstances of that meeting. He was also shocked by the changes in her appearance. The first difference he noticed was a Zyne eye tattoo on the top of her right cheek. Up close, he could also make out the tattoos on her upper right arm. Two snakes twined around a skeleton hanging from a noose. At the top of her bicep, they reared outwards with their jaws wide-open ready to strike. They were cobra snakes—number one on Freddy's list of reptiles to avoid.

Dragging his attention away from the snake tattoos, Freddy tried to look Dr Bufon in the eye. 'I'm pleased to meet you again, Dr Bufon, but I'm not sure what you mean. All I know is that a lot of really strange stuff has happened since I saw you last. I hope you don't mind me asking you this, but what is it exactly that brings you here?'

'Don't talk to her,' yelled Lucy. 'She can't be trusted!'

Dr Bufon's eyelids fluttered as if warding off an insect. 'Honestly, if you can't say something nice . . .' she began. Her attention seemed to be suddenly taken by Freddy's hair. 'You know—some people don't fancy red hair, Freddy, but I find it absolutely adorrrable.'

Reaching forward she ran her fingers through Freddy's hair and shivered. At the same time, she attached a micro-recording device about the size of a grain of sand to his quivering scalp.[31] Even Lucy, who was watching her like a hawk, did not notice. Dr Bufon then placed her hand

---

[31] I asked Freddy why this recording device was not also fitted with a micro-transmitter. He answered that Zyne technology in the communication area was so advanced that any transmission would almost certainly have been intercepted by multiple sources.

briefly on Freddy's chest and felt the rapid beat of his heart before returning it to her pistol grip.

'It is very important that you surviiiive this little tournament Freddy,' she continued. 'When you do, we will talk, and you can aaask me anything you want, and I promise IIIII'll tell you everything I know. Unlike others I imagine.' Her eyes fluttered like bats towards Lucy. 'Will that satisfy you?' Her hand moved from her pistol to Freddy's chin. When he could not reply she nodded his head for him.

'Take caaaarre, Freddy.'

She cast a withering glance at Lucy, which reminded Freddy of the way they looked at each other when they had crossed paths on the Arnhem Escarpment. Freddy's head suddenly felt very heavy without Dr Bufon's hand there to support it. It remained slightly extended as he watched her re-ascend the stairs to the balcony. The Beta Zyne had watched everything with a blank face. When Dr Bufon returned to her position alongside him, he once more addressed the crowd.

'And now it is time to welcome our Zyne Champions!'

23. The Tournament of Blood

In the clouds that shrouded the top of the Alpha Tower, a dark object dangled from under the Control Disk. At first, it was no more than a dot—like a soaring bird. But, as it descended, Freddy could see that it was a platform enclosed by a wire safety cage. By the time it was halfway down, he could see the Zyne champions inside the cage. The crowd roared louder and louder as it approached. Louder than Freddy had thought it was possible for beings to roar.

'Makes my entrance look a little lame,' said Freddy after he figured out what was happening.

'Your entrance was great,' said Lucy.

Four words and Freddy found himself swinging like Tarzan on a vine back to thinking that she was not the worst person he had met. At that moment, of course, his thinking was swayed by the fact that they were about to enter the Tournament of Blood as teammates. They needed to rely on each other like never before.

As the Zynes descended on their platform, the cage that had been casting a crisscrossed shadow over them since their arrival, was lowered into place.

While this was happening, Zyne Guards removed the non-competitors and the Moschops.

'I really wish I were in there with you—bad back and all,' shouted Haji making his way from the arena. Then, as a last thought, he turned back and said 'Don't trust anyone, but especially the Zynes.' Then, noticing the cage was almost down, he left the arena with an extra zip in his step.

The next thing Freddy heard was a giant clunk as the cage hit the ground. Now the only way out was the Channel of Blood, which flowed under the base of the cage to the area where Haji was now seated. This area was called the Pit. Once there, the eliminated competitors faced the vilest ridicule from the Zyne spectators. The nastiest remarks were replayed to them on a special screen fixed to the front of the cage.

Freddy counted 22 teams of combatants including his own. That made 66 challengers. Most of them, like Freddy, were gazing with wide eyes around the arena.

Everything seemed to be floating and blurry around the edges. Feeling dizzy and needing to focus on something, he gazed at Koia. She seemed cold and hard but still beautiful in his eyes.

Noticing Freddy staring at Koia, Lucy turned and studied her more closely. 'They all look alike to me, but isn't that the one that almost pulled me out of the *COY?*' she asked.

Lying to Lucy was too fraught with danger, so Freddy answered, 'Yes.'

Lucy opened her eyes wider and turned to Freddy. 'Is she the one you were looking forward to being cannibalised by?'

That was not how Freddy liked to remember his relationship with Koia, but he answered, 'Yes.'

'You are a naughty boy, Freddy,' she said.

It was not the answer he expected. He turned to check her expression, but it gave nothing away, so he let it slide. There were too many other things to worry about at that moment. The descending platform was one of them.

It had almost reached the top of the cage, and Freddy could see the champions more clearly. Even so, he thought his eyes were playing tricks on him. Firstly, he could only see two of them. Surely if the challengers were allowed teams of three the Zyne champions would be allowed the same number? At the same time, he noticed that they seemed to be blue and—

'By the way,' said Lucy, 'we possibly should have told you earlier, but the champions are a little different from normal Zynes. Their bodies are tattooed with images of beings they have defeated, and—as you can see—they have additional limbs grafted to their body.'

'They have four arms,' gasped Freddy.

'Yes,' said Lucy, 'and four fists.'

Freddy shuddered at the alien appearance of the Zyne champions. Their hexapedal forms made them look like giant bugs. He was almost sick by now with the slow churning of his stomach. The sound of the crowd was so loud that it had become a uniform roar as numbing as silence. Freddy looked across to see how Lucy was faring. She was saying something to him, but he could not hear her over the roar of the crowd.

'What?' he shouted.

'Stay out of the way!'

Freddy nodded but he could not see how that was possible. They were going to be in a cage.

A metallic sound turned his attention to the top of that cage where a gate was opening to allow the platform to enter. The Zyne champions were now close enough that he could see some of the animals and Tribals tattooed on their gleaming bodies and even faces. Their torsos were bare but beneath this they wore different coloured pants—one blue, the other yellow. Freddy assumed this was to assist the crowd in knowing which was which.

As the platform hit the ground, the voice of the Beta Zyne boomed, 'Let the Tournament begin.'

'Good luck, Little—' began Gruntenguile.

But before the sentence was finished, Freddy heard a thud, followed by an enormous gasp as if someone had just

151

had their lungs emptied by a violent impact. He turned just in time to see Gruntenguile collapse to the ground.

Standing over his flattened body was the third Zyne who had just swung into the arena on a rope from nowhere. He wore long Zyne pants like the others, only his were red. Above these, he wore nothing but rippling muscle and tattoos.

Freddy's first thought was to run but his legs would not move.

He had expected an unfair fight, but he had not expected it to be this brutal.

24. The Zyne Champions

Freddy could not see any of the other mayhem erupting around the cage at that moment. All he could see was the red Zyne advancing towards the flattened Gruntenguile.

He wanted to do something, but his legs would not move.

The red Zyne was a brute. Three times Freddy's size and massively muscled. He stood over Gruntenguile, leaned forward and grabbed his throat.

He had to save his crusty manservant, but, before he could force his body to move, something curled around the red Zyne's neck like a lasso. It was an arm, and the lithe muscles on that arm told Freddy that it belonged to Koia. This was confirmed a second later, when her head appeared over the red Zyne's shoulder. The brute was taken completely by surprise. Challengers do not normally seek out the Zyne champions, preferring to fight against easier combatants until they had no choice but to confront the Zynes.

Koia's bicep bulged around the red Zyne's throat. She pulled her elbow in tight with her other arm to apply more pressure. The problem was that the tighter she pulled, the more enraged the red Zyne became. He reached over his shoulder to get a hand on Koia, but she arched her head back to keep clear of his grasp. His lower arms felt back for her legs, but he could not reach them. While this was happening, Freddy regained his senses, but he was still not sure what to do. The rules forbade him from assisting Koia, and there were no free combatants.

By now, the red Zyne's face was almost as red as his pants. It looked like Koia might choke him out when suddenly, spying one of the bollards in front of him, he rolled forward and slammed Koia into it. This broke Koia's grip and at the same time the red Zyne pushed himself up with his four arms and sprang to his feet. Turning around, he launched a vicious kick at Koia's head, but she rolled clear and took the blow on her back. She staggered to her feet. The red Zyne had no qualms about fighting a woman and he charged in to finish her off. He had forgotten about Freddy, and Gruntenguile, who was still lying flat on his back. The red Zyne had assumed he was out cold but Tribals are a tough breed, and Gruntenguile was a particularly tough Tribal. As the red Zyne ran past, he spun around and swung one of his legs into his path. His bony heel smacked into the red Zyne's ankle like a wrecking ball and brought him smashing to the ground.

'Freddy,' yelled Gruntenguile, 'find an opponent—preferrably one of the Pygmy Tribals—before one of the Zynes picks you.'

Yes, of course, thought Freddy. Why had he not thought of that himself? He cast his eyes around the arena. Of the sixty-six combatants who had started the contest, about ten were already eliminated. The two most recent were washing down the Channel of Blood to the roar of the crowd. The other eliminated challengers had already been fished from the Channel. They sat, huddled in the Pit, copping the crowd's abuse. The two flat-capped Wanderers sat in the first seats. The second the contest started they had run to the Channel and dived in. The others were Tribals who all looked happy to be where they were despite the taunts of the crowd. There was no sign of Lucy and the thought raced through Freddy's mind that she may have already been badly hurt and taken from the cage by one of the air ambulances hovering overhead.

Then he looked up and saw her on the netting at the far end of the arena. She was climbing to the top of the cage with Polydora in hot pursuit. It was funny to see Lucy fleeing from the younger and smaller Amazon, but Freddy knew it would not be funny once Polydora got hold of her. Lucy's tactic was to avoid early elimination by staying clear of the other competitors, but the roof of the cage was dangerous.

Then, just as Freddy was getting his bearings, someone jumped on him from behind.

Gruntenguile saw this out the corner of his eye, but there was nothing he could do. He had his hands full. The red Zyne's ankle had completely shattered, and if there is one thing a Zyne cannot handle, it is pain. Springing to his feet Gruntenguile stood over the red Zyne who lay screaming on the ground. Then, grabbing the red Zyne by his good foot, he dragged him towards the Channel of Blood.

The red Zyne weighed about as much as a well-fed Anteosaurus but Gruntenguile was inspired. The Zynes had enslaved his race for eons, and he was about to drag one of their champions into the Channel of Blood and eliminate them from the tournament. The red Zyne was made powerless by his pain. His hands squeezed his injured ankle to ease the agony.

Luckily, they were close to the channel, and Gruntenguile soon dragged him to the edge. Stepping to the side of the red Zyne, he pushed with all his might until he rolled like a felled log and tipped over the side into the Channel of Blood with a big splash.

The red Zyne was eliminated.

'Bon voyage . . . grrrnnt,' cried Gruntenguile.

The roar of the crowd was deafening.

The red Zyne floated away on the hyper-saline fake blood, but he was not destined for the shame of the Pit.

An air ambulance flew in and a medic pulled him from the Channel and placed him on an open stretcher in the rear of the vehicle. The crowd cheered their scorn for Gruntenguile. Zynes are the worst losers in the universe.

Freddy heard this and assumed that one of the Zynes had been victorious. He could not see anything because he was pinned to the floor of the spaceship by Koia, who, seeing that the red Zyne was out, had gone for Freddy. She twisted him around and for the second time sat on his pounding chest.

'I was kidnapped,' pleaded Freddy. 'I was looking forward to . . . whatever—' The rest of his apology was silenced by Koia grabbing hold of his jaw. She held it so tightly that, for a moment, Freddy thought she was going to snap his neck. Then her knees came forward and pinned the fleshy part of his arms. That hurt, but that was it.

Once in this position, the pressure eased, and Freddy realised that Koia was only pretending to attack him to buy time for them both. A smile broke over his face, but a frown from Koia told him that was not a good idea. The next thing he thought was that he could not wait to tell Lucy. She had been slandering Koia for weeks, and now it seemed that her feelings for him were real. Not that you could tell from her face. Apart from one wink that told Freddy to play along it was pure Amazonian ferocity. Freddy was not sure how long they remained locked in that position. The danger was, of course, that if it went on for too long the crowd and judges would sense that it was a sham. During this time, Freddy could see the top of the cage where Lucy was scurrying like a suminia up a tree to escape Polydora.[32] Her tactic of keeping out of harm's way by climbing the cage was now looking like it was not such a great idea. A fall onto the adamantium floor of the spaceship from that

---

[32] Suminia were one of the first arboreal creatures. They evolved opposable thumbs, 200 million years before monkeys.

height would be certain death.

The other thing Freddy noticed was an increase in the cheering to a cyclonic roar. A few seconds later, the face of Gruntenguile appeared over Koia's shoulder. He wanted to yell to him that Koia was on their side and was only pretending to strangle him, but he could not move his jaw.

Gruntenguile grabbed Koia and pulled her off Freddy.

Freddy had just enough time to gasp, 'She was just holding me! She's on our side.'

At the same time, Gruntenguile looked up and saw the yellow Zyne racing towards him. His tattooed face glistened with sweat and flecks of blood.

'Any suggestions?' asked Gruntenguile.

'Yes,' said Koia. 'Attack!' Twisting out of Gruntenguile's grasp, she ran towards the charging yellow Zyne. When they were about twenty feet apart, she dived into a star flip. This broke the yellow Zyne's rhythm, and he staggered to a halt just as Koia came out of her flip and landed back on her feet. She launched herself at the yellow Zyne, going straight for his eyes, digging her strong fingers and sun-hardened nails deep into his eye sockets.

The yellow Zyne roared, clutching his eyes in agony.

The crowd cheered.

Koia was not sure about what to do next, but it did not matter. From the side, Agrosios the Angry launched himself at the yellow Zyne, knocking him to the ground. Agrosios then threw himself on top of the yellow Zyne, but he was no pushover and quickly wrapped his four arms around Agrosios and applied a double bear hug. A lesser man would have passed out, but Agrosios was well prepared for this situation. Lucky for him, he had been abandoned in the wilderness as a baby and raised by bears. He wrapped his arms around the yellow Zyne and pulled tight.

Koia thought about helping him, but there were too many lasernators already in position. Instead, she looked for a fresh opponent. Unfortunately, the closest one was the blue Zyne who was running directly towards her. He was their alpha champion. She had been eliminated by him in a previous tournament and should have been intimidated, but Koia did not know the meaning of that word, despite her otherwise excellent English. She glared defiantly at the blue Zyne flying towards her like he had been shot from a space cannon.

In the Tournament of Blood, it is not a good idea to focus entirely on one thing. Your side vision is what keeps you alive. A Swamp Tribal had also seen the blue Zyne charging and, thinking that he meant to fight him, attacked Koia first. Catching her off guard from the side, he threw her to the ground.

Freddy had seen enough of what was happening around him to know what this meant. Koia was fighting the Swamp Tribal. Agrosios was battling the yellow Zyne. Gruntenguile by now was struggling with a Pirate Tribal. There was only one opponent left for the blue Zyne.

That was Freddy.

The blue Zyne also realised this and decided to put on a show for the crowd. He slowed down and walked in prancing steps towards Freddy like he had all the time in the world. His purpose was simple—to terrify Freddy for the amusement of the crowd. Fear is the only thing that Zynes love more than violence. He slammed his calloused fists together with each step.

Freddy could not help noticing that the blue Zyne was larger than the other Zyne champions. He was also a lot bluer. As well as wearing blue pants, his bare upper torso was completely covered in tattoos. As he got closer, Freddy saw that the tattoos included many animals but also the battered faces of many Tribals challengers. These tattoos served their psychological purpose. Freddy was awe-struck by the sheer number of the blue Zyne's past victims. So numerous were they that the tattoos had encroached onto the blue Zyne's face which was otherwise square-jawed and quite good looking.

The blue Zyne's showy advance had one drawback. It gave Freddy a few seconds to think.

A lot can flash through your mind in that time.

25. Running, Darwin (northern Australia, January 1934 AD, 250 billion years later)

A sticky heat was fighting a light breeze drifting in from Fannie Bay and winning. Instead of relief, the breeze carried the rotting smell of the mangrove flats lining Darwin Harbour. It was so humid it was hard to fall over.

Freddy thought about stretching but he was too young to be bothered. He started running straight down the middle of the street.

The only other person awake was Professor Dupler. He stood in the front yard of his house next door wearing oversized cargo pants and a white singlet. Hose in hand, watering his front lawn. He flicked the hose upwards to give Freddy a friendly squirt as he ran past.

'A bit hot for running isn't it?' he asked. Not that he was surprised. He was used to the strange habits of the O'Toole household, and Freddy was as regular as clockwork with his morning runs.

Freddy smiled in reply to the Professor's question. His father was timing him, and he needed to keep moving.

The only noise in the street was the hoarse bark of an old brown dog called Rooper.

'Roop . . . roop . . . roop . . . roop . . . roop . . . rooop . . . rooooop.'

Soon young Freddy passed all of the neat bungalows that lined his street and reached the mangroves. A buzzing confusion of green springing from a black bog.

Here he paused as he did every morning. He looked steadily for a while at the path ahead. Then he ran forward and sprang into the mangroves like one of the stray cats that preyed on the seabirds there at night. He landed with his left foot on a large buttress root. Using his knee as a spring, he bounded ahead to another root, landing on it with his right foot. In this manner, with his eyes fixed on the path ahead and trusting in his side vision, he leapt from mangrove to mangrove, and avoided the stinking black bog beneath. The mangroves were about thirty yards across at this point, and Freddy believed that it augured well for his day if he could make it through without slipping into the foul-smelling black mud. He had almost made it that morning when a root that had held firm for years gave way and sent him sliding into the bog up to his knees. Splotches of black sludge flew even higher, splashing a map of the Dutch East Indies across his face.

'Blazes!'

He recovered in an instant and sprang back onto the next root that could take his weight and continued through to the end of the mangroves.

He emerged onto a white pebbled beach overlooking Darwin Harbour. Strewn across this beach, close enough to jump between them, were a scattering of large rocks. This was Freddy's gym.

For ten minutes, which had seemed like an eternity when he first started the course, Freddy leapt from rock to rock as quickly as he could, as if each were a bomb about to explode. That was the way his father had taught him to tackle the course during his first ever lap. After his ten-minute circuit of the rocks, he did 50 push-ups and 50 sit-ups before completing the course again. He kept going until he had completed the course twelve times.

When he finished he always thought the same thing: *Why on Earth am I doing this?*

26. What is Learned in Youth, Pangea, 250 Ma

There were no mangrove roots or boulders but there were bollards.

The blue Zyne lunged forward and Freddy jumped like the Crimson Avenger onto one of the bollards to his right.

This evasion infuriated the blue Zyne. Competitors were normally so keen to be eliminated they offered little resistance. The less they struggled the better it was for them. The blue Zyne lurched to his left, but Freddy had already leapt to another bollard. This was a new tactic in the tournament, and the spectators hushed as they wondered how the blue Zyne would react. There was something slightly comical about the situation, but the blue Zyne was not laughing.

'Make it easy on yourself,' he snarled. 'It is only a matter of time before I crush you. The sooner you are floating in the Channel of Blood, the sooner all this will be over.'

What moved Freddy to answer the way he did, he did not know. 'Blurrr!' he blurted, 'You are the ugliest Zyne I have ever met,' and, as if that were not enough, he added. 'Your face would put a Yiaaak off their dinner.'

When it comes to their appearance, Zynes are the vainest creatures in the universe. The blue Zyne roared and threw himself at Freddy. He had only a split second to leap to another bollard.

The next few moments were the most comic in the tournament's long history as Freddy leapt from bollard to bollard with the blue Zyne chasing him. The bollards were there for the Zyne champions to smash their opponents into, and it enraged the blue Zyne to have them used to make him look foolish. As Freddy leapt clear of his attacker, he caught glimpses of the action in other parts of the cage.

The most alarming thing that he saw was that Polydora had caught up with Lucy. They were grappling on the top of the cage.

Agrosios and the yellow Zyne were still wrapped in each other's crushing bear hugs. The yellow Zyne had recovered the use of his eyes and his four sweat-slathered arms were applying a pressure that would have squeezed the life out of most men. Agrosios was squeezing just as tightly.

Koia was dragging the Swamp Tribal she had been fighting to the Channel by his long beard.

Gruntenguile had gotten the better of his Pirate Tribal and was rolling him into the Channel.

The third Amazon, Aella, was grappling a sure-footed Mountain Tribal with calves like watermelons. Apart from that, there remained probably ten other contests still taking place inside the cage.

All of this was seen in an instant as Freddy leapt from bollard to bollard and his energy drained in the thin air, which contained even less oxygen in the foothills than in the lowlands. The strobing lights were also testing Freddy's balance. Seeing his successful evasion, the Zynes had aimed even more lights directly at his eyes. Too many things were against him. He could not keep it up for much longer. Although it was cooler in the foothills, it was still warm, and the increase in moisture in the mountains meant it was also humid. Competitors were slicked with sweat and as slippery as eels.

Eventually Freddy leapt onto a bollard lathered in sweat from having had a challenger pushed hard against it a short time earlier. He slipped and crashed hard on the pavement, cracking his head on the adamantium. He wished he had not been so unkind to the blue Zyne a few minutes earlier as, a second later, the blue Zyne threw himself on top of Freddy and pinned him helplessly to the pavement.

'You're mine now, you blood-head Earthling.' Instead of pummelling Freddy, however, the blue Zyne paused. 'What are you looking at?'

Freddy did not hear him. He was staring at a tattoo in the middle of the blue Zyne's forehead. It was, he assumed, the face of one of his past victims.

It was his father.

27. From the Jaws of Victory

'I thought he beat you?'

The blue Zyne pinned Freddy's chest with two hands. Another strangled his neck. A fourth was clubbed into a fist held over his right shoulder. A battered Tribal was tattooed between each bony pair of knuckles. That fist was about to pound Freddy's face, but it froze at his question.

To understand what happened next, however, it is necessary to know how things had progressed in other parts of the cage.

The battle between Agrosios and the yellow Zyne had been a stalemate. Watching them bear hugging each other for so long, the crowd were losing interest. As chance would have it, Agrosios had been in the same situation once before when wrestling a bear on the rocky slopes of the Parnonas Mountains in eastern Sparta. What he did then was to roll until the bear got so dizzy it released its hold. It was worth a try so Agrosios started rolling. He headed straight for the Channel, reached it, and then rolled back. He did this a few times. The crowd was torn between this spectacle, Freddy's athletic escape from the blue Zyne, and the dramatic struggle on the top wires of the cage.

When Agrosios stopped rolling, the yellow Zyne was so dizzy he could no longer keep his grip on Agrosios, who jumped to his feet as steady as an oak tree. The yellow Zyne staggered to his, wobbling like a one-legged drunk. Agrosios placed a finger on his chest and, with the smallest of flicks, sent him splashing into the Channel of Blood.

'Spartaaaaaaaaaaaaaaaa!' screamed Agrosios.

The crowd cheered.

Thinking they appreciated his efforts, Agrosios raised his arms and shook his fists, but his showboating did not last long. He was there to fight Zynes, and there was still one on his feet somewhere. Searching the arena, he saw less than a handful of contests. The Pit was almost full with eliminated challengers. Another air ambulance was about to land and collect the yellow Zyne who was clinging to the side of the Channel, choking on the bloody liquid.

The two Amazons were fighting a pair of Desert Tribals. Koia had hers in a stepover toehold. Swiftly releasing this grip, she dragged him to his feet and pushed him to the Channel in a full nelson. Once on the edge she released the hold and threw him in. One more down! A short time later Aella's opponent suffered the same fate. Under the rules of the tournament, Aella and Koia should have then fought each other. Amazons, however, are not fond of rules. They looked fiercely around the arena for another opponent.

The play of lights had already attracted the attention of Agrosios to the spot where the blue Zyne was sitting on top of Freddy. The Zyne's fist was cocked. His bicep bulging. One blow could knock Freddy's head off his shoulders, but the fist was paused in mid-air. Agrosios ran towards them. Tackling an already engaged combatant was not technically within the rules, but he was a Spartan— and an angry one at that. He did not sweat over details. Just as the blue Zyne was about to release his punch, Agrosios flew at him. He was just about to grab the blue Zyne's descending fist when he was struck from behind. The yellow Zyne, for reasons the judges were never able to properly explain, had been allowed to re-enter the arena. This seemed outrageously against the rules, but there really was only one rule: 'the Zynes must win'.

The yellow Zyne took full advantage of catching Agrosios off-guard and smashed him into a bollard. Agrosios' chest hit the bollard with a pain like being struck by lightning and, straight away, he knew that he had busted a couple of ribs. Clutching his chest in agony, he glared at his attacker.

The crowd booed.

The yellow Zyne stepped forward to finish off Agrosios.

The blue Zyne released his fist.

Freddy closed his eyes and looked forward to being unconscious.

He did not care anymore. The weight of the blue Zyne's bony knees pushing hard into his lower ribs had become so unbearable that he could not imagine anything worse. He did not even brace himself for the impact. As it turned out, he did not need to. The blue Zyne's fist was halfway to Freddy's face when two feet, one on either side, kicked into the blue Zyne's ribcage, and he lost balance. His fist scraped the side of Freddy's face and slammed with a crunch of broken knuckles and phalanges into the adamantium floor of the spaceship. Grabbing his broken hand, he screamed loud enough to wake the extinct. Opening his eyes, Freddy saw Koia on one side of the blue Zyne and Aella on the other. Amazons do look alike in the way that all really fit people do, but Freddy was struck by the similarity between the two of them and it came to him in a flash that Aella must be Koia's mother.

Each Amazon grabbed an upper arm to drag the blue Zyne off Freddy and into the Channel. Two on one was a breach of the rules, and Zyne guards with lasernators already poised at their shoulders ran into position. The blue Zyne struggled but his spirit was broken by the damage done to his right hand. A splintered shard of his proximal phalange poked through the pinkish red flesh of his middle finger. Despite this, the Amazons could not budge him. His legs were anchored to Freddy.

'Move, Freddy!' It was the first time Aella had spoken to him. 'We must drag him to the Channel while he is still in shock from the pain.'

'And before we're lasernated,' added Koia.

Drawing his knees up and wedging his feet into the floor of the spaceship, Freddy pushed hard.

'That's it,' strained Aella. 'Keep it up.'

Looking and feeling like a squashed worm struggling under a large boot, Freddy pushed and pushed as the Amazons dragged and the blue Zyne roared in pain. They had almost reached the Channel when the Beta Zyne nodded the order to fire the lasernators. Aella was hit and almost fell, but the calibration was not enough for an Amazonian warrior in full flight. She fell to the side of the blue Zyne, wrapped her arms around him, and rolled him forward. Freddy rolled with them. There was a huge splash and the world turned red. Freddy tried to breathe and took in a mouthful of the bloody liquid. He choked and struggled to the surface where three faces bobbed nearby. One was the blue Zyne's. He splashed the water with his good hand and cursed all Amazons. Though the continuation of his species depended on them, he would have happily killed them all. The other two faces belonged to Koia and Aella.

'Just let yourself float,' said Aella. 'We're all eliminated but you have done well. Just as I thought you would.'

Any conjecture about why Aella had so much confidence in Freddy was cut short by another huge splash of red.

All the time they had been struggling with the blue Zyne, his yellow counterpart had been grappling Agrosios. Wrestling a Zyne in the Tournament of Blood is never easy, but when you have busted ribs, it is much harder. Fortunately, pain only made Agrosios angrier.

Screaming 'Spartaaaaaaaa!', he charged at the yellow Zyne and wrapping him in another bear hug, pushed him to the edge of the bloody Channel. Once there, he encountered a problem. The yellow Zyne had just as strong a hold on him and he could not throw him in the Channel without sacrificing himself. The pain from his ribs was unbearable.

This time, screaming Greek curses through clenched teeth, he leapt into the Channel, taking the yellow Zyne with him.

Still bobbing about in the waves caused by their entry, Freddy breathed a huge sigh that it was all over, but then he remembered Lucy and looked up to the top of the cage.

A violent din was swirling around the cage and he could hardly hear his own thoughts, but miraculously he heard Lucy. Much later, he realised that it must have been telepathy rather than ear hearing.

'We can't hold on much longer,' she cried.

Many in the crowd also heard her telepathic cry. Thrilled by the prospect of this bloody spectacle, they booed even louder.

Two air ambulances hovered in to collect the eliminated Zynes. The yellow Zyne was short of breath but hopped on the back of his air ambulance without too much difficulty. It took off straight away. The blue Zyne was moving more slowly.

As Freddy watched on, the bushy, black brows of Agrosios suddenly appeared alongside him.

'Can you throw me to that air ambulance over there?' asked Freddy.

'Spartaaaaa!' shouted Agrosios.

Freddy changed tack and demonstrated with his hands the idea of throwing him on to the air ambulance.

Agrosios' face lit with understanding. He locked his hands and Freddy stepped into them.

'Now!' cried Freddy.

'Spartaaaaa…' The pain from his busted ribs dug deep, but he gave it everything he had in him.

Freddy was suddenly a missile. A second later, the blue Zyne, who had just mounted the ambulance, was skittled by Freddy and splashing back into the Channel. Next, Freddy pushed the startled medic into the same place and leapt onto the driver's seat. He pushed the lever up hoping that was the direction it would take him. It did. The air ambulance flew skywards. Freddy was almost thrown off the back. He managed to hold on, but the trouble was that, if he could not stop, he would soon be diced on the top of the cage. His hand fumbled on the throttle and eased it back just in time. The crowd cheered and he gave them a wave. Quickly getting a feel for the controls, he steered the ambulance to just below where Koia and Polydora clung, completely exhausted, hanging on by the very tips of their fingers and the mettle of their spirits.

'Let go and drop on,' he cried. What he was doing was way outside the rules, and he knew that he could be lasernated any second, but he banished these thoughts because there was nothing he could do about that.

Lucy and Polydora let go at the same time, fell, and landed on the back of the stretcher. There was not room for both of them to lie down, so Lucy came forward and threw her arms around Freddy. Polydora sat behind Lucy and held on to her. They were almost settled when a laser beam upset Freddy's concentration. The air ambulance tipped violently to one side.

'Watch what you're doing,' screamed Lucy.

Freddy leaned against the fall and regained the controls in time. He could see more lasernators getting into position. It was time to get out of there.

'Hold on!' Freddy banked the air ambulance and gunned it back to the channel, zigzagging to avoid laser fire. He did not know until much later that Gruntenguile, using a trick of telepathy that he had learned during the last Tribal Revolt, had disabled the Zyne lasenators.

Freddy's landing was not as smooth as his take off. They splashed and tumbled into the bloody liquid. The air ambulance continued on its way, skipping over the surface before crashing into the blue Zyne who by now had received more injuries out of the arena than in it.

Freddy was in not much better shape himself. He was dazed and allowed himself to be washed along the Channel to the now crowded Pit. The bruises below his ribs where the blue Zyne had dug his knees still throbbed. He did not realise until he reached the Pit that he was clinging to Lucy. Once there, the flat-capped Englishmen helped Freddy and Lucy out of the channel. Aella and Koia did the same for Polydora and checked that she was okay. Never has someone so small been so indestructible. She was fine. As the three Amazons sat down and embraced each other, it became suddenly clear to Freddy that they were a family.

Koia then turned to check Lucy who nodded that she too was okay. Then she looked at Freddy. It was a new look from her but no less awkward.

Agrosios hauled himself out of the fake blood at that moment and sat between them.

Freddy slapped his back. 'You did well.'

'Spartaaaaa!'

'You deserved to win—but, don't worry, it looks like everyone has been eliminated.'

'No,' said Lucy, nudging Freddy and pointing back to the cage. 'Not everyone!'

Freddy turned and looked in the same direction. At first, he could not see anyone. The gaudy lights continued to dance across the surface. Then he caught a small movement. Someone was climbing onto one of the bollards. Once on top they balanced unsteadily, and then raised their arms towards the clouds swirling over the Central Pangean Mountains.

'Gruntenguile,' gasped Freddy.

Unfortunately, in his moment of triumph, Gruntenguile forgot about the lasernators. The second they were enabled, Freddy was zapped.

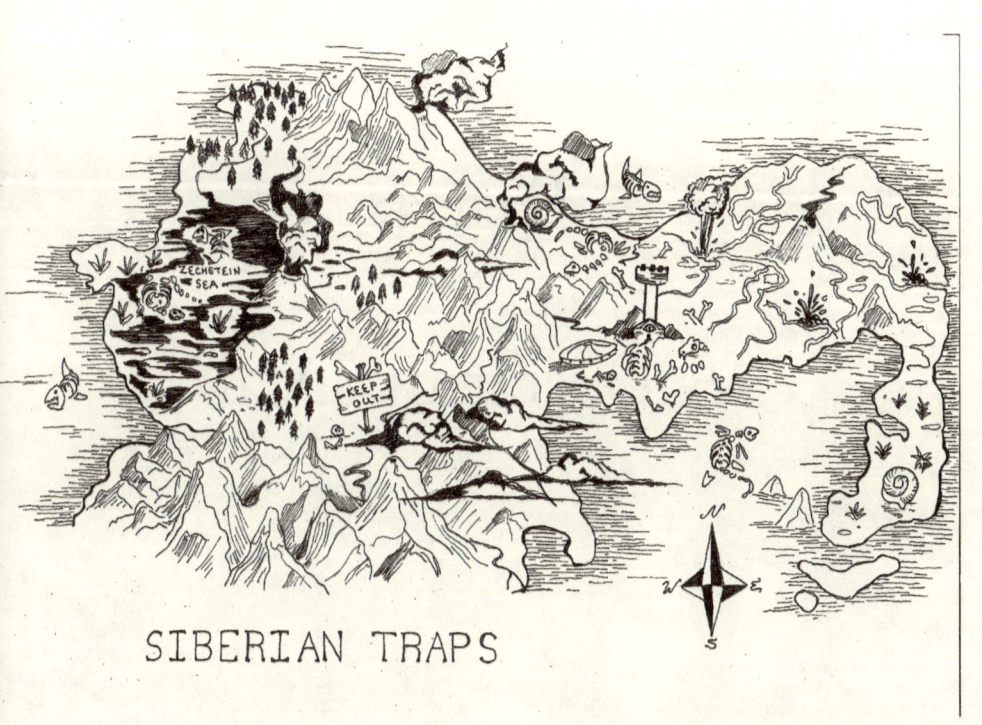

SIBERIAN TRAPS

Part 4:

A Dastardly Deal

28. The Atlantis Brig

Freddy came to in the lowest cell of the *Atlantis* Brig. It was as hot as a furnace, and a slimy liquid, like molten Vegemite,[33] was dripping onto his face.

He did not want to open his eyes, but he did not want to drown in slime either. This proved difficult, as the slime had glued his eyelids together. When he finally did force them open, everything was blurred, and, for a moment, the idea that he might once more open his eyes on Koia raced through his mind. When the outlines of the creature above him stopped shaking he realised that was not the case.

Freddy had never seen a Yiaaak before, but he had no doubt that the creature dripping reproductive slime on him belonged to that unfortunate species. Two flabby, fat-dimpled cheeks ran either side of a large orifice in the middle of what had to be its face. This orifice served as eyes, ears, nose, mouth, reproductive, and excretive organ. It blinked again and dripped a fresh flow of reproductive slime over Freddy's face.

'Blazes,' he cried, rolling to his side. Ripping off his shirt, he shook and wiped off as much of the slime as he could.

Yiaaaks are not socially savvy creatures but they are moderately intelligent and as capable of telepathy and translanguage as any of the so-called, 'higher' species.

'Forgive me. I rather forgot my manners. It's been so long since we've had company. I forgot that some

---

[33] For those not familiar with the eating habits of Australians, this is a black paste not unlike axle grease in texture and taste.

creatures don't enjoy being dripped on. Amongst Yiaaaks it's quite the compliment.' It spoke in the voice of Jungle Jim, plucked straight from Freddy's memory.

'Well, thank you,' said Freddy. 'The sentiment is appreciated, if not the slime.'

'You must have done something pretty bad to be put down here with us,' said the Yiaaak. Stepping back, it raised the ring of tentacles around its shoulders to hide its face.

Freddy was relieved but at the same time slightly ashamed of himself for the feelings of revulsion that the Yiaaak had inspired in him.

'I'm sorry if I . . . overreacted,' he stammered.

'You didn't overreact!'

Freddy wheeled around, reaching instinctively for his missing machete. Someone, or quite possibly something else, was in the cell with them.

Sitting in the corner—presumably to get as far away from the Yiaaak as possible—sat Count Schnauzer, his knees pulled in tight to his chest just as they had been in Doylian Lair.

'Count Schnauzer—what are you doing here?'

For a few moments, the Count was silent. Then he burst into such a crazy cackle of laughter that both Freddy and the Yiaaak took a step backwards.

'What am I doing here? That is good, young Freddy! That is about the funniest damn thing I have ever heard.'

Freddy looked warily at Count Schnauzer. He would sooner have trusted the Yiaaak.

'You don't remember me, do you?'

'Of course I do,' said Freddy. 'We met back at Doylian Lair, but we were separated when the Amazons attacked.'

'Yes, I remember that,' said Count Schnauzer, each word as flat as a hammer-fall. 'But we also met one time before that.'

Freddy continued to stare blankly at the Count. He was

sure that Doylian Lair was the first time he had met him.

'Perhaps this will help.' The Count wobbled to his feet and, stepping into the light, pointed to a scar under his right eye. 'I also had a beard the first time you met me. I shaved it off, because sometimes it's best not to be recognised.'

Freddy looked down at the Count's hand and saw the same cold sausages that he had shaken on the expedition to Arnhem Land the previous year.

'Yes, I remember now,' he said. 'But you still haven't answered my question.'

'Oh yes, what am *I* doing here?' said the Count. 'Not much I'm afraid. After you kicked me senseless, and left me for dead back at Doylian Lair, I was captured by the Amazons. They held me captive in one of their stinking, hide tents for a few weeks before they traded me to the Zynes. Since then I have been stuck in this miserable cell in the salubrious company of our dripping friend here.'

'And where is this miserable cell?' asked Freddy.

'It is in the *Atlantis* Brig, which is in the very lowest level of the *Atlantis*,' said the Count. 'A place from which there is no escape.'

Freddy eyed the Count suspiciously. He seemed a devious fellow but, trapped as he was in the *Atlantis* Brig, surely he had no choice now other than to speak truthfully. 'So, why are you here?' asked Freddy.

The Count raised his eyes at Freddy's directness. 'An interesting question,' he began. 'I'd almost forgotten the main purpose of my being here amidst all the betrayal and incarceration.' Sitting back down, he looked about the tiny cell as if freshly reminded of his situation. 'There are many things I could say in answer to that question,' he said, 'but since time is so precious, and I was unexpectedly interrupted last time, I shall get straight to the most important point. I am here to give you this.' The Count raised his left middle finger and at first, Freddy thought he was making a rude gesture. In fact, he was pointing to his left eye. Freddy looked at that eye but could see nothing interesting or odd about it. He glanced across to the right eye. Apart from being magnified to twice the size by the Count's monocle, it looked the same. For a moment, Freddy feared that the Count was about to perform psychic brain surgery on himself.

'This message was meant to be delivered to you at Doylian Lair,' said Count Schnauzer, 'but at the time I was not sure that you were worth the effort. You have made it this far, so I might as well give it to you now.'

Freddy was baffled and could only think that the Count had been locked-up with a Yiaaak for too long. The Count stared at Freddy and pointed more insistently to his left eye. Moving closer, Freddy knelt down directly in front of Count Schnauzer. Maybe the Count had a grain of sand in his eye that was bothering him. This seemed possible because when he looked closer his eye was covered in tiny scratches but, as he continued to look, something extraordinary happened. The eye flipped around in its socket like an egg in a pan to reveal what looked like a film screen in miniature. A countdown from ten flashed on the eye-screen and, after zero, the tiny image of Professor Dupler suddenly appeared. The background was hard to see on such a small screen, but it appeared to be dense jungle. After a quizzical look towards what Freddy assumed was the camera and a final stoke of his beard, the Professor began:

'If you are listening to this message, Freddy, you have done very well. Congratulations on making it so far. I only wish that I could be there with you.

'You are now, I imagine, in a place called Pangea. A place I have dedicated my life to discovering, and perhaps one day I too will be standing in that same wild and beautiful place.' The Professor paused, and Freddy cast an ironic look around his dingy cell. 'No doubt,' he continued, 'you are wondering why you are there. I know that you suspected it might have something to do with your father. I hope it does—but I don't know.' The Professor paused once more, but his eyes remained fixed. 'I know it will be hard for you to hear this, Freddy, but Pangea is still very much a mystery to me. That is why you are there. I know only that you are in a place of immense intrigue and deadly shenanigans that could have a devastating effect on our Earth and time. I believe, however, that you will find some people there who could do with your help. Not the least of them is the man who is delivering this very message. You are your father's son, Freddy, and, from the moment I saw the look of understanding on your face as we stood in that cave on the Arnhem Escarpment, I knew that you were the one most likely to solve this dark game we are all playing. I would love to tell you exactly what it is you must do, but the truth is that I know as much about Pangea as a Sentinelese tribesman knows about aeroplanes.

'But what I do know is this. When the time comes for someone to act, that someone will most likely be you. You have an instinct for this game, Freddy. I'm not sure how you got it, although, I must say, I have my suspicions. But I do know you have it. This is the last contact I will have with you, Freddy, and, if you ever see me again, do not trust me.

'I knew I was giving a lot for this damn eye.' The Professor pointed to his glass eye. 'For this chance, but I did not know I would lose—' Professor Dupler's mouth remained open but his image suddenly froze and disintegrated into static. Count Schnauzer's eye revolved in its socket, and Freddy was once more looking at the hazel eye of the Count.

'That gives me such a headache,' he said, pressing his fingers to the side of his head and blinking.

'How did you do that?'

'Zyne technology—I agreed to become a messenger between Pangea and modern times years ago when I was still excited by this game. I have been expecting them to take the time-eye back and maybe they will. They don't mind keeping people...' Count Schnauzer looked over at the Yiaaak and added 'and creatures waiting. Although I don't think there's much chance, they still have my old eye.'

'Is that what the Professor has?' asked Freddy. 'A Zyne *time*-eye?'

The Count nodded. 'Yes, one of the older models. Not as advanced as mine. I told him it would take control of him eventually, but he didn't listen. We're all the same. The need to know is just too great.'

'Where did he get the eye?' Freddy asked.

'That, he would not say—I am afraid we're all playing a very close game.'

Freddy walked to the opposite corner of the cell. It was only four paces away. Spaceship brigs are notoriously small.

Frowning, he ran his fingers through his hair, not knowing which point to focus on. 'But I thought Professor Dupler *was not a member* of the Doylians?' he said at last.

'He isn't. Nor am I. The Doylians do not let just anyone into their society. Only when they are sure that you are interested in all of this for the *right reasons* will they talk to you. Professor Dupler was simply someone who was very close to finding out about them and the truth about Pangea.'

'What about you? When did *you* find out about the Doylians?'

'I have been more what you might call a private contractor. I was searching for Pangea, but in the end, the Zynes came for me. I am something of an expert in certain fields that were of interest to the Zynes. They brought me here. I worked for them and later became a time messenger.' The Count pointed to his eye. 'But I became suspicious. These eyes,' the Count once more raised his finger to his eye, 'do more than just relay messages. They take over—cell by cell, thought by thought. Eventually, people live for the eye. So far, I have been able to control mine. But it takes a lot. I often wonder if it's worth it.'

The Count's time-eye remained fixed on Freddy as he spoke.

'So how did you get mixed up with Professor Dupler?'

'I made some mistakes. I needed to fix those mistakes. The Doylians would not trust me because I had been working for the Zynes. Professor Dupler seemed like the only person I could turn to. Some of his work suggested he knew something. I decided to pay him a visit. I discovered, however, that although the Professor had somehow acquired a time-eye, it wasn't a very good one. It didn't allow him to see anything, but whoever gave it to him could see everything he was seeing.'

'You mean they could see me?'

Count Schnauzer nodded.

'The Professor knew the risk he was taking, but it seemed worth it. It always does before the consequences come home to roost. I imagine that whoever gave him that eye also told him about the Arnhem Land cave where we first met. But that was all the Professor knew. Apart from that, he had nothing to back his research other than the vaguest of evidence and wild rumours.'

'When did you meet up with the Professor to record that message?' Freddy pointed to the Count's time eye.

'After the expedition last year, I told the Professor

that I knew a lot more than he could imagine about the discovery he had made.' The Count looked once more to the floor. 'Sometimes we need to talk to someone about the things we've done. Anyway, after I told him what I knew, he convinced me that we had to help the Doylians and that you were somehow important in all of this. I tried to arrange some GT Turbos for an expedition to Pangea, but that proved harder than I had anticipated. In the end, I could only find two, and I needed one for myself. That was why the Professor stayed behind. He believed that Gruntenguile would be more use to you here than he would. Once I had arranged the GT Turbos and located the crystal portal, I returned here, to Pangea, to parley with the Doylians and prepare them for your arrival.'

'Hmmm . . .the Professor wants me to help the Doylians,' said Freddy. 'But I still don't get why you're helping him? Why did you come back here, Count Schnauzer? Forgive me for saying it, but you don't look like the "save the world" type.'

The Count pointed to the scar under his right eye. 'Do you see this scar, Freddy? I did that with my own knife! It was a tattoo of an eye. The same eye as that hatpin you are wearing. It is an old way of identifying others, Searchers, who are seeking to find this place. I should have chosen the hatpin. Or, better still, I should never have come here.'

The Count stared at a point somewhere between himself and Freddy. 'You see, Freddy, I am the main cause of the Dark Cloud. It is my dreadful handiwork, *my* machinery that has caused this catastrophe.' The Count glanced upwards at the adamantium ceiling. 'I should never have come here in the first place, but now I must see my work through. To the very end.'

'If it's a machine that's causing the Dark Cloud, then it can be shut down,' said Freddy. 'Right?'

The Count shook his head. 'It's a little more complicated than that.'

'What do you mean?'

'There are three lock rings. One works. Two are fake. Two of the rings went missing during a Tribals' uprising. They have been missing for centuries, but the Doylians now have one of those missing rings—'

'The ring on Haji's necklace!'

'Precisely.'

'And the Zynes still have the third ring?'

'Presumably, yes. It is kept by the Alpha Zyne, but it is rumoured that in the confusion of the rebellion they lost track of which was the real lock ring. There is no way to check or test it other than to see if it works.'

'So—if I'm getting this right—there is a one-in-three chance that Haji has the real lock ring?'

The Count nodded.

'What if it's one of the two fake rings?'

'Then a booby trap kills whoever is attempting to shut down the tower in a toxic explosion of steaming gases and lava.'

Freddy slumped to the floor.

'A two-in-three chance of being cooked alive,' said the Yiaaak. 'That is a real bummer.'

'Blazes,' said Freddy. 'This just gets crazier and crazier. Someone has to tell me what to do. I can't keep going like this. Where are the people I came here with? Where's Lucy? Haji? Gruntenguile?' He buried his head in his hands.

'Do we look like we're in charge around here?' asked the Count.

Freddy had one more question. 'Do you think my father is involved in all this?'

The Count shrugged his shoulders.

There were too many questions, and not enough answers. Suddenly, Freddy could think of only one thing.

Escape.

He cast his eyes around the cell. The floor, the ceiling, and three sides were plated adamantium. The fourth side was adamantium bars. Forcing himself onto his feet, he walked to that side of the cell. He clenched the bars as he had seen prisoners do in films. A grey corridor choked with eerie echoes ran in both directions. Scrapes and creaks; a strangled howl; a sound like whistling; a faint dripping (possibly more Yiaaaks). Even the sounds could not escape that terrible place.

Then he heard another sound. At first it was only faint, but slowly it grew louder and harder until its hollow echo stamped out everything else, filling the grey corridors like a solid thing.

29. Dr Claudia Bufon

The *tramp-tramp-tramp* of jackboots drew nearer.

His eyes widening, Freddy glanced quickly from the Count to the Yiaaak, but they were no help. The Yiaaak made a sound like squealing tyres and slid to a back corner on its tentacle legs, cringing there with its upper tentacles hiding its head. Count Schnauzer remained slumped in the other corner. Both of them looked so broken that Freddy knew he had to get out of there. He walked quickly around the cell holding his head. He had to do something. He did not know what that something was, but that was no excuse for not doing it. For too long, his life had been a runaway train hurtling towards a collapsed bridge.

The stamp of the jackboots became deafening, reminding Freddy of the beating of the drums in the Amazonian village. He knew they were coming for him. It was best, he thought, not to be pacing nervously. Better to be lying calmly on the hard floor as if it was a feather mattress. He lay down and pretended to be asleep. That proved to be harder to do than he had first thought. The rhythmic slap of the cruel leather on the adamantium floor was made worse by the awful screeching coming from the Yiaaak.

Tramp-Tramp-Tramp-Tramp-Tramp...

This was followed by the spine-twitching sound of scraping metal, which Freddy correctly guessed were the adamantium bars rising.

. . . Tramp-Tramp-Tramp!

Just as Freddy thought the boots were about to march right over the top of him, they came to an abrupt halt and an even more dreadful silence followed.

'Ouch!' The hard toe of one of the boots kicked his rib cage. Much harder than necessary, he thought.

His eyes had not been closed for very long, but it took a few seconds for them to focus. He blinked before opening them fully, shielding the weak light with his hand. The first person he recognised was himself reflected in a black leather boot. That boot extended all the way to the knee of Dr Claudia Bufon. Above this, a toxic haze of cigarette smoke slightly blurred the rest of her figure. Her fore- and middle finger pointed straight at Freddy like a pistol barrel and between them, she held an ivory cigarette holder. The cigarette in the end was a freshly lit Lucky Strike. Raising the holder to her mouth, which was glossy red with lipstick, she kissed a small quantity of smoke into her lungs, before puffing it out. Straight in Freddy's face.

'Congratulations! That was some performance. The most *intriiiiguing* Tournament of Blood I have ever seen.'

Intriguing was just the word that had been running through Freddy's mind, although he had not been thinking about the tournament.

'It sounds like you have seen a few,' countered Freddy. He knew he could not trust Dr Bufon, but, at the same time, he felt that he would always want to.

'Enough,' she replied. 'My work takes me to some interesting places, but I am not always here at this time of year.'

'What exactly is your work?' asked Freddy.

'I work for important people,' she said. 'Those people have important interests here in Pangea, and they like to know what's going on. To that end—whyyy are *you* here and whyyy are *you* seeking an audience with the Alpha Zyne?'

'Who says I want to see the Alpha Zyne?' said Freddy.

'Come, come—let's not waste each other's time, shall we? Why else would any Wanderer willingly expose themselves to the dangers of the Tournament of Blood?'

Freddy had never been good at talking in questions, and he could see he was no match for Dr Bufon. Besides, the only idea he had at that point that could remotely be considered a plan was to work his way into her trust. If he did not do that, he might rot in that cell for the rest of his days. He needed to do *something*, and that meant getting out of the cell. Nothing could be done there.

'The truth is I'm not sure why Professor Dupler sent me on this expedition. The Professor was not even sure himself. He is not as advanced with his research as you seem to be, Dr Bufon. Since arriving, I have been travelling with my companions. *They* believe that something is happening to the north and that—' Freddy paused, fearing for a moment that he was saying too much but not knowing how to say less.

'They think the Zynes might be responsible,' continued Freddy. 'That is why they—we—wanted to meet the Alpha Zyne.' Freddy waited for a reply, but none was forthcoming, so he continued. 'We wanted the Alpha Zyne to give us permission to travel north to see for ourselves.'

Dr Bufon laughed. The sound jangled in the air like chains, then stopped as if the chains had suddenly been pulled tight.

'Why would anything that is happening here, in this time, *250 million years before your time*, be of any concern to you?'

'That is something I'm not quite sure about. I think the answer has something to do with our primitive understanding of time—'

Dr Bufon pushed an open palm towards Freddy. 'Really, Freddy, you must stop believing everything you hear. Life can become so very *confuuusing*.'

She had a point, and Freddy really wished he could trust her.

'But enough of this *chit chat*. You *arrrre* going to get your wish. It is *tiiiime* for you to meet the Alpha Zyne. He is also very interested in meeting *yoooou*.' Dr Bufon stuck her pointy nailed finger into Freddy's bare chest and glanced across at the wailing Yiaaak. 'And, lucky for you, I brought a spare shirt.'

Dr Bufon draped a green prisoner's shirt over Freddy's bare shoulder, swivelled on the sole of her boot and tramped out of the cell before suddenly turning as if she had forgotten something. Peering past Freddy to Count Schnauzer, she said, 'You are also required. The Beta Zyne wishes the pleasure of your company. It will be like old *tiiiimes*.' Dr Bufon then gave a tiny nod of her head, and two of the guards came into the cell and lifted the Count to his feet. The Yiaaak, still screeching, burrowed further into itself.

They marched out of the cell and the bars creaked and clunked shut behind them. Dr Bufon led them at a brisk pace along a labyrinth of corridors. Freddy listened carefully for telltale sounds, but all he could hear was the jarring tramp of boots. As they approached cells, adamantium barriers dropped to conceal the occupants. They made eerie metallic noises as they slid down and slammed on the floor. The echoes bumped into each other up and down the passageway. All the while, Freddy wondered if his father was rotting in one of those cells.

At last, they arrived at the very base of the tower, which formed the central hub of the *Atlantis*. Inside this tower was a large elevator. Freddy guessed it could have carried fifty or more people. It was the only way to reach the Control Disk.

'I hope you are not afraid of heights. The Control Disk is over a mile high.' Dr Bufon did not wait for Freddy's answer. She held out her hand, and a doorway opened before them. Freddy and the Count followed her inside. The jackbooted guards stayed where they were. The doorway closed on them, but they remained visible, if only as distorted shapes, through the semi-transparent wall. Freddy had heard about elevators, but this was the first time he had been in one. Dr Bufon raised her hand, and Freddy suddenly felt like his backside was flying out his mouth.

30. The Beta Zyne

When they reached the top, Dr Bufon once more raised her hand to the door. It opened and Freddy squinted into a flood of hard light. The first thing he saw was—

'Gruntenguile! What are you doing here?'

'Waiting for the party to start, Little Boss. This is where the Tournament Reception is held.'

'No talking,' interrupted Dr Bufon. 'There will be time for that later.'

Freddy was too amazed to speak much anyway. A window encircled the entire Control Disk. On one side, reared the majestic, snow-covered peaks of the Central Pangean Mountains; on the other side, streaky clouds hung, like a tattered, grey blanket, over ancient Africa. The window was so clear that it looked like there was no window at all.

It was like a scene cut from a *Buck Rogers* comic. That was the only place Freddy had seen anything that looked like a computer.[34] A circle of massive screens surrounded a central chamber, spewing a sickly light over their operators. Some threw out 3D images like attacking spirits.

The high-level Zyne technics sitting in front of these screens did so with their backs to the windows and the grand view outside. Their polished pants sat on body

---

[34] The first modern computers were being invented around the time Freddy left on this expedition to Pangea. It was not until the following year, however, that the first electronic programmable computer was developed. This computer, The Colossus Mark One, weighed 20 tons and was used by the British to break German codes. The degree of Doylian involvement in this breakthrough remains a mystery.

sensitive polymer seats that melded into their butts for maximum comfort. Freddy had thought that his arrival might cause a stir, but no one looked up from their work or paid him the least attention.

The upper Zynes were dressed in tight-fitting white tunics and pants and wore the same protective vests as the Zyne guards although Freddy assumed it was more symbolic or fashionable in their case than for the guards. They also wore the same hobnailed jackboots as the guards. The boots of the upper Zynes, however, were lined with the same body-sensitive polymer as their seats.

Only one Zyne took any notice of Freddy's arrival.

Freddy had seen the Beta Zyne from a distance during the Tournament of Blood but was not prepared for how charming he seemed at close quarters. He expected that defeat may have cast a shadow over his face but, if anything, it seemed even more assured.

The Beta Zyne signalled for Count Schnauzer and Gruntenguile to be taken aside. Then he offered his pale hand to Freddy. 'Congratulations! You gave us a real "run for our money", to use one of your expressions.'

Freddy shook his limp hand.

'*We* normally use that expression when we have only *just won* rather than when we have *just lost.*'

'I know the correct use of the expression, Freddy, and it suits the occasion. I forgot that you were knocked out before the official end of the tournament. Your team and your Subzyne teammate—'

'Gruntenguile!' interrupted the fellow of that name who was listening to their conversation some distance away.

The Beta Zyne continued as if he had not heard, '— and the Amazons, were, unfortunately, disqualified.'

'Ruminant manure!' said Gruntenguile pretending to cough.

The Beta Zyne ignored him. 'The winner automatically became the previous competitor eliminated. That was, of course, the . . .' He turned to a subordinate Zyne standing next to him.

'The yellow Zyne, Sir'. The subordinate bowed as he spoke.

'You can't be serious. That's not fair! The red Zyne should never have been allowed to swing in like he did at the start of the tournament, and the yellow Zyne should never have been allowed to re-enter after he had been eliminated. If it were not for that Agrosios would have won for sure. Even *after* all that the tournament was won by Gruntenguile—fair and square.' Freddy could not hide his anger. He had never seen such cheating since his father had taught him how to play cards. As he spoke, he searched the Beta Zyne's face for signs that he might be joking but could not find any.

'Well, who knows?' asked the Beta Zyne, as if sympathising with Freddy's concerns. 'I am no expert, but it seems very unsporting to question the referee's decision after the event. And, to be honest, Freddy, they can ignore a little bending of the rules here and there, but they have to draw the line somewhere, and *attacking the medics* that went a little "beyond the pale", to use another of your expressions.'

'Ruminant manure,' coughed Gruntenguile.

'Lucy and Polydora were about to fall from the top of the cage. Is there a rule against saving someone's life?'

'Let's not get caught up in emotional details. There is really only one rule anyway, and that is that *we can't lose.*' By the time the Beta Zyne finished that sentence, his face had hardened to an expression that closed the matter.

Looking at that face, a feeling of hopelessness wrapped around Freddy's heart like a wet octopus—there was no beating the Zynes.

At the same time, another feeling was also growing in him. It was the same feeling that he had felt when standing before the crystal sword and outside the cave in Arnhem Land. It was a feeling like he had been there before. Maybe, in his heart, he just wanted something to be familiar.

He did not have much time to ponder this, however, because a loudspeaker interrupted his thoughts. It announced in a sharp voice, 'the Alpha Zyne'.

The Beta Zyne turned and faced the chamber behind the circle of screens. A door, unseen before, split in the middle and opened to reveal a dark space behind. Out of that darkness, stepped the Alpha Zyne. There was no mistaking who he was because the symbol in the middle of his breastplate was the alpha symbol, α, from the Greek alphabet. Apart from that he was dressed the same as the other upper Zynes, except for the colour of his suit, which was adamantium silver. The upper Zynes, the Beta Zyne included, lowered their heads as he entered. He walked straight towards Freddy and stuck out his hand.

Freddy glanced back briefly at Gruntenguile and in a split-second saw that he was just as surprised.

Freddy stared at the Alpha Zyne's hand as if it was the first he had seen with five fingers.

Confusion and elation washed over him.

The Alpha Zyne was his father.

With hair!

31. The Alpha Zyne

The letter D formed between Freddy's tongue and teeth but that was as far as it got. A tiny shake of the Alpha Zyne's head, and a sharp look in his eyes was enough to tell him that he was to show no sign of recognition. The same look was thrown over Freddy's shoulder to Gruntenguile.

His father's hand hung in the air for a few seconds before Freddy was able to reach out and clasp it in his own trembling hand. It felt real. The skin was a little softer than he had known it, but it was his father's hand. The only real difference was that his father now had hair on his head.

Feelings, long buried, clambered unsteadily from their graves and fought zombie wars inside his head as he touched his father for the first time in six years.

His father shook Freddy's hand twice and then tried to let go, but Freddy could not release his grip. He kept shaking it as if checking it was on tight enough.

'It is a pleasure to meet you, Mr O'Toole,' his father said, giving their hands one final shake. Suddenly realizing that everyone was looking at their clasped hands, Freddy let go.

'You, too, Sir.' The letter D had once more been swallowed.

The Beta Zyne cast curious looks at them both. Something was not quite right, but he could not put his finger on what it was.

Turning quickly to the Beta Zyne the Alpha Zyne announced, 'I will hold a private counsel with Mr O'Toole in my chamber.'

'I would not advise that.' There was a hint of suspicion in the Beta Zyne's voice.

Freddy guessed his father was walking a tight rope for him at that moment.

'Advice declined!' The Alpha Zyne held up his hand to the Beta Zyne, and Freddy caught a flash of a tattoo on the palm. It was the alpha symbol. There was no greater argument in Zyne society than an α tattoo on an upheld palm.

The Alpha Zyne turned and walked back into the darkness of his chamber. Freddy stood rooted to his spot, his hand still outstretched.

'You are meant to follow,' said the Beta Zyne.

'Blazes! Of course,' said Freddy, feeling a bit rattled.

It took some effort to move his legs, but he finally convinced them to follow his father into the Alpha Chamber and the door slid shut behind them.

Inside, Freddy found himself standing before a man he knew as well as anyone but did not know at all. He was not sure what he expected his father to do. Maybe embrace him. Even football players did that sometimes but there was no embrace. Instead, he stood at arm's length and looked him over.

'You could do with a little more meat on those bones,' he said at last.

'Nutrition capsules don't really stack on the weight,' said Freddy.

'And that hair never came good.' His father ran his hand over the top of Freddy's ginger mop and shook his head. Freddy's scalp tingled at the long-lost touch, but it did not last long. His father withdrew his hand and checked his palm as if worried the orange colour might have rubbed off. Looking up, he continued. 'I imagine you have a few questions.'

'A few questions?' cried Freddy. 'I've got six years of questions!'

'Let me anticipate some of them and start as close to the beginning as is possible.'

Freddy's father had never been very emotional, but Freddy was shocked at how calm he was after such a long absence. Freddy on the other hand could barely stand upright.

As his father spoke, Freddy tried to separate his memory of Colum O'Toole from the Alpha Zyne that stood before him.

'Let's start with the good news. *You're not human!* You're a Zyne, just like me—and a rather important one at that.' His father paused for a moment and seemed disappointed at Freddy's limp reaction. 'Hmmm . . . You are a bit lacking in Zyne history, so I should tell you that our ship,' the Alpha Zyne gestured around him, 'crash-landed here several centuries ago—to use a human measure of time. I am the sixth generation born on what you call Earth, and I hope the last to reside on this decaying lump of dirt. Our time draws near.'

'Why leave? Why not stay here?'

'That is spoken like an Earthling who has never been anywhere else. This planet was not even on our long-list. Life here is too fragile. This is a brittle clod of rock and water spinning way too close to a sun that, one day soon, will cook it to a crisp.'

'But this planet is still alive and going well—okay, at least—250 million years from now. You know that. You've seen it for yourself.'

'You don't want to be up and moving every few hundred million years. Besides that, the atmosphere here ages Zynes—and all creatures—much more rapidly than our intended destination.' The Alpha Zyne cast a wan look around his chamber. Three walls, including the wall through which they had entered, were covered in screens that showed various parts of the *Atlantis*. These screens changed every few seconds, and the Alpha Zyne could telepathically conjure up whatever part of the spaceship he chose. One screen remained the same, however, and that was the one showing the goings on in the main operating room of the Control Disk. On that screen, Freddy could see more challengers gathering for the tournament reception. He was relieved to see that Haji and Lucy had arrived. A short distance from them stood the three Amazonian champions. They were choosing between different coloured hydration capsules served by pale lower Zynes wearing pale yellow tunics.

So distracted was Freddy by the screens that it was a while before he noticed the fourth wall of the Alpha Chamber. When he did, he took a step backwards.

'It's a while since you last saw that, Freddy,' said his father turning to the crystal sword protruding from the fourth wall.

Freddy nodded as he gazed for a moment at the tip of that terrifying instrument. Shivering, he drew his eyes away.

There was nothing else in the room except a swivelling chair, which sat in the very centre. He briefly wondered what his father must do with his time before a question that had been building inside him over many years finally spilled from his lips. 'Are you sure you're *really* my father?'

A shadow crossed the Alpha Zyne's face. 'Yes,' he replied.

'What about my mother? Was she who you always said she was? Did Jane O'Toole really die in a car crash in Ireland?'

'You probably should ask just one question at a time. It is a no and a yes so far.'

'What do you mean?'

'I mean your mother was not who I said she was, but, yes, Jane O'Toole did really die in a car crash in Ireland. Although I can't even see why that's relevant.'

A leaden weight lifted inside Freddy. He had spent his life grieving a mother that he had never had. 'So Jane O'Toole was not my mother?' He looked steadily at the Alpha Zyne's stony features. 'If what you're telling me is true, I am guessing now that there was a real Colum O'Toole.'

His father turned around and stepped away from Freddy, becoming a dark silhouette in front of one of the screens showing the crowd gathering for the tournament reception.[35] When he spoke, it was to the screen, not to Freddy.

'When I visited the time where you have lived most of your unfortunate life, I needed an identity. I was surprised by how caught up everyone was with having a name. Most of the higher civilisations don't bother with such primitive notions. It is enough for a Zyne to know their rank. Anyway, this fellow, O'Toole, was a Wanderer here in what you Earthlings call Pangea. He was my size and looked remarkably like me, although not quite as good looking. He was also bald. It was for that reason that I shaved my head in your time. Anyway, this O'Toole fellow also had a respectable job that took him to remote places where no one knew who he was or what he was doing. Not only that, he was proving to be quite a nuisance here. Stirring up the Subzynes and even competing in our Tournament of Blood. He almost defeated our blue Zyne. Had him out cold! If our guards had not blasted him with lasernators O'Toole would have dragged him to the Channel of Blood.'

[35] It was customary for Zynes to hold any event that might involve social pleasantry as early in the day as possible. This allowed them to get it out of the way so they could get on with more important things.

198

'How can you cheat like that?' asked Freddy.

'Oh, it's not cheating, Freddy. You have not quite understood yet that the first rule of our society is that Zynes must win.' The Alpha Zyne smiled. For a moment, Freddy thought he was going to ruffle his hair, but, at the last second, he drew his hand back to his side. 'Anyway, my point is that this human was perfect for the scheme I'd hatched. All I had to do was terminate him—to be on the safe side—return to his time, and assume his identity.' Freddy's father smiled like he'd just shown his son how to mend a puncture on his bike.

'Terminate?'

'Yes, you know; the nice word for kill—'

'You killed a man—to assume his identity?'

'Yes, it worked a treat.'

'But you can't just kill people.'

'Why not? It's not like I didn't have a *reason*, and he wasn't a Zyne. He was a human. Humans kill other species all the time *and most times eat them.*' The Alpha Zyne shuddered. 'Besides—I didn't do it myself—I gave the job to the Amazons. They were unusually cooperative, and I can only assume that O'Toole had fallen foul of them for some reason or other.'

Freddy stepped back, horrified by what he was hearing, but as much as he wanted to ask more questions about the murder of Colum O'Toole there was an even bigger question he needed to ask. 'What about my mother? I have got one, haven't I?'

'Why do you ask? I assume you know how Zynes collaborate with the Amazons to produce our offspring.'

'My mother was an Amazon?' Freddy looked over the Alpha Zyne's shoulder at the screen where he could see the Amazons attending the reception just outside the Alpha Chamber. Then he felt his biceps. 'Hmmm . . . What was her name?' he asked.

Freddy's father turned around and smiled at his son's silly question. 'I certainly didn't want to know her that well, and what does it matter anyway? In Zyne society, the only thing that matters is the father. The mother is simply a vessel. The sooner we liberate ourselves from them altogether the better. You will understand that when you get more used to Zyne ways. Don't worry, we will dehumanise you soon enough.'

For a while, Freddy was unable to speak.

'I guess the next question is why?' asked Freddy. 'Why would you want to travel to the mid-twentieth century and leave me there?'

As he was asking these questions, Freddy's eyes flitted to every corner of the room. There was no way out. Even if he could make it out of the Alpha Chamber, which seemed impossible, the Control Disk was heavily guarded, and the screens showed how crowded and well secured the rest of the ship was. The tournament was over for another year, and every Zyne had returned slavishly to their work.

'I don't know how much you have learned about our ways,' said the Alpha Zyne. 'Not much I imagine if you have been spending your time with rebel Subzynes and Wanderers. They are not our biggest fans. However, let me assure you that you have a lot to be proud of in being a Zyne. Our society is highly successful, and the key to that success is Zyne thinking. Whatever is logically best for our society as a whole is implemented without reference to any primitive emotions, and one of our core Zyne practices is controlled selection.'

'Of people?' asked Freddy.

'No, Freddy, of Zynes. There's a lot you have to learn but do concentrate. Anyway, this controlled selection happens in two phases. The first is in the selection of the Amazon for reproduction. The second is in the weeding out of any offspring who do not fall within certain parameters. Size is one factor. Small babies are culled. This is very important to us. The standard measure of weight in Zyne society is the minimum accepted weight for a new-born.'

'Are you saying that I was sent away because I was a runt?'

'No, that was just an example. There are other criteria as well. One of them—a very important one—is hair colour.'

The Alpha Zyne paused; waiting for a response, but Freddy was not capable of one. Had his father just said 'hair colour'? He replayed the sentence a few times in his head. Surely, he had not heard correctly.

'I was banished by my own father for being a red-head?'

'You make it sound like a bad thing,' said his father. 'The gene for red hair has been linked to an increased tendency towards non-conformity, and our society is not prepared to take that risk. The gene is almost extinct, but occasionally it comes back, as it did in your case. Mutations do occur. Blood-heads we call them. Anyway, the point is that blood-heads are not allowed in our society. Our laws are very strict about that. It is the job of the Amazon bearers to take care of the elimination; however, your bearer did not eliminate you. It was not until I arrived to collect you at three years of age, as is the custom, that I realised the problem. Then, for reasons I can't explain, I was unable to eliminate you myself. For a while—the only time in my life —I did not know what to do. If there is a truth close to Zyne truth, Freddy, it is blood truth. My blood runs in you. Nowhere else.'

His father stared at one of the screens for a moment before continuing. 'It was not long after that the pesky Wanderer, O'Toole, fought in the Tournament of Blood and started stirring up trouble. I saw an opportunity to, as you say, "kill two birds with the one stone". I had O'Toole eliminated and used his identity to take you forward to his time for safekeeping until we could come up with a cure.'

'You mean a cure for red hair?' asked Freddy.

'Of course,' continued his father. 'We're always coming up with new things. I thought our medics could surely come up with a cure for red hair. The difficulty was that the cure had to be effective at the level of DNA, so it proved a little trickier than I had at first thought.'

Freddy stared wide-eyed at the Alpha Zyne.

'Anyway, where was I?' he continued. 'Oh yes, I arranged a meeting with this O'Toole after the tournament and pretended to listen to all his blah-blah concerns about the environment and his sad old planet when, in reality, I was "casing him out", as you Earthlings say. Once that was done, I visited the Amazons and hired them to dispose of O'Toole. Then I shaved your head and brought you back to the *Atlantis*. I brought you here to this very chamber.'

Looking back at Freddy he added, 'it seems like yesterday.' He turned again and took a few steps towards the crystal sword. 'We stood here.' They both stared at the tip of that terrifying instrument for a few moments. 'I remember thinking at the time that if you could survive the sword then you deserved to live. That you deserved to be a Zyne. I realise now how ridiculous that thinking was. My thinking had become quite primitive.'

His father turned back to Freddy and added, 'This planet does that to you after a while.' Then he turned back to the crystal sword. 'I had never used the crystal sword before. It is more like a museum piece, a symbol of our first-time travel breakthrough, but I had no choice. It was the only way to get to O'Toole's world without anyone knowing. Ever since some of them went missing, we have had to book the GT Turbos weeks in advance and every flight is recorded—the red tape is ridiculous!

202

The Beta Zyne *and* the Zyne Council must clear all GT Turbo flights these days, and there was no way they would have given me clearance to take my mutated blood-head offspring to a future time. That is not Zyne thinking!'

His father looked briefly at Freddy to see how he was enjoying the story so far and seemed to mistake the look of shock on his face for spellbound interest. He turned back to the screen. On that screen, Freddy could see the Beta Zyne placing a bone wreath around the neck of the yellow Zyne who did not look one bit embarrassed.

'I held you up. Like this. I lined up our hearts and ran through the sword. My last thought was that neither of us would survive, but, sometime later, I awoke to a tapping on my head. I opened my eyes, and it was you.'

'Was it in the cave? In Timor?'

'It was—'

'Then why didn't I come back to this portal?' asked Freddy.

'Good question. The answer is simple. These old things are so dodgy you are lucky if they work at all. There are only three of these portals left in this time. The one you see before you, the one in Amazonia, which was your point of arrival—'

'How do you know that?' asked Freddy.

'Don't worry. I have ways of knowing everything.' His father smiled like maybe he didn't want to know everything. 'The third sword portal in this time has fallen into the hands of Swamp Subzynes. In future times there are several. Travellers can use telekinesis to direct them to a particular portal; however, it does not always work. The worst case I have seen was a Crossblood whose head ended up in Victorian London and the rest of him in

Renaissance Machu Picchu.[36] It terrified the Incas so much they abandoned the city the next day ...' His father chuckled before pulling himself together and continuing. 'Anyway, where was I?'

'The cave in Timor,' said Freddy.

'After the cave, we trekked to the coast and got a passage on a mission boat to Australia. Once there, I contacted Professor Dupler who had corresponded with O'Toole but never met him. Before the meeting, I added to what I had already learned from O'Toole by reading all of his articles and his book, *The Coincidence of Mysticism*. Really, he should have called it, *The Nose That's Sitting in the Middle of Your Face*. When I met Professor Dupler in Darwin, he had no reason to believe I was anyone other than who I said I was. I gave him no cause to doubt anything I told him, and he was too busy with his work to worry about oddities in my behaviour as I pretended to be human—which was not always easy. That damn Professor, for example, was always complaining about your daily training. I wish he was there today to see how it all turned out.'

'What about Gruntenguile?'

'Before I left your time, I briefly returned and hired Gruntenguile. It was easy because he thought I really was Colum O'Toole, and O'Toole is such a hero to rebellious Subzynes like Gruntenguile. He thought it an honour to serve me.' The Alpha Zyne chuckled once more at his powers of deception. 'You can't beat Subzynes for loyalty, and there are not many creatures that would accept a contract written on a Gorgonopsian skull.'

---

[36] The ruins of Machu Picchu can still be found in modern day Peru. The city was part of the Inca Empire and was built around a crystal sword time-portal in the fifteenth century. The headless body incident, however, freaked them out and the Incas abandoned the city overnight. It is not known what happened to the portal.

'What does Gruntenguile get?' asked Freddy.

'Nothing—that's the beauty of signing a contract with a Subzyne. It's all about their pledge, and let's give Gruntenguile his due—you are alive.'

'So Gruntenguile thought you really were Colum O'Toole, just like everyone else?'

'Yes, just like everyone else.'

Freddy ran his hands through his ginger mop and thought for a moment. 'You didn't have the heart to kill me because I had ginger hair, and I guess I should be eternally grateful for that, but I still can't see why you stayed. Why didn't you just leave me there and return straight away to Pangea?'

His father kept his eyes trained to the Beta Zyne on the screen before him for a few moments. 'In life, Freddy, we cannot always explain everything, and, besides, that is not really important anymore. The fact is I did stay—for seven long Earth years. I have to say I enjoyed parts of it although I found talking to Earthlings most annoying. They just keep repeating things, like "hello", and "how are you?", and saying your name every time they see you like you might forget. It was also boring at times because no one ever wanted to fight. It is mostly all talk and eat with Earthlings. Anyway, I stuck it out for as long as I could. I thought I owed you something because—outside a miraculous cure—you were never going to be a real Zyne. It seems crazy when I look back on those times, though, as I have said, my Zyne thinking was somehow over-ridden.' The Alpha Zyne glanced over his shoulder at Freddy and added, 'Since that time I have returned to pure Zyne thinking. I would never do it again.'

Freddy studied his father's reflection on one of the screens.

'I don't believe you,' he said.

'What do you mean?'

'I mean I don't believe you have returned to pure Zyne thinking.'

'And why do you say that Freddy?'

'Because someone gave Professor Dupler a time-eye. Who else would have done that if it wasn't you?'

'It could have been anyone. Those old time-eyes are like whiskers on a Subzyne.'

'How do you know it was an old one?'

The Alpha Zyne looked hard at Freddy and did not reply.

'And another thing,' said Freddy, 'how did you explain being away for seven years?'

'I didn't have to. I returned to the same time that I left—not a second later, not a second older. You would never have known who you really were if the Professor had not been so obsessed with finding out about all this—and he is not the only one snooping around our affairs. There are others. Your companions, for example.' His father turned, and for the first time held Freddy's gaze for a few moments. 'Don't worry, we know all about the Doylians.'

'What about Dr Bufon?' asked Freddy seeking to steer the conversation in a new direction.

'Now that's different. She is someone with whom, the Beta Zyne assures me, we can do business.'

'What sort of business?'

'That is not your concern.'

Freddy looked back to the screen in front of the Alpha Zyne. The yellow Zyne was making a speech and pointing out the red and blue Zynes. He could not have done it without them and so forth. Lucy and Haji listened with twisted faces. Gruntenguile coughed in the background.

'What are you going to do with us?' asked Freddy.

The Alpha Zyne turned his back on the screen and faced Freddy. 'I am going to give you what you want,

Freddy. I am going to take you all to the north and show you what you want to see. Want to see what's causing the Dark Cloud? I'll show you.'

'How do you know that's why we're here?'

'Because I know everything, Freddy.'

Freddy's mind stretched back over his journey. Who could he really trust? Especially knowing the extent of Zyne technology. He did not doubt what the Alpha Zyne was saying. It seemed pointless to even think about defeating them.

'If you know that is what we want, why are you taking us?' asked Freddy.

'Why? Because there is nothing that any of you can do about it . . .' Then, turning back to the screen, he added 'and I could do with an outing.'

32. The Zyne Party

As far as Zyne parties go, the reception was in full swing.

Beings bunched like bananas in the same groups in which they arrived.

The first group Freddy noticed when he left the chamber were the Amazons. Standing in a close group, they cast grievous looks at the upper Zynes. They glanced at Freddy as he left the chamber, but the expressions of Amazons are as inscrutable as cats. Freddy looked directly at Koia but could not hold her gaze.

The next group he noticed were the two flat-capped Wanderers. They were deep in conversation with a high level Zyne. Standing alongside them was Agrosios, and the flat-capped Reggie and Bertie.

The Zyne fighters stood closer to the centre, near the great bank of flashing computer screens. Standing with the Zyne champions was Dr Bufon. She had brought her own drinks to the reception and was swilling a bubbly beverage from a long glass. This glass was narrow at the bottom but ballooned out at the top. If, as Freddy assumed, it contained alcohol, it contained a lot.

On the opposite side of the room stood Gruntenguile and Lucy. Her bottom jaw almost fell off its hinges when she saw Freddy emerge from the Alpha Chamber with the Alpha Zyne. Her shock turned to something else when she noticed that Freddy's first impulse had been to look towards the Amazons.

Haji stood some distance away, trying to work his way closer to Count Schnauzer. He was talking to a blank-faced Zyne technic while glancing in the Count's direction. The Count did not return these glances. He stood to the side surrounded by guards, gazing hungry-eyed at the trays of nutrition capsules being offered to everyone but him.

Apart from this, scattered groups of higher ranked Zynes were either fighting or discussing fighting in small groups.

None of the all-Tribals teams were there.

'You may mingle with your friends,' said the Alpha Zyne leaning close to Freddy's ear. 'Say nothing about what I have told you. I will tell everyone soon enough.'

Before Freddy could take two steps, Dr Bufon, as she was so clever at doing, stepped from nowhere into his path.

'You continue to *surpriiiise* me, Mr O'Toole. It may be that you have as much to tell me as I have to tell you.' As she spoke, she ran her fingers once more through Freddy's hair and removed the micro-recording device she had planted on his scalp before the tournament. Freddy tingled under her touch and searched for something that Buck Rogers might say but before anything came to mind, she was gone.

After seeing Freddy enter the room, Haji abandoned his conversation and tried to intercept him, but Dr Bufon had beaten him to it. Now that she was gone, he grabbed Freddy's arm and led him to Lucy and Gruntenguile.

'We'd given you up for dead,' said Haji. 'You never quite know how those lasernators are set. They can kill you just as easily as tickle.'

Lucy was less concerned for his safety. 'What were you doing in there with the Alpha Zyne? Is there something *you* haven't told *us*?'

Freddy had not agreed to the Alpha Zyne's order to to keep quiet. Even so, he still felt bound to do as he had said. The trouble was that it was hard to dodge Lucy's questions. Luckily, at that moment, his father raised the alpha tattoo on his palm and silenced the crowd.

'Zynes, and visitors, welcome to our reception for the Tournament of Blood victors.' The Alpha Zyne waved his hand towards the Zyne champions.

Gruntenguile cast a haughty look in their direction and coughed.

'Now is a time, however, not to think in terms of winners and losers.' The Alpha Zyne first looked towards Freddy's group, then Agrosios, after saying the word 'losers'. 'Now is a time to come together, and what better way to do that than to marvel at the greatest wonder of Zynedom on this miserable planet. I know some of you are especially interested in this. Therefore, I have decided to take you all on a special journey to the wastelands of the north, known to Wanderers as Laurasia.'

Through all of this, Lucy looked awkwardly at Freddy.

'Why are you looking at me like that?' he asked.

'I don't know. Maybe it's because you have been accusing *me* of holding out on you about what is going on in this little game, and now I find you are all chummy with the Alpha Zyne.'

'I can't say anything right now. You'll just have to trust me.' The words hung in the air, sounding like an echo of Lucy and Haji's pleas to him over the past weeks.

'Let's go take a look, shall we? Beta Zyne, set a course for the Probe Tower immediately.'

Dr Bufon choked on her drink, and the Beta Zyne looked like he did not think it was a great idea, but the Alpha Zyne had his palm raised. 'Yes, your Alpha,' he replied. The Beta Zyne relayed the instructions to a Gamma Zyne technic sitting at the nearest computer console. He relayed some instructions to a group of Delta Zynes, and the flight deck rippled for a few moments with further instructions and the pressing of buttons and the turning of knobs. There was a lot of leaning forward to check gauges, sharp orders, and brisk replies before, a short time later, the Control Disk seemed to become a living thing.[37] It shivered and gave a hydraulic groan and then a roar like a landslide swelled beneath them and filled the space inside the Control Disk until it quivered. With a mighty clunk, the Disk detached from the tower before rocketing across the *Atlantis* and up the sheer, grey and white slopes of the Central Pangean Mountains.

Everyone lurched backwards except the Alpha Zyne who, smiling grimly, gave one more order. 'Let's take the scenic route.'

---

[37] Zynes preferred telepathy but backed it up with verbal communication for double security on occasions such as this.

33. The Control Disk

Freddy stood alone staring out the window of the Control Disk, watching the monstrous grey slopes of the Central Pangean Mountains fly past. They were a spectacular sight, but Freddy hardly noticed them. His father's words were racing through his head like a slaughter of Gorgonopisians through a herd of Lystrosaurs.[38]

'If there is a truth close to Zyne truth, Freddy, it is blood truth.'

Out of their whole crazy conversation that was the only thing that seemed to make sense.

Freddy, like most boys, had bled before. His blood was red and ran just as freely as anyone's blood. Was Zyne blood any different? Did it matter whose blood flowed through your veins? Or was it just your blood?

He looked over to where his father was also standing alone. He stood just as Freddy remembered him standing in days gone by. Hands on hips and gazing into the space between things like he was posing for a statue.

He had found his father but felt no closer to him. If he was a Zyne, as his father said, why didn't he feel like one?

'You're not *thiiiinking* again are you, Freddy?'

'Dr Bufon!'

That wily woman had once more managed to sidle up to Freddy without him noticing.

For the first time, Freddy avoided her eyes. He looked instead at the snake tatoo on her right arm. She had a way of flexing her muscles that made the snakes look as if they were alive.

---

[38] Interestingly, the collective term 'slaughter' is applied in modern times to iguanas, who look remarkably like Gorgonopsians—except they are only a fraction of the size.

'What do you want from me?' asked Freddy.

'I'm *sooo* glad you aaasked, Freddy. But, first, it is time for me to *surpriiiise* you.' Dr Bufon held up the micro-recorder she had planted in Freddy's hair. 'Before the tournament, I didn't just pop down for a chat, Freddy. I placed this micro-recorder in your hair, and it has revealed some very interesting information. The *moooost* interesting being that you are the Alpha Zyne's long lost and illegal blood-head son. Do you know what that means, Freddy?'

Freddy shook his head.

'It means that you reeeeally need to be a good boy if you want Daddy to keep his job. Because I can asuuure you—it is a much sought after position.' Dr Bufon turned in the direction of the Beta Zyne who was looking directly at them. He shared a cryptic smile with Dr Bufon before returning his attention to a row of computer screens.

Some distance away, Gruntenguile turned around to check on Freddy. Noticing that Dr Bufon had ambushed him yet again, he called out to him. 'Freddy, why don't you come over here with me?'

'What a tempting offer,' said Dr Bufon, screwing her nose. 'But, before you go, Freddy, I should answer your question. What do I want from you?

'Just to be sensible.

'I have a big deal about to go through, and this little joy ride is holding things up. I work for some very powerful and quite tetchy people.' She poked a pointy fingernail into his chest before continuing. 'So far in this game you have been very lucky, Freddy, but luck has a way of running out in Pangea, and you're out of it.' Her hand slithered upwards and she traced with her fingernail the L-shaped scar beneath Freddy's eye, before making her way back to the Beta Zyne.

Grunenguile watched Freddy carefully as he made his way across the room.

'What was she after?' he asked.

'I am not entirely sure,' said Freddy. 'Just giving me a warning that she knew about the Alpha Zyne being my father.'

'Grrrnnt . . . The Alpha Zyne being your father, must come as quite a shock to you,' said Gruntenguile. 'I know it was a shock for me. I had never met the real Colum O'Toole, but he was a great hero to the rebel Tribals.'

Freddy looked at his loyal manservant. He had known him for only six years, but it seemed like a lifetime.

'Who should I trust, Gruntenguile?'

'Grrrnnt . . . The same people you have always trusted: you first, me second.'

'Should I tell Lucy?'

Gruntenguile looked across at Lucy. She had her head on an angle as she always did when thinking deeply. 'Maybe not just yet,' he said, 'but we should join them. There is safety in numbers, and I am still under contract.'

*

For the final thousand feet of the ascent all that could be seen outside was a grey swirl of choking cloud. It was a relief when they finally burst through the top of the cloud, and an awesome vista opened ahead of them. For a while, no one said anything. Freddy thought he'd had his fill of breathtaking sights, but nothing could have prepared him for the show of raw power erupting over the skyline of ancient Laurasia.

'Can we stop that?' asked Lucy.

The question hung in the air until she turned her eyes to Count Schnauzer who had joined them on the viewing deck.

'It is much worse than it looked the last time I was here,' said the Count. 'The biggest explosion from our time was the eruption of Mt. Tambora on the island of Sumbawa in the Dutch East Indies in 1815. That was about 800 megatons of TNT. If this blows, it's impossible to say how big the explosion will be maybe 1,000 teratons of TNT.'

'Would that destroy the planet?' asked Freddy.

'It depends,' said the Count. 'If it happens sooner rather than later, it might just save the planet. It would, I hope, provide an outpouring of lava, large enough to cap the plume beneath. If it is allowed to continue as it is now, it will either suffocate the planet or—one day—it could explode so violently the Earth might be torn apart.'

The further they went, the worse things got. Smoke blackened the air and sulphurous gases fizzed on the side of the Control Disk.

'How far can we travel into this toxic cloud?' asked Freddy.

'Far enough.' Count Schnauzer's voice at his shoulder sounded like the last echo. This was his creaton, his legacy.

Below them a dead sea, scummed over like a diseased eye, suffocated the groaning landscape.

'The Zechstein Sea,' said Haji. It lay like a ghostly corpse across most of what in Freddy's time would become Europe. A masterpiece of death.

Past the Zechstein Sea they soared once more to cross the Ural Mountains, which were, at that time, a much higher range. When they descended on the other side, the smoke thickened, and the Control Disk could go no further. They slowed and hovered over a desolate plateau looking for a landing spot. Alternating frost and fire had fractured the rocks into a shimmering plain of shards dissected by lava flows, which looked like the exposed veins of the Earth. From a distance, the surface was white-specked and as they drew closer, Freddy realised they were the bones of animals torn apart and scattered by the fierce winds.

Freddy turned to Count Schnauzer. A cold sweat had broken across his brow.

'When we put the thermal rod down, we knew there was some chance of a mantle plume, but we didn't expect . . . this.'

Freddy had never thought much of Count Schnauzer, but he reached out at that moment, and placed a hand on his shoulder. 'Blazes,' he said, 'what part of the modern world is this?'

'Siberia.'

34. The Siberian Traps

They landed on a shrapnelled ledge overlooking a maze of lava flows splashing and spitting against steaming islands of fractured rock. Sulphurous gases oozed from hellholes and encrusted the tortured rocks like leprosy. The air shimmered with heat and disorder.

Freddy, like most boys in those days, had an idea of what Hell might be like if he should ever have the misfortune to go there. This was it.

Delta Zynes, seemingly blind to the hellish scenes outside the window of the Control Disk, handed out safety equipment. Facemasks to protect against the mephitic vapours. Silver suits to shield against the heat.

Once they were ready, an eye-shaped door slid open on the side of the Control Disk, and the Alpha Zyne led the way down the ramp with an air of casual invincibility, like he was going out to bat.

The others followed more cautiously. Sparks and pieces of molten lava flew like fireflies. A low rumbling broken only by more violent eruptions shook the air, and the earth under their feet rattled like old bones.

Only the Alpha Zyne seemed at ease. As he walked, the smoke seemed to clear in front of him and a platform emerged. It was little more than an encrusted scaffold of adamantium pipes. The Alpha Zyne mounted the platform and peered into the distance. Freddy followed his line of sight across the steaming flows of lava. At first, he could not see anything due to the thick flurry of gases, but a violent burst of wind suddenly cleared the air a little. Shrouded in a pall of hissing vapours, Freddy could just make out a metal tower. It rose about a hundred feet in the air where it was crowned by what seemed to be turrets or the upturned teeth of a skull. From the base of the tower ran a pipe similar to those in the *Atlantis*. It was about twenty feet in diameter and ran in a southerly direction before disappearing into the broken terrain.

Freddy shuffled across to where Lucy and Haji were standing either side of Count Schnauzer. 'Blazes! What do we do now?'

Turning to Freddy, Count Schnauzer whispered in a quivering voice, 'There is a panel on the front of the Probe Tower with the eye symbol of the Zynes set into it. In the pupil of the eye is a crescent-shaped notch. The ring locks into that notch, and a quarter turn to the right locks down the Probe Tower forever. There is no reversing the lock down. Once locked; it stays locked. Locking the tower will be the final act of Zynes on Earth. The *Atlantis* cannot take off until it stores enough of the Earth's energy, and the tower is shut down.'

'The problem is,' said Haji, 'if we wait for the Zynes to store enough energy and lock this thing down there will be no life left on Earth.' As he spoke his hand rested on the spot where his shirt bulged slightly over the ring.

'Don't you fools see?' hissed Count Schnauzer, sweat sliding down his trembling face. 'It is hopeless. That is why he has brought us here. He is mocking us! It is as if he knows we have one of the false rings.'

'Shut up Schnauzer,' said Haji, glaring fiercely. 'We have no time for doubts. The Doylians have strived for years for a chance like this. Yes, our ring may be—most probably is—one of the two false rings. Maybe there isn't a real lock ring at all, but we are here right next to the Probe Tower and for the fate of the world and all eternity and the love of God, we must at least try.'

Freddy had never admired Haji so much as at that moment. He felt inspired by his fighting spirit.

Then, Haji turned to Freddy and grabbed his hand. Before Freddy realised what he was doing, Haji slipped the ring on Freddy's middle finger.

'What are you doing?' asked Freddy.

'You are the one who is going to lock it down. I can't get across there with my bad back.' Haji stretched and grimaced.

'No way! Why is it always me that has to save the world? Why is it always me?'

Freddy was struggling to keep his voice down and the Zyne champions cast suspicious looks in his direction. He clasped his hands behind his back to conceal the ring.

'*Seriously! Why me?*'

Stepping in close to Freddy, Lucy curled her arm around his back. Squeezing his arm, she said, 'Because you *can*, Freddy! *You can!*'

The Alpha Zyne gazed with distant eyes at the Probe Tower. To him it was more than just an extraordinary piece of engineering. It was the only way to reunify his species. Deep in the next galaxy, the other spaceships in the Zyne Armada had already landed. Chances were they had already given them up for dead. Inter-galactic space travel is never easy, even for the most advanced civilisations.

Freddy felt Lucy's hand on his arm, and the ring on his finger. He looked out across the maze of lava flows and jagged rocks. He looked down at his battered boots, which were opening up at the sides. Then he turned back to Lucy. 'What about the lasernators?'

Gruntenguile grunted and tapped the side of his nose. 'Leave that to me.'

'What if the Zyne champions come after me?'

Haji winked at Agrosios and said, 'Leave that to me.'

At that very moment, the Alpha Zyne turned and faced the group.

Freddy had just made up his mind about what he was going to do. It was simple really. The fate of his planet was at stake, but the sight of his father's face stopped him. How could he betray his own father? His own blood?

His father's voice boomed over the thunderous sounds of the exploding landscape. 'Behind me you see the Probe Tower—'

The Beta Zyne stepped forward. 'Do they really need all the details? That they are even here is surely enough.'

The Alpha Zyne raised his palm. A hot gust of wind blew across the plain and feathered their faces with grey dust.

'You should have more faith in your species Beta Zyne. This tower will not be stopped until we have drained every joule of energy we need to get the *Atlantis* back in space and on our way.'

Lucy pushed her mint-scented lips close to Freddy's ear. 'Go now,' she urged.

Freddy took a half step forward but then froze. His father was looking directly at him.

'Don't do it, Freddy. Do not betray your own kind at the urging of an Earthling girl. Remember whose blood flows through your veins! Remember above all else—you are a Zyne.'

The words hung and spun in the hot air.

Lucy's hand tightened on Freddy's arm.

Dr Bufon shared a sneaky glance with the Beta Zyne. '*Reeeally*. How is that possible?' Pinching her ivory cigarette holder in front of her face, she squinted at the Alpha Zyne through curling blue smoke.

The Beta Zyne stepped forward and asked the same question. 'How is that possible?'

'Never mind now. I will explain later,' said the Alpha Zyne, holding his palm towards them, 'but, believe me— *he is a Zyne.*'

'That is not true!'

All heads turned in the direction of a new voice. Except Lucy. She did not take her eyes off Freddy.

Freddy was not aware of this until Lucy confessed to him some time later, because his attention was fixed on the person who had dared to challenge the Alpha Zyne. It was the Amazon, Aella.

'*You* may have long forgotten, Alpha Zyne, but I am Freddy's bearer.'

Lucy was still holding Freddy's arm. Squeezing it tighter with each new revelation.

'Well, good for you,' said the Alpha Zyne. 'But what if you are?' He shared a smug laugh with the Zynes gathered about him. The very existence of bearers was a source of embarrassment to most Zynes.

'I know that you are not the boy's father, and that he is *not* a Zyne. He is a Crossblood. Not your usual kind but an Amazonian Crossblood.'

'Don't be ridiculous! The only Crossbloods are the result of Zynes spreading the glory of Zynedom.'

The other Zynes laughed at this well-used Zyne joke, but the Alpha Zyne did not chuckle as heartily at his own joke as he had in the past.

Aella held the Alpha Zyne's gaze until he was forced to ask the question that he wanted so much to ignore.

'If what you say is true, which Wanderer do you claim is the father?' Freddy noticed a tightening of the Alpha Zyne's voice, and a half memory stirred in him of the last time he had seen him so agitated.

'That, I will not say.'

'No!' cried Freddy. 'Say for my sake.'

Aella's eyes met Freddy's. They were fierce eyes—there is not much an Amazon can do about that. But they were not as forbidding as they had seemed during the tournament. Freddy knew that she was his mother.

'For your sake, Freddy, I will say. Your father is the Wanderer with the strange voice. The one *you* …' Aella turned to face the Alpha Zyne, 'ordered killed. His name is Colin O'Toole.'

'Are you sure you don't mean Colum?' asked Freddy.

'Hmmm, I think you're right. It was Colum.'

Freddie looked from Aella to Koia and then to Polydora. He didn't want to ask the next question but if he didn't, no one else would.

'And are Koia and Polydora your daughters?'

Aella nodded.

'That makes them my *half-sisters, right*?'

'No—full-sisters,' said Koia. 'Why do you think we were being so friendly?'

'Koia is also your twin,' added Polydora.

Lucy's hand was like a tourniquet on Freddy's arm. If she had not been gripping him so tightly he may have fallen over.

As Freddie stared from Aella, to Koia, to Polydora, everyone else turned their attention to the Alpha Zyne. He was unable to speak for some time. 'Don't you mean his father *was* Colum O'Toole?'

'I mean what I say, Zyne.' Aella turned to Freddy. 'Your father lives still with the lost Wanderers in Babel.'

In a flash as sudden and sure as a lightning strike, Freddy saw everything exactly as it was. He did not feel like a Zyne because he was not a Zyne. He was a Crossblood, of sorts, and . . . Freddy stopped and reined his thoughts in, recalling the Professor's final instruction to him: 'When the time comes for someone to act that someone will probably be you.' This was surely that time. Freddy pulled his hat down as tight as it would go. Turning, he picked out the Probe Tower through the sulphurous gases fuming from the lava flows. In less than a second, he decided on a path and took off. The first lava flow was the widest, and he needed some height to get across. He jumped up onto the viewing platform and leapt like a fleeing Cynodont over the top rail. The lava hissed and fizzed beneath him, but he paid it no mind. He bounded across the narrow islands of jagged rock, his eyes fixed on the path he had chosen and trusting his instincts to keep him out of the lava.

He had no idea of the scene he had left behind.

Agrosios seized a crutch from under the red Zyne's arm. The red Zyne collapsed. Stepping forward he waved the crutch in front of the yellow and blue Zyne. His ribs were still hurting from his recent injury, but he made the wrenched look on his face appear like anger rather than agony. At the same time, Gruntenguile immobilised the lasernators. Without them, the Zynes were helpless.

Freddy saw none of this as he bounded across the melting terrain towards the tower. Loose rocks rolled and slipped under him. Still he kept his feet. He had almost made it when he landed on a brittle ledge that gave way under him. Falling forward he slid along the length of his forearm grazing it a dimpled red. There was no time to feel pain. Picking himself up, he looked dimly at the blood oozing from his arm. His blood. No one else's. There was not far to go but the loss of momentum was not good. He retraced his steps and took off once more. He leapt and made it across the final lava flow and clambered up a rocky slope to the tower. Up close, it was glowing red from the tremendous heat of the lava pumping inside. His eyes raced over the surface of the tower, but he could not find a panel anywhere. Alarmed by this he glanced back at Count Schnauzer. Why had he trusted him? His heart was beating its way out of his chest. It took everything within him and a deep breath to not give in to despair. His thinking had gone haywire. He had to calm down. Looking back at the tower, he ran his eyes slowly over the surface once more, and this time he saw something.

'Blazes!' he cried. It was the Zyne eye, almost hidden by a yellow-green scum. Then, looking closer, he saw the crescent shaped notch, held his clenched fist above it and inserted the ring. His heart almost stopped beating he felt such a rush of relief. Then, for some reason that Freddy could never properly explain, he glanced back at the Alpha Zyne, the being who had once been his father. The father he had been searching for in his heart for the past six years. The once blank mask of his face was marred with an emotion. It looked to Freddy like sadness, and he was gently shaking his head. This could have meant that he did not want Freddy to save the Earth because he did not care one fig about the entire planet, but somehow Freddy knew that was not his reason. He had the wrong ring and was about to be scorched in acidic steam and die an agonizing death in the most awful place the Earth had ever known. Pulling the ring out of the crescent notch, he sat down on the jagged rock at the base of the tower. He slid the ring from his finger and threw it into the molten lava at his feet.

Haji collapsed to his knees clutching his head. 'It's gone forever,' he said.

Lucy clutched the braided horns on her head.

The Beta Zyne stepped onto the platform and placed a triumphant hand on the Alpha Zyne's shoulder. Looking up, Freddy saw him laughing like the Devil across the smouldering landscape. The face of the Alpha Zyne, however, was as calm as buried rock. Looking across the wasteland at him, Freddy realised for the first time the enormity of his own self-absorption. How could he have been so blind all those years ago that he could not see that the man who was caring for him as a father was not even one of his own species?

This was followed by an awful feeling that, somehow, it was all his fault.

Somehow, it was he, Freddy O'Toole, who was responsible for the extinction of the Earth. How could that be? He sat down and squeezed his head to stop it from exploding.

The crowd standing on the ledge above the lava field saw Freddy's defeat and gazed at him with various emotions. The Zynes were triumphant. Dr Bufon could not disguise her delight.

The other non-Zynes were downcast. The game for them seemed to be over. The only non-Zyne not giving way to despair was Gruntenguile.

Brain sucking is a skill, as far as I know, that very few of even the most advanced creatures have mastered. It had taken Gruntenguile years of practice to develop this skill. In its most advanced form it involves sucking all of the irrelevant thoughts from a being's mind until the only thought remaining is the one they need. It is very handy, especially if you have lost something. Brain sucking was what Gruntenguile was doing with Freddy at that very moment. No one suspected anything because Gruntenguile looked no different when he was performing this procedure.

The first thing Freddy noticed was that he suddenly did not know what he was doing there. He looked across at the beings staring back at him and had no idea who they were. And so it went, as memory after memory was razed from his mind. As these memories flew away, he was better able to recall what was left and these mostly involved the Alpha Zyne in the time when he was Freddy's father.

He saw himself picking up the bright-coloured Easter wrappings after his father had eaten all the chocolate eggs.

He saw himself unwrapping a bottle of Blarney whiskey and a cigar almost as big as himself, for his fifth birthday.

Then he saw his father's fury at having lost something and suspecting that Freddy was responsible. Was it a ring? The memories kept peeling away, one by one, exposing long buried layers of recollections until Freddy saw the thing his father was looking for—and yes, he had taken it, but he dared not tell him. He dared not because it was somewhere that he could not get it back. He had swallowed it. He had swallowed the lock ring, and he knew that it was still inside him. As soon as Freddy realised this, Gruntenguile immediately reloaded his other memories.

Looking across at the Count, Freddy recalled his trick from their second meeting in Doylian Lair. Placing his hand on his stomach, he silenced his mind and the rest of the world. Then he moved his hand slowly in small circles, working it through the taught flesh of his stomach wall. The skin parted like ripe fruit, and Freddy pushed his hand further through the slimy stomach sac until his fingers were feeling their way around the inside lining. At first, they found nothing but sticky dissolving capsules, but this did not worry Freddy. He knew it was there and he found it. His fingers touched something hard and round and then felt the crescent edge of a crystal. Freddy pinched the ring tightly in his fingers and pulled it from his stomach. The flesh slid back in place, and the psychic surgery was completed. He held the ring in the air, but he was too far away for any of the onlookers to see what he had in his hand. Only the Alpha Zyne guessed what it must be, and he collapsed to his knees.

Freddy placed the bloodied ring he had pulled from his gut on his middle finger and once more turned to the tower. He drove his fist into the Zyne eye and the crescent moon locked in. He twisted his fist a quarter turn and the eye turned with it as easy as breathing.

Then, nothing happened. Seconds that seemed like ages ticked by, and Freddy wondered whether the ring he had just used was a fake. Then the unthinkable raced through his mind. What if he had destroyed the real ring? As his heart sank at this thought, an awful grinding sound erupted from somewhere deep within the Earth. Freddy looked back at the others. They were turning to run for the Control Disk, except for Haji, who was already halfway up the ramp, and the Count, who seemed transfixed by the scene before him.

The grinding sound rapidly became a deafening roar. There was no time left to lose. Freddy sprang forward and ran for the Control Disk.

About him the streams of lava were rising. The gases seemed suddenly thicker and began leaking into his mask. He felt sick and dizzy at the same time. The smoke was so thick by the time he made it back to the viewing platform he could hardly see where he was going. He could only just make out the entrance to the Control Disk. Seen through the thickening smoke and showering sparks it was a dark eye slowly closing. Freddy raced up the ramp. Halfway up he dived and rolled inside just as the door was closing. Looking quickly back at the devastation he had just escaped, Freddy saw for a brief moment the silhouette of a solitary figure.

'Count Schnau—' cried Freddy, but it was too late.

The door slammed shut, the Control Disk took off, and in the same instant, the Probe Tower blew.

35. Cataclysm

The Alpha Zyne glared at the group standing before him in the Alpha Chamber. It included the Beta Zyne, all of the humans on board, and Gruntenguile. There was at least one reason why he would like each being present executed on the spot.

For a long while, he was silent. Not knowing where to start. His eyes slid from face to face, eventually settling on Freddy's.

'Well, at least I know now what happened to that ring,' he said at last. 'I thought it was lost for good, although you never know when and where things are going to turn up.'

Freddy looked warily at the Zyne who, for most of his life, he had believed to be his father. The Zyne who had also believed the same lie.

'Things are never as bad as they seem—' began Freddy.

'*What?*' said Dr Bufon. 'Are you serious? You have just destroyed the most complex deal in the history of deals, and you say—'

'That's enough, Dr Bufon,' said the Alpha Zyne. 'I am still in charge here.'

'Not for long,' interrupted the Beta Zyne. 'You may not be the blood-head's father as you thought, but we know all about your little visit to the future. And what you left there.'

The Alpha Zyne said nothing, but he could not help glancing at Freddy.

The Beta Zyne shook his head. '*We* needed no assistance. *We* recorded every second of your meeting with Freddy earlier today. You give a very neat summary of all your crimes against Zynedom.'

Dr Bufon looked sideways at the Beta Zyne every time he used the word '*we*'.

The Alpha Zyne looked down at the α symbol on his breastplate. He was not ready to concede defeat just yet. 'What you say may well be; however, until a full Zyne Council is held, I am the Alpha Zyne. Until then, I would advise you to not exceed your status, Beta Zyne.'

The Beta Zyne glanced at Dr Bufon. Dr Bufon glanced at the Alpha Zyne.

'Perhaps, Dr Bufon,' said the Alpha Zyne, 'you can explain your little deal to Freddy and his friends while I decide if anyone here might be useful to the future of Zynedom.' The Alpha Zyne stepped away from the others to watch a screen showing the exploding maelstrom still chasing the Control Disk across the ravaged landscape.

Dr Bufon turned to Freddy. 'You naughty, naughty boy. Do you know what you've done?'

Stepping to Freddy's side, Lucy answered for him. 'Saved the Earth from extinction is what he has done.'

Dr Bufon withdrew her lasernator from its sheath and twisted its calibration knob. 'This is now set at obliterate, and, if I hear from you again, it will be for the last time. Now, I'll repeat my question. Do you really know what you have done?'

'I have destroyed the Probe Tower—but, someone had to. Otherwise it would have destroyed all life on Earth.'

'As it is it will take millions of years for the planet to recover,' added Haji.

Dr Bufon pointed her lasernator at Haji and cocked both her brows and the weapon before continuing. 'Well, hooray for you, Freddy.' She walked towards him, briefly glancing at one of the many screens lining the Alpha Chamber. She did not look at the devastation. She saw only the reflections of Freddy and the other spoilers of her dastardly deal. 'Do you know what I do, Freddy?'

'Aren't you an anthropologist?'

'Pooh no! I gave that up years ago. I work for a living now, Freddy. I do deals. Do you think I would come all this way to study some smelly culture? For what? To write a book that nobody understands. So I can teach a course to a bunch of *cardigan-wearing students*? No, Freddy! I was here for the deal of the ages. I'll tell you about it because,' she glanced across at the Alpha Zyne, 'I guess we need to kill some time before we kill you.'

She slithered like a snake that had learned to walk to the opposite side of the chamber. The screens there showed Zynes in other parts of the Control Disk going about their business.

'Do you know what makes the world go round, Freddy?'

Freddy shrugged his shoulders.

'Deals!'

'I'm afraid I must pull you up on that one,' interrupted the Beta Zyne. 'It actually goes round because it formed in the accretion disk of a cloud of hydrogen that collapsed down from mutual gravity, and needed to conserve its angular momentum—'

'*It's a metaphor*,' said Dr Bufon, glaring at the Beta Zyne. Turning back to Freddy, she continued. 'The explosion you have just witnessed was powered by concentrated geo-thermal energy. It means little to you, Freddy, but those from more modern times may know something of its potential,' she said, turning towards Haji.

Haji nodded. 'Some military scientists are aware of its destructive potential, but it is still not widely known. I am guessing now that you are brokering a deal for geo-thermal technology for your client?'

Dr Bufon smiled and nodded her eyelashes.

'And your clients, if I am not mistaken, are the Axis Powers.'

'Hooray! Someone is starting to get it. Yes!'

'If they get the geo-thermal technology, what do the Zynes get?'

'The third lock ring. Like so many precious things, it has just fallen into my boss's hands. He has been collecting Pangean artefacts for years ever since he got his hands on one of their bio-freeze bags. More recently, however, he got really lucky. First, he found a GT Turbo, then he got his hands on a Zyne Timesmitter. It allowed him to communicate directly with the Zynes.'

Flying debris had smashed the rear camera to pieces, but the Alpha Zyne continued to gaze at the flickering static.

'This is how,' continued Dr Bufon, 'my boss first learnt about the lock ring. He has been searching for it ever since. In the end, he had to invade Russia to get it, but you do what you have to. He knew that the Doylians had been playing about in Pangea for years and had already discovered one of the rings. The Alpha Zyne, however, seemed confident from the very start that it was one of the fakes. He didn't tell us why, but we now know. That meant that the chances of our ring being the correct ring were one in two. It was worth a queen's ransom to the Zynes, but my employer still needed a tough negotiator on the ground. That's where I came in.

'My first job was to track down the ring the Doylians had already found. It may have been a fake, but we needed to be sure. We thought that Professor Dupler was a Doylian, so I invited myself on his expedition to the Arnhem escarpment to check him out. I learnt two things. One—that he was not a Doylian. Two—that he was not interested in dealing with third parties.'

'Not your kind of third parties,' said Freddy.

'Yes,' continued Dr Bufon. 'The Professor, like all of us, made his choices and, like all of us, he will live or die by those choices.' Dr Bufon lit a Lucky Strike and blew a mouthful of smoke in Freddy's direction. While one hand flourished her cigarette, the other dropped to the handle of her Walther P38.

She continued. 'I was also keen to find out about your father. From what I could gather I concluded that he was most likely a Wanderer and, most likely, dead. Strangely, it did not occur to me for a minute that the Alpha Zyne might have been impersonating him 250 million years after his time.'

Dr Bufon blew another ring of smoke in Freddy's direction.

'I also concluded that you, Freddy, were of no use to us, but that you could have been a nuisance. That is why I tried to put an end to your meddling mission. But it seems that good henchmen are hard to find these days.'

Dr Bufon shook her arms over her head. The cobras climbing her biceps came to life with the movement.

'After the expedition to Arnhem Land, my boss told me that he was confident that he was about to acquire one of the rings. That's when I came here, and started negotiating. My client wanted Schnauzer and the geo-thermal technology that he had helped the Zynes develop. The Zynes would give anything for one of the missing lock rings. What could be simpler? I was getting close to wrapping everything up when things started to get sloppy and . . .' She stepped closer to Freddy. 'Let me tell you something, Freddy—when you are pulling off these sorts of deals you can't afford for things to get *sloppy*. You need things *tight*.' Her voice shrieked like a seabird chasing chips. A shock of hair fell across her face. She blew it away, but it flopped straight back. Then, turning away from Freddy, she began circling the Alpha Chamber.

'But now our ring is worthless. Not only that—Count Schnauzer is dead . . . but . . . but . . . but . . .' Doctor Bufon's hair was looking more dishevelled with each 'but'. 'Let me tell you all something for real. The rubber is still on the road, and this deal is *not dead*, and it won't be dead until I say it is.'

'No, it won't be dead until *I* say it is,' interrupted the Alpha Zyne, taking his eyes off the dead screen and swivelling around to face Dr Bufon. 'But first, Freddy, let me show you something.'

The Alpha Zyne stepped up to the screen he had just been watching. He pressed its surface and a computer display appeared. His fingers danced over some icons on the screen and a storage box popped down from the ceiling. Reaching into it he pulled out Freddy's backpack—the same one that he had left behind 250 million years later in Timor. 'Yes, Freddy, we have been all over you like the hair on a Tribals' back ever since you left on this expedition.' He turned to Dr Bufon and handed her the backpack. 'Would you like to see what Freddy has brought with him on this pointless expedition to save his and your miserable world, Dr Bufon?'

Dr Bufon untied the top of the backpack and turned it upside down. The contents needed a good shake before Freddy's spare clothes and the chocolate bar, still in the bio-freeze bag, fell from the open end of the pack. Dr Bufon reached down and picked up Freddy's chocolate bar. 'I had the backing of the Axis Powers *and* the Zynes and their immense technology at my fingertips. You had a change of clothes and a chocolate bar.'

'I think I have almost made up my mind what to do with Freddy O'Toole and his Doylian friends,' said the Alpha Zyne. 'However, before I pronounce my sentence, would you like the pleasure of eating that chocolate bar in front of Freddy?'

'I would love nothing more,' said Dr Bufon.

'You wouldn't mind sharing with the Beta Zyne?' added the Alpha Zyne.

'Not at all,' said Dr Bufon ripping the wrapper from the chocolate and breaking it in half—almost. She handed the slightly smaller half to the Beta Zyne. Then, turning to Freddy, she said, 'I bet you have thought about this chocolate many times over the past weeks as you have been dining on snake stew and tasteless nutrition capsules.'

She was right. Freddy's mouth was watering, and he was almost fainting from the distress of having to watch someone else eat his chocolate.

The Beta Zyne grabbed his slightly smaller half of the chocolate, threw it in his mouth, and swallowed it whole. His higher body temperature melted it almost instantly. Doctor Bufon, however, made more of a show of enjoying her chocolate directly in front of Freddy. As she popped the last piece of chocolate in her mouth, she turned to see how the Beta Zyne was enjoying his chocolate when, to her surprise, he collapsed in front of her. She did not look surprised for long because, a few seconds later, she too collapsed.

36. Almost Back

'Well—that was lucky . . . grrrnnt,' said Gruntenguile. Freddy looked to the Alpha Zyne. 'It was the Snapahuties' poison dart. You knew, didn't you?'

'Knew what?' asked Lucy.

'That a poison dart hit my backpack. It must have pierced the chocolate—'

'Dart, yes; poison, no. The Snapahuti use an anaesthetic chemical. It causes nothing more than a temporary loss of consciousness. By the way, they weren't planning to eat you. They were simply guarding the portal as per my instructions.' Reaching forward, the Alpha Zyne plucked the half-moon pin from Freddy's hat. 'This is not just for decoration or identification. Once you were out of Professor Dupler's sight I needed some means of keeping an eye on you.'

'This is a *time-camera?*'

The Alpha Zyne nodded.

Kneeling down, Lucy felt for a pulse on Dr Bufon. 'How long will they be out for?' she asked.

'Ten to fifteen minutes for the human,' said the Alpha Zyne. 'For the Zyne, maybe less.'

Freddy was not worried about the two laying on the ground. He was staring at the Alpha Zyne. 'Just when I start thinking I understand some things . . . Why did you give the chocolate to Dr Bufon and the Beta Zyne?'

'I have been thinking. The rules of this game we are playing seem to have changed. I now find myself about to face the Zyne Council for treason. I can already guess the outcome of that event.'

'What?' asked Freddy.

'The *Atlantis* Brig—if I'm lucky.'

'But won't this get you into more trouble?'

'Yes, it will, but it was the only way I could think of to give you time to escape.'

'But, why?'

The Alpha Zyne looked briefly at Aella before returning his gaze to Freddy. After a long breath, he answered, 'You may not have my blood coursing through your veins—bad luck about that by the way, but never mind—even so, for seven years I was your father. An appalling one by Earth standards, I am told, but I was nevertheless your father. That is something, and at the moment I can't think of anything else that I have.'

'He did hire me to keep you alive,' added Gruntenguile.

'Well, thanks, I guess,' said Freddy. 'But we are still trapped. There's no way to get out until we return to the *Atlantis*.'

'He's got a point, Guv,' said Reggie or Bertie. They had both been poking about the chamber since Dr Bufon's collapse looking for a way out.

Everyone else grunted and nodded their agreement.

'There's no way *we* can escape, but there is a way for *you* to escape,' said Lucy.

'What do you mean?'

Freddy turned to Gruntenguile. He stared awkwardly back at Freddy.

'Why are you looking at me so weirdly?' he asked.

Gruntenguile nodded his head at something just over Freddy's right shoulder.

Freddy ignored him and looked back at Lucy. She too nodded at something behind Freddy.

Unable to ignore them any longer, Freddy turned and found himself looking directly at the tip of the crystal sword.

'What the ... blazing blazes,' said Freddy. 'You're not

thinking what I think you're thinking?'

'That depends on what you think I'm thinking, Little Boss.'

Freddy turned from Gruntenguile to Lucy.

'It's the only way,' she said.

'But you said yourself, it's incredibly dangerous—'

'For most Zynes and almost all people Freddy,' said the Alpha Zyne, 'but not for you! You have already used the sword successfully. Most travellers who use the sword successfully the first time survive repeat journeys. You have already used it twice with no ill effects.

'Most?' asked Freddy.

'Most, including you, Little Boss—but you'd better hurry.'

The Beta Zyne was showing signs of stirring. Soon he would wake and sound the alarm.

'*But why is it always me?*' asked Freddy.

'Your Earthling friend has already told you,' said the Alpha Zyne. 'Because you can.'

'I still don't know that I can trust you,' said Freddy. 'You are still a Zyne, after all.'

'I am what I am—and I owe some of that to you. All I can give you is this chance. Take it before I change my mind.'

Freddy nodded.

'Sadly, you are not a Zyne, Freddy. Your real father is someone I would still rather like to kill; however, you are in a very sad way, all that I have.'

'What will happen to everyone else when the Beta Zyne wakes up?'

'That will be up to the Zyne Council, but, don't worry, they will create several sub-committees to deal with this issue. It will take forever. By then you will be back to do whatever you can. Now—say your goodbyes.'

Freddy nodded and turned to the Amazons.

Aella looked hard at Freddy. She had dealt with human goodbyes before and did not like them.

Taking out his pocket watch Freddy held it in front of her. 'Have you seen this before?' he asked.

She stared at it before taking it from Freddy's hand and running her fingers over the engravings on the back.

'Is it my real father's?'

'Yes, it is,' she replied. She stepped forward and grabbed Freddy. He flinched. Aella normally hugged men to squeeze then into asphyxiation or at least submission, but that was not how she hugged Freddy. She let go and his sisters did the same. First, Polydora sprang onto Freddy like a monkey. The ill will he had previously felt towards her washed away in an instant. After Polydora let go, Koia stepped forward and wrapped her muscular arms around him.

'So what was going to happen *tonight*—that time back in the tent?'

'Mother was going to tell you about your father and who you were. We thought it was best for you to get your strength back before we told you.'

'How did you even know?

'We hacked your guardian's time-eye.'

The Beta Zyne groaned and rolled to his side.

'There is not much time, Little Boss.'

'There never is,' said Freddy, 'but what little there is I will use.'

Turning quickly to Agrosios, Freddy belted his huge chest in a manner that would have upset anyone else. 'You are a great fighter, and we could not have done this without you.'

'Spartaaaaa!' said Agrosios.

'We plan on teaching the lad a little more English, when we get the chance,' said Reggie or possibly Bertie.

Either way Freddy shook both of their hands.

'Make sure you return home, or the chances are—none of this will ever happen.'

'Don't worry about that, Guv,' said the other. 'We can't afford the payout if we stay.'

Freddy stepped before Haji, and they too shook hands.

'I'm sorry I wasn't more help to you in the clinches, bad back and all.'

Next, Freddy stood before Gruntenguile. He looked more disgusting than Freddy had ever seen him. His beard was horribly singed. It looked like a scorched badger's backside. 'I always thought you were the worst manservant in the world. Now it turns out that you are the best manservant in two worlds.'

'I do my best—within the terms of my work contract . . . grrrnnt.'

Doctor Bufon groaned and Gruntenguile urged Freddy to hurry.

Nodding his head, he made his way to Lucy whose hair had completely unravelled.

'I'm sorry about the spaceship comment. It was so dark. I couldn't see properly.'

'What?'

'My comment about your hair being like a spaceship—I'm sorry.'

Lucy touched the L-shaped scar below Freddy's eye. 'Wherever you find yourself, ask some questions.'

Freddy's brow creased. 'I have got one question—*your father?*'

'You have just broken your record for the dumbest time to ask that question. For now, let's just say that he is not Colum O'Toole or the Alpha Zyne.'

Freddy winked and tapped the brim of his battered hat. He slid the lock ring from his finger and flipped it to the Alpha Zyne.

Catching it, he placed it on his finger. Then he reached into the same box from which he had grabbed the backpack and took out Freddy's machete.

'You may need this,' he said, passing it to Freddy.

Freddy swung it about a few times and placed it back in its sheath.

'You're not coming with me?' he asked.

'Not this time.'

He turned and faced the crystal sword.

'Would you like a push, Little Boss?' asked Gruntenguile.

'No,' said Freddy. 'I've got this.'

Born and raised on Yorke Peninsula – the ill-shaped leg that supports Australia – Don Henderson, in cahoots with his siblings and army of cousins, knew few boundaries, and, from an early age, developed a quirky sense of adventure.

Don worked as a roustabout in woolsheds and as a stock agent before enrolling at The University of Adelaide, where he majored in English Literature. He taught high school English in South Australia, Victoria, Arnhem Land, and Japan. He indulged his passion for writing in various ways, most notably as the founder, editor, and sole scribe of the *Tarcoola Times*, and, later, as a sports writer for the *Whyalla News*.

After attending a conference where the speaker lamented the lack of high interest books for boys he wrote *Half the Battle* (2006) and *Keepinitreal* (2009), published by Scholastic. A third novel, *Macbeth, You Idiot!* (2009), was published by Penguin.

He couldn't stop imagining a high adventure book set in an incredible world, so, when he returned to serious writing a few years ago, he enrolled in a creative writing PhD at The University of Adelaide and set to work on *Pangea and almost back*.

Don lives in the Adelaide coastal suburb of Largs Bay with his wife, Alison. He teaches English at a nearby high school.

In this time-traveling adventure, Freddie O'Toole is searching for
his father, who has disappeared in a plane crash several years earlier.
His guardian sends Freddie on a secret expedition to Timor where
Freddie and his crusty manservant, Gruntenguile, are chased by
Snapahuti headhunters. After a narrow escape, they discover portals
that take them back to Pangea and then to ancient Africa where
Freddie becomes a contestant in the Tournament of Blood. He meets
the leader of master aliens, the Zynes, who unlocks the secret of his
missing father and a dastardly deal between the Zynes and the Axis
Powers in World War Two.

Full-throttle dieselpunk adventure!

What a sensational ride Pangea is . . . as it twists and turns, careers around
wild unexpected corners from the very start, yet is consummately controlled
by the invisible strings of [Henderson's] narration. I love the synthesis of every
conceivable thing in the mix – hints of *Lord of The Rings*, *Star Wars*, epic classical
heroes (á la *Raiders of the Lost Ark*), legends and myths, esoterica, science, para-
science, geology, geography, anthropology, history, social iconography, bread and
circuses, time travel and . . . Freddy!
– Kingsley Allen

A wild adventure ride packed with non-stop action, intrigue, extraordinary
creatures and memorable characters. Great fun!
– Michael Gerard Bauer

Cover design: Ty Brookhart

Book design: David P. Reiter

Glass House Books
ISBN 978-1-922-33248-6
ipoz.biz/ipstore

www.ingramcontent.com/pod-product-compliance
Lightning Source LLC
Chambersburg PA
CBHW020756250626
47155CB00003B/1098